*Rachel started at the sound of
Spence's resonant voice behind her.*

She pivoted around to see him standing in the
doorway.

"I didn't mean to scare you." He sounded mildly
contrite, but the teasing glint in his eyes contradicted
him.

"No, that's all right. Have a seat," Rachel replied
equably.

Rachel realized this was the first time she had seen
him without a jacket, with nothing to conceal the
angular lines of his build. He was an undeniably
great-looking man.

*So what? You're his caseworker, for crying out loud.
Better get it together.*

He was going to have to prove himself, for Katie's
sake. Rachel wouldn't let him sway her with his
charm. But the way he looked at her, the blue of his
eyes deep with a smoky warmth... the way his smile
seemed to wrap itself around her...

Dear Reader,

Welcome to Silhouette **Special Edition** . . . welcome to romance. This month we have a wonderful selection of books for you, and reading them will be the perfect way to get into that summertime spirit!

June is the month of brides, so this month's THAT SPECIAL WOMAN! selection is right in tune with the times. *Daughter of the Bride,* by Christine Flynn, is a poignant, warm family tale that you won't want to miss.

We've also got the action-packed *Countdown*— Lindsay McKenna's next installment of the thrilling MEN OF COURAGE series. And you won't want to miss *Always,* by Ginna Gray. This tender story is another book in Ginna's wonderful series, THE BLAINES AND THE McCALLS OF CROCKETT, TEXAS.

June also brings us more books by favorite authors— Marie Ferrarella, Pat Warren—as well as a compelling debut book by Colleen Norman.

I hope that you enjoy this book and all of the stories to come. Have a wonderful June!

Sincerely,

Tara Gavin
Senior Editor

Please address questions and book requests to:
Reader Service
U.S.: P.O. Box 1325, Buffalo, NY 14269
Canadian: P.O. Box 1050, Niagara Falls, Ont. L2E 7G7

COLLEEN NORMAN
A FAMILY TO CHERISH

Silhouette ®

SPECIAL EDITION ®

Published by Silhouette Books
America's Publisher of Contemporary Romance

Dedicated to my husband, Richard, and my family

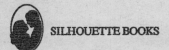

SILHOUETTE BOOKS

ISBN 0-373-09894-4

A FAMILY TO CHERISH

COLLEEN NORMAN

Having worked in the field of mental health for over a decade, Colleen Norman believes in the power of hope. And she believes romance fiction especially reminds us that it's possible to dream, to hope, even in life's toughest moments.

A native Oklahoman, Colleen has won several writing awards, including the Heart of Oklahoma Award. She holds a Bachelor of Arts Degree in Letters, and a Master of Education in Guidance and Counseling. Besides reading, her interests include taking long walks, horseback riding, gardening, hiking in Colorado's Rocky Mountains in autumn and, closer to home, exploring the Kiamichi Mountains. She continues to juggle a full-time job with her writing career.

Colleen currently lives in southeastern Oklahoma with her husband, and she is a devoted aunt and godmother.

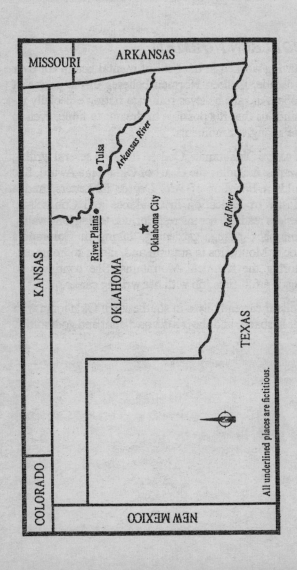

MISSOURI

ARKANSAS

KANSAS

Tulsa

Arkansas River

River Plains

Oklahoma City

Red River

OKLAHOMA

TEXAS

COLORADO

NEW MEXICO

All underlined places are fictitious.

Prologue

Late February

Automatic doors swung open at the touch of Rachel Moran's stride on the mat leading into St. Joseph's Medical Center. She jarred snow from her boots with a few stamps of her feet. The air held an antiseptic cleanness and its warmth took the chill from her cheeks and nose. A single chime heralded a call for Dr. Johnson. Going to the elevator, Rachel pushed the fifth-floor button and rode upward in silence.

The call had come in this morning. A little girl, between four and six years old—both her parents had been killed last night when their rented moving van slid off an icy bridge on the interstate outside of the city of River Plains. The child had miraculously been thrown clear but her parents were trapped inside when it burned. The fire destroyed all family possessions and identification. For a moment, Rachel closed her eyes against the pain she felt for this child, this little girl so alone, so bereft.

At the fifth floor, she stepped off the elevator and walked down the corridor to the pediatrics ward. She stopped at the nurses' station. "I'm Rachel Moran, the social worker from Children's Protective Services. I was called about a little girl admitted here last night, first name Katie. She lost her parents in an accident."

The charge nurse checked her patient roster. "Room 512. And Dr. Shelby wants to talk with you, too. Let me call and tell her you're here."

Rachel nodded and moved to the window at the end of the hall. *Terrible day to be on call,* she thought, grateful she'd had the foresight to purchase chains for her car. Such heavy snowstorms were unusual for Oklahoma, especially late in February. The city was already covered in an eight-inch blanket of snow, with the promise of more throughout the day. A treacherous crust of ice beneath the snow made travel even more dangerous.

"Rachel, I'm glad you're here."

Rachel turned to greet Dorothy Shelby with a smile. "Dorothy, how's the little girl?"

"Mild hypothermia, sprained left wrist, multiple superficial contusions over her face and body. She was extremely fortunate."

"Do we have any new information on relatives?"

Dr. Shelby shook her head. "The highway patrol called. They still haven't been able to locate any next of kin. They traced the plates of the van to Springfield, Missouri. The van was rented to a Sam and Julia West and their destination was a town about a hundred miles south of River Plains. Apparently, they were in the process of moving. So we called child welfare," she added, using the more common name for Rachel's department. "In a few days, Katie will probably be stable enough for release."

"With no place to go," Rachel finished for her, sadness for the child gripping her heart. "If we can't locate any relatives soon, I'll make arrangements to have her placed in foster care."

They walked to room 512. Dr. Shelby paused outside the door. "She'll probably be asleep."

"I won't be long. I just need to see her, even if it's only a quick glance."

Alone, Rachel walked into the darkened room to the second bed. She leaned against the metal guard railing. The little girl was almost lost in the white sheets. Cornsilk blond hair trailed over the pillow in a bedraggled braid. Ugly bruises darkened her small features, her expression stilled in troubled slumber.

Rachel blinked against the hot, stinging tears blurring her vision. In a very personal way, as much as she tried to fight it, this child's tragedy tapped a pain of her own, one from what seemed a lifetime ago.

She swallowed thickly to relieve the constriction binding her throat and through sheer force of will shoved back the tears and the pain. If she could make a difference in this child's life, then maybe all that had gone before would have some meaning.

Hours later, the tears came, tears for the child whose world had been shattered in a split second by fate, and tears for a childhood long past that existed now only in her memory.

Chapter One

Early April

Spence Garrett opened his eyes to the misty glow of dawn through open bedroom windows. The quiet of the room settled over him. He looked at the other side of the bed, at the pillow untouched in the night, at the unrumpled bedding. No Victoria this weekend, he thought. He felt peaceful, and maybe a little relieved.

In one week, the spring jury docket would begin, bringing with it twelve-hour workdays. He had told Victoria he wanted the next couple of weekends to himself. She'd pouted as usual, but she'd been a pretty good sport about it.

"You're going to turn into a fuddy-duddy old judge before you even turn forty," she'd teased. He knew she was disappointed. He also knew she wouldn't have a problem occupying herself without him. *Homebody* wasn't a word he would use to describe Victoria, or even himself. But recently he had found a certain appeal in the idea. Maybe he just needed some time to himself.

The sheets slid from his bare skin as he swung his feet to the floor. The country air was cool, almost chilly, but it felt good. He took a quick shower and as he toweled off, he looked at his face in the mirror. He looked rested for once, he thought. His blue eyes were clear, with none of the late-night redness that weekend mornings usually brought.

He was getting too old for the nightlife Victoria thrived on, Spence decided. He rubbed the blond stubble shadowing his chin and jaw. Not that thirty-six was old. But he was tired of the endless engagements, the dinners, the parties, the charities.

Still, public exposure held a certain importance in his life, apart from Victoria's desires. After almost two years as the elected associate district judge, he now had his eye on a state supreme court appointment. The politicking was moving to a different dimension, but it still meant dinners, parties, charities...to a point. But not this weekend. Spence grinned at his reflection. Complete self-indulgence this weekend, he told himself.

He pulled on a pair of worn sweatpants and half walked, half jogged down the stairs, whistling in rhythm with each step. After putting freshly ground coffee on to brew, he made the three-quarter-mile walk down the graveled driveway to his mailbox for the *Sunday River Plains Times* newspaper.

Spence settled in a chair on the wooden deck skirting the back of his home. He savored the coffee and the solitude while he sifted through the paper.

A photograph caught his attention. For a second, Spence wasn't sure why he was even looking at it. It was in the Living Section, a photograph of six or seven children clustered around a fire truck. Young children, preschool age. Then his vision zeroed in on the little girl in the middle. He'd seen her only in one other photograph and never in person. Hell, he hadn't even been sure she'd existed until a few weeks ago, when his mother had called to tell him she'd received a letter from his sister, Julia.

The letter. A letter of reconciliation after nearly six years of silence. But no one had been in River Plains to open it in February when it had arrived. His mother had wintered in Arizona for Christmas through March, and he had vacationed in Colorado on a skiing trip the month of February.

Sam and Julia must be somewhere in the city, Spence guessed, perplexed. Why hadn't Julia called? But then, she hadn't called in six years. He'd forced himself to quit worrying about her years ago, for his own sanity. But now he didn't know whether to feel angry or concerned. The letter had said they'd be coming through River Plains in February. That was it. Nothing more than Julia writing of her desire to leave the past in the past and to start over as a family. She'd even enclosed a small photograph of her small family. Maybe she'd changed her mind. Again.

The coffee suddenly tasted bitter. What in the hell was going on? Spence tore the photograph out of the paper. This time, he was going to find out one way or another, whether Julia liked it or not.

Rachel flipped open her appointment book and checked her schedule for the day. No office appointments this morning, just time blocked off for ever-present paperwork, then lunch, then out in the field to make home visits to several foster families. It was going to be a typical, hectic Monday, with or without any emergencies.

She pushed back from her desk and walked around the corner to pull open the drapes. The bland beige fabric parted to reveal a large, glassed-in partition, which framed the view of the main office area. She looked at the pool of social workers, their desks lined up in rows, presenting a picture of unceasing industry. The glass muted the drone of voices and clatter of typewriters. Rachel felt thankful for the privacy of her office, necessary for confidential interviews with the families and children with whom she worked. Still, the familiar dissatisfaction settled over her.

"You look excited to be here this morning."

Rachel glanced over her shoulder to the tall, red-haired young woman in the doorway. "Don't I, though."

Leslie Powell walked into the office and dropped into the chair directly opposite the desk. "The ubiquitous pile of paperwork, I see," she commented unnecessarily, eyeing Rachel's desktop. "I have one just like it in my office."

Rachel grinned and returned to the chair flanking her desk, now in full view of anyone in the outer office who might look in her direction. "Sometimes I think the main bureaucratic yardstick used to measure productivity is the amount of paperwork generated by any one person."

"You're such a cynic."

"I'm tired of it. I'm fed up with reports in triplicate, office politics and bureaucracies in general. Where do the people we're trying to help fit in?" Rachel stopped to take a breath. "Sorry, Les. Sometimes I get so frustrated."

"I know," Leslie said with a sigh. "I feel the same way. And I know those are some of the reasons that you're leaving. How are your plans coming?" She couldn't quite keep the reproach out of her tone.

"In just over two months I'll be on my own in private practice as a family and marriage therapist. I've been doing pretty well with it so far on a part-time basis. And I've been talking with St. Joseph's Medical Center about doing some social-work consultation with them on a contract basis." Rachel almost felt guilty at the look of resignation on her friend's face.

Leslie's smile looked halfhearted. "I know this is something you have to do, but you know I'll miss you."

Rachel looked away. This was the hard part, leaving friends behind. She'd worked with Leslie for more than seven years in child welfare. But leaving behind the kids she worked with would be the hardest. Kids like Katie West. Especially Katie. Her background was still a mystery.

Her name was Katherine West and she turned five years old last December, and that was about all Rachel knew about her. There had been no response to the February news coverage of the accident. It was as though the family had come from nowhere. Apparently, Sam West had been something of an itinerant carpenter, going where there was work, living an untraceable life-style with his family. The highway patrol had been left with only the charred remnants of the Wests' limited possessions and personal records, with no hope of reconstructing them and no family photographs to circulate. Rachel was all Katie had. And leaving Katie behind would be like leaving a part of Rachel's heart behind.

Rachel changed the subject, not wanting to think about losing Katie. "You look like you've already had a long morning."

"I guess I have. I've been on the phone about everything this morning. You know, doctor appointments, dentist appointments, foster kids who need shoes, their hair cut, you name it. Too much to do and not enough time to do it."

Rachel exchanged knowing smiles with her friend. The buzzing of the telephone intercom interrupted the conversation. She tapped the flashing button. "Yes."

"Call for you on line four," came the receptionist's crisp voice. "Brenda White from Meadowvale Preschool."

"Thanks, Jean." Rachel picked up the receiver, tucked it under her chin and punched into the line. "Hi, Brenda."

"Rachel. I'm calling to let you know that Judge Garrett just called me a few minutes ago asking about Katie West."

Rachel shifted forward in her chair and grasped the receiver, at the same time motioning Leslie to stay. "Judge Garrett," she repeated in a questioning tone. She frowned, perplexed. Why, after all this time, would Judge Garrett suddenly take an interest in Katie?

"At first, I assumed he was the judge presiding over her juvenile court case," Brenda continued, sounding bewildered.

"Renwick's her juvenile judge. Garrett's an associate district judge, but he only handles juvenile cases on occasion when Renwick's out of town," Rachel clarified, her frown deepening.

"Well, that's what I thought, but he caught me off guard. It's not every day I have a judge calling me about one of the kids," Brenda replied dryly. "He said he'd seen the article in Sunday's paper about our visit to the fire station. He wanted to know who Katie's parents were. That's when I knew something wasn't quite right. I know he's a judge, but I didn't feel comfortable telling him anything more than to talk to you." As the principal of the school, Brenda was always very cautious, Rachel knew.

"Do you know when I can expect to hear from him?"

"I'm surprised he hasn't called already. He sounded pretty determined. And I think he was upset about it."

Upset about it? Great. She hated dealing with angry judges over her cases, although it rarely happened. "Thanks for letting me know, Brenda." Rachel hung up the phone and stared at it a moment, wrestling with the implications of the call. She looked at Leslie. "It seems Judge Garrett has taken an interest in Katie West."

Leslie's eyes widened with instant interest, then narrowed just as quickly into a slight frown. "Why?"

"I don't know. I'm not sure I like this. It doesn't make any sense."

"And it would be Judge Garrett of all people," Leslie grumbled. "The last time I had to face him in court on one of my cases, he did more cross-examining of my credentials than the D.A. or the defense attorney. He acted like he didn't think I knew my job...."

Rachel had never had a judge question her credentials beyond what the district attorney, or one of the assistant D.A.'s and the other attorneys, asked. Child welfare workers were generally accepted as expert witnesses in their field. Except by Judge Garrett. *"And exactly what kind of specialized training did you say you have, Ms. Moran?"* he'd asked her a year ago, the first time he'd presided over one of her cases, his blue eyes that arrogant, icy cool so many of her colleagues found intimidating.

Rachel hadn't felt intimidated. She'd felt annoyed. Then she'd chalked it all up to his lack of experience in hearing such cases, looked him in the eye and spelled out her credentials for him, detail by detail, in a voice as sleek and quiet as a pond on a windless, winter day. He'd returned her gaze and for just an instant, the corners of his mouth had twitched as though he was trying not to smile at her aplomb.

And that annoyed her more.

Because everything was a game with lawyers. This she'd learned from her four-year relationship with Hugh Mitchell. Hugh had come from a hardworking, middleclass River Plains family, and when Rachel had met him, he'd wanted more from life than his job as an accountant gave him. It was not fulfilling enough, he'd confided in her. And he'd seemed conscientious. He'd put himself through his first four years of college. She'd admired his perseverance. She'd identified with it. And she'd seen him through his three years of law school, supported him financially, helped him through his difficult days. After all, law school was tough. They'd planned to marry once he'd graduated.

Then he'd landed a position with Brinkley and Rappaport, the most prestigious law firm in River Plains. Hugh had convinced Rachel they should wait one more year, until he was established in the firm. The year lasted only six months. And he didn't marry Rachel. He married the daughter of one of the senior partners. The perfect ending to an elaborate manipulation. Lawyers were so good at that.

Oh, it hadn't been so unexpected. Rachel had felt inklings of uncertainty when Hugh had postponed their marriage, when he'd grown increasingly distant.

Now Rachel wondered if Spence Garrett had known. After all, he'd worked at Hugh's law firm at the time.

Leslie's grumblings filtered through, bringing Rachel's attention back to their conversation. "Well, I hope to God Judge Renwick doesn't go on vacation any time soon."

Rachel smiled wickedly. "Maybe you should find out what Judge Renwick's vacation schedule is and be gone when he's gone."

Leslie wrinkled her nose in mild irritation. "Thanks a lot, Moran. Not all of us enjoy going to court like you do. I honestly think you like going head-to-head with that guy."

Leslie often referred to Judge Garrett as "that guy" with eloquent discontent. Rachel couldn't help but grin. "I can't say that I *enjoy* court. I guess I just know what to expect."

"That I suppose you would know," Leslie conceded. She glanced at her watch. "Oops, I've got to go. I've got an interview in five minutes. And I know this sounds hopelessly selfish of me, but I'm glad it's you and not me who has to deal with Judge Garrett. Bye." She stood up and was out the door with a wave of her hand.

Rachel smiled after Leslie's departing figure. But the doubting thoughts returned. What did Spence Garrett want? Had she mishandled the case in any way? She thought it through as objectively as she knew how. No, given what she had to work with, she'd done all that could be done.

Come on, Moran. There's probably a perfectly good explanation for the judge's sudden interest. Why should this be any different from any other inquiry about a foster child?

But Katie *was* different, and in a very personal way Rachel couldn't ignore. The memory of the day she'd told Katie her parents were gone and would never be able to come back for her welled up in her mind. And the image of wide, frightened young eyes, the stark pain, the confusion in the little girl's face, all came into focus, squeezing Rachel's heart with remembered pain.

Rachel had understood Katie's fear and confusion. For the other foster children Rachel worked with, there was often the hope and chance of their reuniting with their families, of a better life with the people they loved, and who loved them. But for Katie, it would never happen, just as it had never happened for Rachel.

She closed her eyes against the memory of the eleven-year-old boy huddled in a corner chair at the county sheriff's department, his arms around his younger sister after their parents had been killed in a car accident on an Arkansas back road. They'd waited for someone to take them home. But they'd never gone home. There had been no one left to care for them, just as now there was no one to care for Katie.

Rachel remembered her brother David's attempts to hide his fear, but his reed-thin body had trembled, giving it away, and they'd held on to each other for dear life. Next had been the succession of foster homes, one after another after another until she'd lost track of how many, and finally the worst one.

Rachel felt her neck muscles tightening with tension. She opened her eyes to dispel the images and shrugged her shoulders to ease the tension creeping down her shoulder blades. Usually old memories stayed buried, but her worries for Katie were bringing them back at inopportune times.

Work was usually the best antidote. Rachel focused on the stack of manila file folders, reminding herself there were at least two reports that had to be ready for juvenile court in the morning.

Her peripheral vision caught a movement in the outer office. She looked through her window in idle curiosity.

It took her a moment to realize that it wasn't increased activity that distracted her. It was the brief pause in work among staff as heads came up to observe some object of interest. Rachel followed the direction heads were turned in. The trail of vision ended at the receptionist's desk. Even from across the expanse of the office, Rachel could see the man standing there, impeccably dressed in a charcoal gray suit, distinguished, purposeful.

Judge Garrett.

Surprise pulsed through her. She couldn't ever remember one of the judges coming to the office.

Her telephone buzzed. "Yes," Rachel answered, her eyes still on him.

"Judge Garrett is here to see you." The receptionist's voice held a note of awe.

"Thank you. I'll be right out." Rachel took a careful breath and sat back in her chair. She was surprised to find her heart was pounding.

Relax, she told herself, irritated with this uncharacteristic nervousness. *This is just routine.* But she knew better.

She didn't want to keep the judge waiting. With a fortifying breath, she pushed up from her chair, smoothed imaginary wrinkles from her skirt and strode from her office to greet him.

* * *

Spence Garrett remained standing in the waiting area. He didn't know what was going on but he was damned sure he didn't like the fact that apparently his niece was in welfare custody.

A young woman walked down the hallway toward him. He knew her.

Rachel Moran.

She moved with an air of confidence and directness that had always commanded his attention. Lustrous dark brown hair, as dark as her eyes, cascaded to just past her shoulders in striking contrast to her ivory skin and delicate features. The red jewel-neck blouse and slim black skirt she wore, though conservative by design, didn't hide her utterly feminine allure.

He hadn't seen her very often in the past year, and then only at the courthouse. In the years before, he'd seen her with one of the newer attorneys in River Plains, Hugh Mitchell.

Very attractive woman, he thought, and not for the first time. And not for the first time, he felt that current of awareness when his eyes met hers.

She extended her right hand to him as she walked up. "Hello, Judge Garrett. It's good to see you again." Her voice was soft, her tone polished and professional.

The delicate scent of flowers commingled with a faint, feminine spiciness, drifting to Spence's nostrils and making him think of jasmine and roses.

Spence closed his hand around hers. Her fingers curled around his palm in a gentle but firm grip. Her hand felt warm and small, her skin satin smooth. Such a simple touch to be so distracting, he thought. The dark of her eyes seemed to deepen in faint surprise as though she, too, felt the potency between them. "Ms. Moran," he acknowledged.

Her name glided out in a rich, smooth tenor. Rachel was startled by the kind of crazy warmth that shimmered over her when her gaze met his. His eyes were a brilliant, gray-studded blue that always seemed to catch and hold her attention. She had to tilt her head back to keep eye contact. His height was a good six feet next to her petite five foot four.

It wasn't the first time she'd felt that charge of energy traveling between them, but it was the first time she had difficulty ignoring it. There was an intensity about it that seemed different....

And she had forgotten how handsome he was. But that wasn't what absorbed her attention. Suddenly, she realized what was.

He reminded her of Katie.

His honey-blond hair, styled meticulously back from his forehead, was a bare shade darker than Katie's golden hair. His perfunctory smile tilted his mouth up at the corners and deepened the grooves lining his cheeks, like Katie's. And those eyes. The same blue as Katie's. But his features were wholly masculine with strong, sculpted lines.

The curiosity and interest in his eyes mirrored her own response. His expression softened for the tiniest moment, and she realized he felt this vital energy between them as much as she did.

Rachel felt a pinch of self-consciousness and pulled her hand away. "We can talk in my office," she suggested. Her voice sounded so normal, as if this were an ordinary meeting, but she couldn't have felt less so.

Spence Garrett gave her a nod of agreement, the moment dissipating between them as if it had never happened. He followed her lead to her office.

Rachel paused to close the door behind them, indicating for him to sit in the chair across from her desk. She drew the drapes closed before sitting down.

She let her hands rest loosely clasped in front of her. "How may I help you?" she asked, her tone neutral and calm, but she tensed in anticipation.

Spence didn't relax into his chair. His posture was taut, although the only indication of emotion was in the faint tightening around the corners of his mouth. "Why is Katherine West in welfare custody?" His words were direct and controlled but edged by an undercurrent of emotion.

The question itself confused Rachel. Hadn't he read the papers? The sense of foreboding returned, arresting her curiosity. "I need to know what your involvement with her is," she replied quietly.

Spence studied Rachel's face briefly. He reached a hand into the inner breast pocket of his suit jacket, pulled out a small photograph and handed it to her across her desk.

Rachel cradled the picture between her hands. It was a family portrait of a man and a woman with a small girl perched on her lap. The child was unmistakably Katie. Rachel's throat tightened with the realization she had never seen Katie smile with such joy. She looked at the woman, lovely, blond, with the same distinctive eyes and smile as the judge seated across from her now. The man in the picture seemed out of place, with his dark hair and rugged looks, but there was no mistaking the expression of love on his face for his wife and child.

Understanding weighted Rachel's heart. She looked up from the photograph to meet Judge Garrett's gaze. "Julia is your sister," she said in a quiet voice, bewilderment making her voice hesitant. She hadn't known he'd had a sister. But then, she'd never been privy to his personal life.

"And Katherine is my niece." Clipped words finished her thought for her. "Are Sam and Julia in some kind of trouble?" Barely concealed anger added a roughness to his resonant voice, but his eyes held worry.

Shock jolted through Rachel. *My God, he doesn't know.* It seemed incredible to her. Jumbled questions raced through her mind. How could he have not known? Surely someone, a friend of the family's, anyone, would have recognized their names in the news coverage of the accident.

But they hadn't.

Rachel collected herself. The answers to her questions would wait. He needed to know.

Chapter Two

Rachel pushed back from her chair and moved from behind her desk to sit in the chair positioned a few feet across from him. "Judge Garrett," she began, then hesitated, wanting to choose her words carefully, fighting the sudden dryness in her throat. She intertwined her fingers in her lap, then opened them in a slight gesture. "I'm so sorry. Your sister and her husband died in a car accident in late February."

The anger and worry drained from Spence's expression and his face blanched with the shock of her statement. He brought his clenched-up hands to rest against the bridge of his nose, but not before Rachel glimpsed the moisture glistening in the corners of his eyes.

On impulse, she shifted forward to the edge of her chair and reached out to him, touching his arm in an effort to console. He didn't pull away. They sat together for a long moment.

The only sounds in the small office were the whispery rush of chilled air through the vent in the ceiling and the faint whir of the aging digital clock on the bookcase against the wall. Spence unclenched his fingers and rubbed his hands across his face as if to rid himself of the pain clouding his features. He dropped his hands to dangle between his knees in a gesture of defeat.

Without a second thought, Rachel reached out to hold his hand, feeling drawn to him in a way she didn't quite understand. It was then that he looked up at her, grief etched into his face. His fingers tightened around hers for a brief moment before he pulled away.

Rachel looked at him intently. "Is there anything I can get for you? A glass of water?"

He opened his mouth to answer but his voice caught and he shook his head. He cleared his throat. "No, thank you." He stared at the wall behind her for a few seconds, then returned his gaze to her. "What happened?"

Rachel quietly recounted the accident. She felt deeply touched by his sorrow but there was no way she could spare him the stark reality of his loss. "I'm surprised no one recognized their names in the papers at the time of the accident," she finished, her voice gentle.

She sensed him pull back from her almost immediately, a certain tension falling between them.

Spence sat back in his chair and looked away from Rachel, reeling from the deluge of emotions. Julia dead. His niece, whom he had never met, miraculously alive, and unhurt, at least physically. And he hadn't known of any of it.

How could he explain Julia when he didn't really understand her himself? The twelve years separating their ages had separated their lives. How could he explain the changes in his parents after Julia's birth? Or the constant arguments between his mother and Julia? Or his powerlessness to change any of it? He wasn't used to having to explain his family's most intimate problems to anyone, much less to a social worker. But this social worker evoked feelings in him he couldn't begin to sort through.

He looked at the photograph still on the desktop. "I was in Colorado the month of February. Our mother wintered in Arizona up until a few months ago. Julia had written Mother a letter, with this picture enclosed." He stopped, contemplating his next words. "Without a picture of my sister, no one connected Julia West with Julia Garrett."

Rachel's dark eyebrows pulled together in a slight frown, not understanding. But she stayed silent, encouraging him to continue with a nod.

Spence's chest felt tight with emotion. Some of it had to be told, he knew, however uncomfortable for him, because of the circumstances. Rachel Moran deserved that much. But as for the rest, he didn't believe any purpose could be served by dragging his family's private matters out into the open. Certainly not for the welfare department's scrutiny.

"Julia spent her teenage years out of state in boarding schools. I don't think she really had any friends in River Plains." He paused, his glance going to the photograph. "About six years ago, Julia had a . . . disagreement with our parents over her plans to marry Sam West. She was eighteen. It was a rift that was never resolved. Julia cut off contact with us. It wasn't something that was discussed outside of the family. All anyone else knew was that Julia lived out of state."

Rachel again felt him receding from her, from the brief intimacy they'd shared.

It was a simple, reasonable explanation and one that was clearly very difficult for him to share with her. Rachel felt sadness for him. Julia's death had robbed him of the chance for their reconciliation, the chance to make amends, the chance to make their family whole again. "Judge Garrett," she began, wishing there was something she could say that could make a difference, but knowing there was nothing.

He regarded her tender, concerned gaze. A ghost of a smile touched his lips. "You look so sad," he said.

His observation and the openness in his eyes caught her off guard. "I—I do feel sad. Sad for you, your family, Katie..." She hesitated. She felt disconcerted that her own feelings were so evident. And that Spence was so aware of them even in his own time of sadness.

She felt the distance they'd maintained between them over the years sliding away in the wake of the moment. No games, no manipulations, those things suddenly so meaningless in the face of mortality.

They both sat for a few quiet, somber minutes. Spence looked tired, unexpectedly vulnerable. The urge to reach out to him, to hold him, to comfort him somehow, surprised Rachel. But then, the man she beheld wasn't at all what she'd expected. The Spence Garrett she'd known in earlier years was an arrogant young attorney, always very much in control, very much a part of River Plains's best—the circle Hugh Mitchell had aspired to, the circle in which Rachel had never really belonged. Spence Garrett seemed now very much...human.

"I'll take custody of my niece as soon as arrangements can be made," Spence said abruptly, breaking the silence. The gray lights in his eyes were dulled by pain.

"Judge Garrett," Rachel began, suddenly feeling awkward as his manner shifted back to the businesslike tone she'd expected from the beginning. "We couldn't locate a will. There's no legal document designating godparents or anyone Katie would have gone to live with in the event of a tragedy like this."

"Julia lived like there was no tomorrow," he muttered with a disparaging shake of his head. "Sam West was raised in a children's home. He didn't have any family I know of. My mother and I are Kath—Katie's only immediate relatives."

"There are some procedures we'll need to complete before Katie can be placed in anyone's custody, even a relative's," Rachel explained carefully. "I'll just need to get some information from you and your mother, to determine where Katie will live. And I'll need to do a home study."

At the startled look on his face, Rachel gave him a reassuring smile. "It won't take long. It's routine."

Spence frowned. "I would prefer you direct any questions you have to me. I don't want my mother bothered with any of this."

Rachel's smile dimmed a little. "If Katie's to live with her grandmother or you, I'll need to do at least a minimal home study and help Katie adjust to the change. I can assure you I'll be very discreet. As you know, all records are confidential," she explained in a quiet voice.

Spence stared at Rachel, considering the position she was firmly maintaining. Suddenly, he'd had enough; this intrusion was too much. He stood abruptly, thrusting his hands into his trouser pockets, and turned away from her. "Has my niece been in only one foster home since her case was adjudicated?"

Rachel didn't like the imperious inflection in his tone. She frowned at the broad expanse of his shoulders. "Yes, one," she answered, her compassion gone. Damn, what was he thinking about doing? Manipulating the law to his own advantage?

He turned toward her, giving her a frosty, sideways glance. "Then you must know that under state statutes you aren't required to get court approval to place the child in a second foster home."

"That doesn't preclude a simple home study," Rachel asserted in as modulated a voice as she could muster. *He can't be thinking this through very clearly,* she decided, *considering the shocking news he's just received.*

"The point is, I do not want my mother's privacy, the family's privacy, infringed upon in any way. Julia's death will be a difficult enough burden to bear without the welfare department prying into... into our suitability," Spence replied pointedly, his stare icy. "I'll have it arranged myself, if necessary."

At that, anger flared in Rachel's chest. She stood and moved behind her chair, gripping the top of the backrest with her hands. She looked at him directly, taking a settling, considering breath before she answered him in a deadly quiet voice. "Judge Garrett, two days after Katie's mother and father were killed in the accident, she was put in a foster home with two adults who were complete strangers to her. She's lived there for nearly six weeks. Now she's faced with being uprooted again to live with relatives she doesn't even know exist." Rachel paused, her eyes fixed on his. "Now, you tell me, Judge Garrett, what would you suggest is in Katie's best interest?"

He lifted his hands in a halting gesture. "Don't patronize me, Ms. Moran. I intend to do what's in the child's best interest. I'm simply telling you I won't tolerate an invasion of the family's privacy in the process." But even as he spoke, the glitter of anger in his eyes dimmed. He looked away from her for a moment, his mouth thinning into a tight line that deepened the grooves in his cheeks. A muscle flexed in his jaw.

This was going nowhere. Rachel thought again of the tremendous emotional strain the man had to be under. She moved to stand behind her desk. "I don't think this is a good time to be discussing this—"

"There's nothing to discuss," he interrupted.

Rachel ignored his biting assertion, knowing in fact their discussion was not over. Now simply wasn't the time. "Judge Garrett, I'm very sorry about your loss. I know finding out about your sister's death in this way has to be difficult. I only want to help you and your family with this," she told him, her voice quiet.

When Spence swung back to meet her gaze, anger still glimmered in his eyes, but there was something else there, something she couldn't identify. He rubbed the back of his neck, seeming at a loss for words.

Rachel reached for a business card from her desk, picking up the family photograph at the same time. "Please, call me soon about setting up a time to meet Katie, and let me know if there's anything else I can help you with," she offered, handing the card and photograph to him.

Spence tucked them into his inside breast pocket. "I'll be in touch. I want you to make any and all arrangements only through me," he instructed in a terse voice, then turned and strode from the office.

Rachel let her body drop into the cushion of her desk chair. She felt riddled with emotion and her mind teemed with unanswered questions.

His refusal to let her talk to his mother bothered her. A disturbing spark of awareness took hold in her mind. Maybe there was something about his family he didn't want her to know. If he had nothing to hide, then why else would he be so difficult? And she wondered what exactly had caused Julia's estrangement from the family. It looked as if she was going to have a battle with the judge on her hands.

She should have known. Lawyers were experts in the art of argument. In Hugh's first months with the law firm, which were also Rachel's last months with him, she had listened to his courtroom war stories on Fridays after work at Compositions, a local jazz bar and favorite after-hours gathering spot for River Plains's legal best. She'd listened to how he and his colleagues manipulated interpretations of the law to fit the needs of their cases, how they played on semantics, how they would nitpick irrelevancies to throw the opposition off. It was a game they played for big money and they played it very well. She'd seen Spence there on occasion in the days before his judgeship, always with an attractive woman on his arm, always with his fair share of stories.

That's what made her angriest about the entire encounter with Judge Garrett. She knew his type and she still let him get to her. He'd made her feel so many different things all at once. Compassion, frustration, anger, disappointment . . . and worst of all, attraction. She was disappointed to learn he was the sort of person to use his judicial position for personal gain. But that didn't lessen the vibrant charge of energy still circling them, making her wish he were many things he'd probably never be. . . . And she knew that was the height of foolishness.

Rachel pressed her fingers against her lips. *I must be losing my mind.* She squeezed her eyes shut, disgusted with herself.

You're thirty-two, not some silly teenager. A child's welfare hung in the balance, and for a moment her common sense, instilled some twenty years before, had been eclipsed by her fascination with this man. For a moment, he had made her forget a family as prominent as his own, a family that had once almost destroyed her, that had destroyed her brother. She would never allow another child to suffer the same way.

Whatever had happened between Julia Garrett West and her family was ultimately the reason Katie was in welfare custody now. And it was possible that whatever problem existed then was still present. And where did Spence Garrett fit into it?

If he wanted to make a battle out of Katie's placement, so be it, Rachel thought. She had nothing to lose. Katie had everything to lose if Rachel didn't do her job right. She'd be ready for him.

Spence leaned a shoulder against the frame of the French doors opening onto the herringbone brick terrace, his arms folded loosely across his chest. Before him, the garden stirred beneath the warm spring sunlight and cool breeze. The delicate blooms of azaleas had opened in varied shades of reds. Lanky rosebuds and willowy dogwoods gave mottled shade to the lawn.

He watched his mother, balancing herself with a cane, move stiffly amid clusters of tulips, jonquils and irises. Strands of silver hair curled from beneath the straw hat shading her face. Her cream-colored slacks and blouse hung on her thin frame. Too thin, he thought. At times, her gait seemed unsteady, more than just stiffness from the mild osteoarthritis from which she suffered. As far as he could discern, her health problems weren't as great as she seemed to think. But pain was a subjective experience. And that was a medical issue between his mother and her physician.

He had canceled his docket for the day and immediately driven to his mother's home with the news of Julia and her small family. Jacqueline Garrett hadn't let him see her tears, waving him away from her, and had spent the first few hours after she'd received the news alone in her bedroom. Now she moved round the yard, tending to the roses, her solace.

Spence straightened and walked out into the late-afternoon sunlight. Jacqueline didn't look up when her son came up beside her to walk in slow cadence with her step.

He strolled with her in silence. How had it all changed? Being twelve years older than Julia, Spence had been caught up in the momentum of adolescence and academics when his sister was born and hadn't had much awareness of the subtle deterioration of his family. When Julia was six, he was entering college. When she turned ten, he had graduated from the University of Oklahoma with his bachelor's degree in economics and had gone to work in Washington, D.C., for a United States senator. When she turned fifteen, he'd gone off to law school. And when Julia turned eighteen, Spence was just graduating with his law degree from Harvard and was on the verge of marriage. He'd returned to River Plains to take a plum position with Brinkley and Rappaport. By then, Julia was already gone, leaving behind no forwarding address.

He simply hadn't taken the time out of his life to understand what was happening to his family, to see how serious it really was, until it was too late. Maybe he hadn't wanted to see, he thought, a grim realization that made him pause.

Jacqueline halted and stooped carefully to give a dandelion a futile, frustrated tug. It was only one of several weedy clumps invading the flower beds.

"I need to get that boy out here to get rid of these things," she muttered, referring to the high schooler she paid to do odd jobs for her after school. She was trying desperately not to think of Julia, not to feel the pain, Spence suspected.

"We need to talk, Mother," Spence said, his voice gentle.

Jacqueline straightened, with the support of Spence's hand at her elbow. She angled her head up and he could see the grief-deepened lines marring her refined, still lovely features, the unnatural brightness in her blue eyes. She gave a mute nod.

He'd had some time to think since the morning's conversation with Rachel. And in observing his mother today, her unsteadiness, the undercurrent of irritability he felt in her, he was realizing just how limited his choices were. "I think Katie should live with me."

His mother frowned. "But, Spencer, you're not married. You don't have a wife who can take care of her. And she's such a young child. She should live here. Have a woman to care for her." At her son's questioning look, she shifted her weight to stand more steadily.

"Mother, I think you're doing remarkably well under the circumstances. But I also think a five-year-old child would be too great a strain for you."

She stiffened. "Louise can watch her during the day."

"That's part of the problem. Louise is only here during the daytime. What about nights? And weekends? And Louise wasn't hired to take care of a child in the first place. She's here to help you."

"But you would have to hire a woman to help, too. What difference would it make whether it was you or me?"

Spence put his hands on his mother's shoulders. "I think you know what some of the differences are." He spoke with a firmness that brooked no argument. He didn't want to have to detail her physical problems, real or exaggerated as they might be.

His mother looked away, seeming to consider his reasoning. Her shoulders slumped in concession—and perhaps in relief; he couldn't be certain. "Oh, Spencer, I wish things were different. I wish I still had my health. I wish I could have Julia back...." This last ended on a whisper, her voice brimming with emotion.

Spence put an arm around her. "I know. I wish we had her back, too."

They continued their slow stroll around the yard, side by side, letting the changes in their lives settle.

Jacqueline straightened. "When do we meet her?"

"In the next day or two."

She sighed. "I'm flying to Tulsa for my treatment tomorrow morning." Jacqueline called her physical therapy her treatment.

"You can meet her as soon as you get back."

"I suppose so. I think I made a considerable amount of progress in Arizona. The climate, you know," she said. "I hope this new therapist will be good."

Spence knew his mother preferred out-of-town therapy, believing that better care could be found in the two larger cities of Tulsa and Oklahoma City. He suspected the venue didn't matter, but as long as she believed she was improving, he didn't want to argue the point. "How long will you be gone this time?"

"Until this weekend. I'll probably be exhausted." She sighed. "Maybe meeting her next week some time would work. After I've had time to rest...."

Spence again felt a twinge of uncertainty. But he nodded. "Let me know. I'll have it arranged."

"I want to see her often, you know."

"You will."

"When will she come to live with you?"

The recollection of the morning's discussion with Rachel brought a sense of compunction with it. "I think there will be some formalities to take care of first." He wanted to be as tactful about the matter as possible.

"Such as?" His mother stopped and turned to face him squarely, lifting a finely penciled eyebrow an inquisitive fraction higher.

"Ms. Moran—she's the welfare worker—will probably want to talk with me about a number of things." Spence hesitated, then decided to confront the issue head-on. "She may want to talk with you, too, since you're Katie's grandmother and you'll be spending time with her."

"Ms. Moran, the welfare worker," she repeated with a hint of distaste in her tone. "Why?"

"It's part of the home study they complete before placing children in someone's custody."

His mother stared at him for a moment and thumped her cane on the ground petulantly. "My God, Spencer, we're not a common welfare family," she exclaimed, her expression one of utter disbelief.

Spence found his mother's attitude annoying, although he wasn't at all surprised by it. Jacqueline was a proud woman, too proud at times—the wrong times. "It's a routine procedure."

"I think it's patently ridiculous. Your father would never have stood for this if he were still alive." Angry tears glistened in her eyes, and she turned away.

His patience ebbed. "What Dad would or would not have done is irrelevant." The one thing his mother could do to irritate him was to compare him to Frank Garrett. At this point in his life, it didn't usually bother him. But today was not a usual day. More quietly, he added, "Everything will be handled confidentially."

Jacqueline would not be mollified. "You're a judge. Why can't you do something to simplify the process?"

"The good name of the family alone isn't enough to bypass the system set up to care for homeless children," he answered bluntly. He felt the pinch of guilt at his own self-righteous words. He had implied to Rachel he would not be above such a tactic. Regret at his unreasonable statements distracted him for a moment.

He tried again. "This isn't some embarrassment you have to endure, Mother. It's part of the process of helping Katie adjust to a new home. And I would imagine she's going to need all the help she can get." *He* was going to need all the help he could get.

"But the welfare department? Can't we work this through a private agency?"

Like the out-of-town agencies you and Dad tried with Julia's problems? As far as Spence could tell, nothing had been gained in doing so. Maintaining the outward appearance of the model family had always been so important to his parents, too much so. The public airing of private linens simply wasn't done. Spence had to admit he wasn't looking forward to having a social worker peering into his family's private affairs, either. But he didn't see that he had many other viable options. "Not under these circumstances."

Jacqueline threw a hand up in dismissal of the entire conversation. She pivoted around the support of her cane and started at a diagonal across the lawn toward the house.

Spence didn't call after her because he knew she probably wouldn't answer him. He understood, too, that the shock of Julia's death had left his mother's emotions raw.

Before he left, he stopped in the living room, where Jacqueline stood at the baby grand piano, looking at the collection of family photographs clustered atop it. "I'll call you as soon as I know something."

She lifted her chin in acknowledgment, her arms folded tightly across her chest. Spence could see she was staring at the photograph of his father. He could see the struggle in her eyes. And then he saw the crystal tumbler, one-fourth-filled with what was probably straight scotch, sitting next to the photograph.

"What are you doing, Mother?" he asked quietly, indicating the glass with a nod. The glass confirmed some of his suspicions. He wondered just how much she was drinking these days. He rested his hands akimbo.

Jacqueline's lips trembled, but she tilted her head stiffly. "It's not enough to hurt anything.... I just needed something to help me relax." Her voice had a thickness to it that bordered on a slur. Tears hovered at the corners of her eyes.

Spence was silent, debating how much to press the issue. It was only afternoon, too early to be drinking.

Jacqueline shifted uncomfortably under his scrutiny. "My only daughter is dead, Spencer. Can't you grant me a little peace?" Anger edged her tone.

"There's a difference between finding peace and drinking at the wrong times for the wrong reasons, Mother," he told her quietly.

Her eyes flashed with anger, but tears squeezed from her eyes. She looked very tired and very vulnerable.

Spence rubbed the back of his neck. Today wasn't the day to reason it out with her. "We'll talk about this another time, Mother."

He left her to her thoughts and memories.

He drove through the elegant neighborhood that had been his playground as a child. Branches of silver maples arched together to canopy the street. Sunlight filtered through the young spring leaves to spatter bordering lawns.

Ironic that such a peaceful neighborhood could house such turmoil. It hadn't always been so. Spence looked back on his boyhood years with fondness. The change seemed to have begun in the years after Julia's birth. During his college and early work years, his family contact had been limited to holidays. But still he'd seen his father grow progressively more short-tempered, argumentative and dissatisfied, and Frank Garrett had never been a very tolerant man.

His mother had seemed overly involved with every nuance of Julia's life...overly controlling, demanding perfection where perfection was impossible. Spence had never thought twice about her after-dinner drinks. Now he wondered if her drinking had been a problem even then.

He slowed to a stop at an intersection. He rolled down the window, needing fresh air, and let his elbow rest halfway out the window as he accelerated into the turn.

Now there was a new life in the family depending on what Spence had to offer her, and he had to question what that was. Money? There was plenty of that thanks to his father's wise oil investments years ago. A home? He'd built his country home under the belief he'd never remarry, never have children, although at times those thoughts resurfaced. He lived there alone.

Spence made an arbitrary left turn, heedless of the direction of his route, struggling with the enormity of the problem that had dropped into his hands with no warning. He had never felt less prepared to deal with a situation and he wasn't used to that.

I just want to help. Rachel Moran's quiet words came back to him. But he'd seen the questioning light flicker in her dark eyes at his resistance. He didn't want to let her into his life and she knew it.

But she hadn't pressed him for any substantial explanation, waiting in the fragile silence of the moment, instead, responding only to his grief. And he recalled the soft touch of her hand and the surprise he'd felt at his desire to hold her, to let her hold him, as if her very touch could somehow have eased the pain.

A stillness settled over him at the realization a woman he barely knew had touched his soul in a way the woman he'd chosen as his wife never had. He hadn't thought much about Diane in years, but now he remembered her reaction to the news of his father's death. Diane had simply asked in a restrained voice if there was anything she could do. To ask her to hold him had never crossed his mind, and she hadn't offered.

He wondered again, as he had so often, on just what their relationship had been based. Diane was dazzling, a studied beauty, the perfect wife for a successful attorney in his native Oklahoma. She'd been relentless in her pursuit of him. But once she'd won him and his heart, it seemed their relationship changed. She'd grown bored with their marriage, bored with him, he supposed. They'd divorced by mutual consent four years ago. Any illusions Spence had harbored about relationships had died along with his marriage. For him, relationships had become no more than pleasurable diversions, with no commitments, no pain.

But something had stirred inside him this morning with Rachel. Maybe it was just that he'd always been aware of her, from the first night she'd walked into Compositions with Mitchell two years ago. Offhand, she wasn't what he would call stunning. She wasn't the type of woman who would normally catch his attention. But she had. Immediately. He remembered very little of that winter night except for Rachel. She had arrived with the glisten of melting snow in her hair. Their glances had connected on a current of awareness. She'd seemed annoyed by it. He'd been intrigued by it—and by her annoyance. She was observant, reserved, sexy and not interested in anyone but Hugh Mitchell. Spence had been surprised a few months later at Mitchell's involvement with and subsequent marriage to Sandra Brinkley. But that's how love went. Their paths hadn't merged again except occasionally in court.

He knew from her reputation and his own experience that she was stubborn and opinionated when it came to children. And who was he to disagree with her? Since when had he become an expert on kids? As far as he could tell, she hadn't been intimidated by his judicial status or the foolish threats he'd made in a moment of anger.

She only had to know what he chose to tell her, he reminded himself. She didn't need to know Jacqueline Garrett's problems. And if he had to have a social worker, let it be Rachel Moran.

Chapter Three

Paul Burris shifted his posture to a more comfortable position, his chair creaking beneath his weight. "You think he'll cool down in time?"

Rachel sat across from her supervisor in his office. She lifted a hand in a gesture of ambivalence. "He's had twenty-four hours to think it over so far. It's hard to say. I don't know him well enough to even guess."

Paul pulled at his chin reflectively. "There may be nothing to it. It wouldn't be unusual for a family of the Garretts' stature to be offended by the prospect of a welfare study."

"Maybe." She shook her head in mild disagreement. "I don't know. Obviously there were some serious problems if Julia left the family. I just don't know what they were."

"You're good at your job, Moran," Paul allowed. "But I don't have to tell you he could go over our heads if he continues to take exception to your position."

"I realize that. I know he could try to call the interview we had yesterday adequate for placement." The possibilities were grim. Rachel knew there were workers in the hierarchy of the department who might agree with him. Having Paul's support was a good start, though.

Rachel looked at the man who was thumbing through Katie's file. He'd bowed his head, revealing the gray streaks in his thinning black hair. He rarely called her by her first name, a habit she attributed to his years in the military. She knew he didn't like touchy situations, but he'd been with the welfare department some eighteen-odd years and had seen and dealt with worse ones than this. She respected his ability as a social worker although they didn't always agree on matters. All in all, she couldn't have asked for a better boss than Paul. She'd miss him when she left.

Paul closed the file and let his fingers tap over the top of it. He looked back up at Rachel, his expression thoughtful. "Remember one thing, Moran. Intuition is invaluable, but without empirical evidence to back it up, it won't stand up in court. And considering you're up against a judge..." He shrugged expressively.

She raised an eyebrow at his caution. "You're the expert. Most of what I've learned, I've learned from you."

Paul chuckled at her loaded compliment. "So if this whole thing blows up in your face, you can blame it on me?"

"Don't worry, it won't." She hoped.

"It could get rough. Garrett's an influential man."

This time, Rachel shrugged. "So maybe I'll be leaving the department in a blaze of gunfire. I'll take full responsibility for whatever happens."

Paul winced. "My retirement isn't too far down the road, Moran. Please, don't do anything to jeopardize it."

Rachel smiled at the only half-humorous worry in his expression. "Have I ever let you down?"

"No, but there's always the first time."

"You have my promise, Paul."

"Just be very careful. And keep me informed."

"I will." Rachel stood, smoothing the lines of her navy suit jacket, the pleats of her skirt falling to swirl just below her knees. She reached for Katie's file, then left his office, pulling the door closed behind her.

She hoped Paul's faith was well-placed. She had encountered angry parents while investigating allegations of abuse. But she understood their underlying fear and the threat she represented to them. She always went to homes with the attitude of social worker, not policewoman. Her quiet, nonaccusing approach got her an interview every time. But with Spence Garrett, she wasn't sure of anything.

The receptionist hailed her. "Here's your mail," Jean said, handing Rachel a stack of letters.

"Thanks." Rachel proceeded toward her office at a slow pace, sifting through the envelopes.

One return address, the state of Idaho, Vital Statistics, immediately grabbed her attention. She slid a finger under the flap of the envelope to tear it open and pulled out the enclosed letter. She halted in midstep to skim over it. Attached to the letter was a certified photocopy of Katie West's birth certificate. Rachel scanned the document and saw Julia's maiden name, Garrett, and her birthplace, Adams County, Oklahoma.

So it had just been a matter of time until the joint searches between her department and those in other states turned up the essential lead they'd needed. Even if Spence hadn't shown up, all Rachel had to do was request Julia's birth certificate from the Oklahoma division and locate her parents in River Plains.

Rachel wondered if things would have been any easier if the letter had come earlier, but it was a moot question. But she felt a pull of sadness for Spence, having found out about his sister as he had. Was there any easy way?

Once back in her office, Rachel poked the certificate into Katie's file. She had other cases needing her attention and she directed her thoughts to the children she needed to follow up on this morning. She slung her purse over her shoulder and left to make home visits, putting her thoughts about Katie to the back of her mind.

It was almost lunchtime when Rachel returned. She stopped at Jean's desk to check for messages.

The receptionist peered up at her over the top of horn-rimmed glasses. "I'm glad you're back. Paul wants to see you in his office right away."

"Okay," Rachel said, suppressing a grimace. She hoped Paul wasn't in one of his talkative moods. She was starving and she had only half an hour for lunch today.

Paul stood when Rachel entered his office. "We were just beginning," he said in greeting.

Rachel suddenly realized someone else was in the room.

"You've met Judge Garrett," Paul continued, indicating the visitor behind her with an open gesture of his palm.

Surprise and curiosity fluttered in her chest. But when she turned to acknowledge the judge, she kept her expression impassive. "Judge Garrett," she said with a polite nod.

Spence stood and extended his hand to her in a brief, warm handshake. "Ms. Moran."

His smile was one of practiced perfection, a politician's smile, Rachel thought somewhat uncharitably. But his eyes held hers for a distracting moment, and when she turned away to sit in the chair next to his, she felt vaguely uncomfortable.

She smoothed her skirt over her knees and clasped her hands in her lap. She hoped she looked more casual than she felt.

Out of the corner of her eye, she noted the expensive glint of the judge's gold cuff links and tie clasp, the precise, tailored lines of his gray pin-striped suit. He had that polished look of success and success to come, a look that had always struck her as meaningless. *So, what's he really like?* she wondered. Or was this all there was to him?

Paul sat behind his desk. "Judge Garrett is here to discuss placement of his niece. We haven't discussed any details yet. The judge arrived a few minutes before you got back from the field." Paul looked at Spence. "I understand you've already talked with Ms. Moran about this to a small degree."

"We have."

"Have you given any more thought to placement for your niece? I believe you were talking about her living with her grandmother?"

Spence shook his head. "No. I've decided to adopt Katie myself."

Rachel looked at him in surprise. Paul spoke up in clarification. "You mean to say you and your wife?"

"No, I'm divorced. I meant exactly what I said."

Rachel listened with absolute attention. This was an interesting twist she hadn't anticipated. She'd guessed he'd go with the grandmother. Most of the single men she knew wouldn't want to adopt a kid on their own, related or not. She glanced over at Paul. He was almost squirming in his seat. He hated nontraditional placements. She tried not to smile and decided she'd better help her supervisor out.

She shifted in her chair to face Spence more squarely. "Judge Garrett, I think Mr. Burris is surprised because where a female child is concerned, it's a bit unusual for a single man who isn't the natural father to file for adoption."

"Unusual, but not unheard of, I'm certain."

Correct as he might be, Rachel wondered if he realized the welfare department scrutinized such placements more intensively than traditional ones. After all, just yesterday scrutiny appeared to be the very thing he wanted to avoid. She again realized how much she didn't know about him. "Do you have any children of your own?"

"No, I don't." Spence looked from Rachel to Paul. "Is that a problem?"

"No, not at all," Paul answered. "Placement decisions are based on a number of factors. And we certainly want to place Katie with a relative, and as soon as possible."

"Then we have a common goal," Spence stated, a faint smile easing his expression for the first time in their discussion.

But Rachel wondered if he really knew what he was getting himself into. "What helped you decide for Katie to live with you rather than your mother?"

"My mother has some health problems that are limiting for her," he answered more easily than she'd expected. "I'm in good health and willing to provide for my niece."

Rachel studied his face. Two days wasn't much time to make such a significant life decision, and he didn't strike her as an impulsive man. Still, he hadn't even met Katie. He was just full of surprises, wasn't he? she thought with a touch of dry humor.

Paul cleared his throat and darted a look in Rachel's direction. She returned his glance blandly. She suspected Paul's conservative ideals were a little shaken up by Spence Garrett's proposition. As far as she was concerned, departmental procedures would allow her to evaluate the judge's suitability very closely. She would make certain of it.

Paul pursed his mouth reflectively, then cocked his eyebrows in a concessionary expression. "In that case, we'll work with you in every way we can."

Spence shifted forward, resting his forearms on his thighs. "I assume we have to follow the usual procedure for adoption?" he questioned, looking from Paul to Rachel.

She didn't respond, deciding it would be better if he heard it from her supervisor as a way of backing up her position.

Paul seemed to have read her move and eased back in his chair. "We'll do an adoptive home study to gather the information we need. That will include interviews with you, medical and financial information, and so on. You obviously know the basics, but Ms. Moran can go over the process with you in more detail later. There will also be a review period prior to finalizing the decision. We want to help you make certain adoption is what you really want."

"It's what I want," Spence replied with no hesitation, not seeming the least resistant to Paul's outline of the study.

"Ms. Moran will be your caseworker, as she is the most familiar with your niece." Paul glanced at his watch. "Now, if you'll both excuse me, I have a lunch meeting I need to get to," he finished, pushing back from his chair.

Rachel and Spence arose simultaneously. She turned to him. "If you'll come with me, we can set up a time to talk that's convenient for you." She found her lips curving into a smile, mirroring the one touching Spence's lips as he looked down at her.

"Certainly." As they walked toward the door, he reached around her and opened it for her in a courteous gesture.

Rachel was acutely aware of his nearness, of the spicy, inviting scent of his cologne, of the warmth emanating from his body. His arm brushed lightly against her shoulders, sending a tingle of warmth down her spine. She stepped quickly through the doorway, away from him, feeling disconcerted.

Spence didn't seem to notice her hasty movement, having stopped to shake Paul's hand before following her. It annoyed her to no end that this man, who was exactly what she couldn't stand in men, and whose case she now handled, could affect her so easily. *Just ignore it*, she told herself. Even as she thought it, she knew the command was about as effective as a paper umbrella in the rain.

Rachel led the way to her office, walking at a brisker pace than usual. Neither of them spoke until they stood at her desk.

She opened her appointment book and turned to face him, leaning her hips against the edge of the desk. "When would be a good time for you?"

Spence considered a moment before answering. Rachel found it difficult to ignore how handsome he was, in spite of herself. She dropped her glance and pretended to study her appointment book.

"I have to be back in court for the rest of the afternoon. What about first thing in the morning, say about eight o'clock?"

"That's fine," Rachel replied, making a note in her book, although she doubted she could possibly forget. Glancing up, she added, "I talked with Katie and her foster parents yesterday to let them know we'd found you, or rather, you'd found us. I wanted to give her a chance to adjust to the idea."

His eyes shadowed in thought, and when he spoke, his voice was unexpectedly quiet. "How is she?"

Rachel felt her hard line of resistance to him softening at the concern in his expression. "Death is so difficult for children to comprehend. Katie's at an age when kids begin to understand that it's irreversible. But sometimes they hold on to the hope that their mother or dad or whoever died can somehow come back. I think she's doing as well as can be expected."

"Does she talk much about the accident or Julia and Sam?"

"Not really. As far as we know, she doesn't have a conscious recollection of the accident. But she does have terrible nightmares. Fortunately, she rarely remembers them the next morning."

Spence drew a deep breath. "Is she going to be all right?"

He looked so uncertain, Rachel felt her heart melt a little. She gave him a gentle, reassuring smile. "Yes. She has a lot of fears to work through. I know she's afraid that either I or her foster parents may die and leave her. It's simply going to take some time. It's not something that can be pushed."

Spence blinked as though he had something in his eyes and he rubbed a hand over them. "When can I meet her?" His voice sounded rougher than before.

"When would be good for you?"

"After five in the evenings, unless it's a problem for you. Or I can take a day off."

"No, I can arrange an evening if that's best. What about Thursday, day after tomorrow, after you're through with work?" Rachel suggested. She wondered if she detected uncertainty in his eyes and added, "That is, if you don't already have something planned."

"No, that's fine."

"We can meet here around five-thirty and drive over to her foster home. Usually we arrange a neutral place away from the foster home, but in this situation, I think it would be more comfortable for Katie if we met there." Rachel studied the tightened lines of his face. Something was bothering him. "Unless you have some reservations about that."

"No, I'll be here." Spence paused, smoothing his tie unnecessarily, then shoved his hands into his pants pockets. "Is there anything special I should know or do when I meet her? Something I can do to help her?" he asked, looking suddenly lost.

Rachel felt her heart melt a little bit more at the uncertainty in his expression. "Katie needs someone to love her, as her parents did. That's the best thing anyone can do to help her," she answered, her voice soft with sympathy.

Spence stood in silent thought for a few seconds, then looked at Rachel with an openness that unsettled her. "Rachel," he began, then glanced away briefly. He looked back at her. "May I call you Rachel?" At her slight nod, he continued. "I intend to rely on your expertise. Whatever you think is best for Katie, I'm willing to listen."

Surprise slid through her. She hadn't expected him to make this concession so easily, and she suspected it was a difficult one for him to make. She decided her being straightforward would be best. "Our program is child-focused. I'm glad you feel the same. Otherwise it would have been difficult for us to work together." She paused. "I wasn't sure how you felt."

"I was wrong," he told her. No excuses, no explanations, and she knew he meant what he said. It surprised her.

She smiled up into his eyes, relenting. "Then we'll start all over."

"I'd like that very much," he said. His answering smile wasn't a practiced one, but one that was meant for her and her alone. It sent a soft, warm glow through her that touched something deep within. "I'll see you in the morning." And then he was walking out of the room.

Rachel's shoulders slumped. It was as if his smile and the warmth in his eyes had held her spellbound. And now, as she stared at the empty doorway, the spell was broken, leaving her breathless and even a little disappointed.

In a helpless whisper, she asked herself, "What is the matter with me?" knowing there was no good answer. No rational answer, except that he was an attractive man. She knew enough about him to realize she should keep her distance emotionally, which she'd need to do anyway as his caseworker. But she didn't really know *him*. So why was she acting this way?

Stress, she told herself. It was the only explanation she could think of to account for her weakness to the man.

You can't afford to lose your objectivity. There were too many unanswered questions. Why had he acquiesced to the home study so easily? To keep her focus away from his mother? Or had he finally come to his senses and realized he was in over his head? Realized he needed her help? For Katie's sake, she hoped that was the case.

He could be very charming, very compelling with women, she knew. Especially with that smile and those blue eyes.

Irritation burned in her chest. Of course. He needed her. And he knew it. And he didn't like it. So maybe he was resorting to something he was good at—charming women—to get through the process with as much control as he could. At least he hadn't resorted to calling in markers to try to get the case pulled out of welfare. She had to give him credit for that.

Well, as long as he's willing to be civilized about it, let him be charming. I know the score.

Her stomach growled. She glanced at the clock. She could squeeze in lunch if she hurried. The afternoon still stretched before her and she had a lot of work to get done before her visit to Katie. She would think about Judge Garrett later.

Rachel wondered what she would do without Louis and Mary Edwards. She parked her car in front of their modest, bungalow-style home, located in a tidy, family-centered neighborhood. Their own children grown, the Edwards filled their nest with foster children.

The front door swung open. A small girl, her blond hair pulled into a ponytail with a pink ribbon, stepped onto the porch.

Rachel smiled and waved. "Hi, Katie."

"Hi, Miss Rachel." Katie held the door open for her with one hand, clutching a plump teddy bear with the other. A tiny smile sparkled in her blue eyes.

Rachel stepped into the foyer and closed the door behind her. The homey smell of something sweet baking made her mouth water. "Mmm, something smells good," she said, kneeling to give Katie a hug.

"We're baking chocolate chip cookies."

Rachel rocked back on her heels to look at her. "Well, I'll bet they taste as good as they smell. And how are you?"

Katie shrugged, her gaze fixed on the floor. "Okay."

"Okay?" Rachel gave the teddy bear's arm a squeeze. "How's Bitsy?"

Somberness shadowed Katie's face, her eyes darkening. "She had a bad dream last night. It woke me up."

Mary Edwards came up a few feet behind the little girl, wiping flour from her hands with her apron. She exchanged a telling glance with Rachel. The bear was a cherished gift from Rachel. What few nightmares Katie remembered, she sometimes talked about through the bear.

"She did? Did she tell you what was scary?" Rachel probed in a gentle tone.

Katie clamped her mouth shut and answered with a vigorous shaking of her head, her eyes downcast. "Would you like one of our chocolate chip cookies?" she asked instead, changing the subject.

"Thanks, that sounds good," Rachel said, smiling for Katie's benefit. She pushed herself up to stand. She knew Katie tried to bury her feelings where they couldn't hurt her, but they came out in her dreams. And Rachel knew how much it could hurt.

Mary stepped forward and ushered Katie and Rachel into her bright, cheerful kitchen, always redolent of lemon-scented cleaner and something tasty in the oven. In minutes the three of them sat at the table with a plate of cookies, a glass of milk for Katie, and cups of coffee for Rachel and Mary.

Rachel kept the conversation light and about nothing in particular at first, then steered the topic to the reason for her visit. "There's someone I'd like you to meet, Katie. Remember I told you yesterday you have an Uncle Spence?"

Katie nodded but she looked uncertain. "My mama's brother," she said, hesitating.

"That's right, your mom's brother. He'd like to meet you, too."

Katie fidgeted in her seat. "Okay, I guess."

"I'll be there, too," Rachel said, trying to reassure her.

The fidgeting stopped and relief brightened Katie's eyes. "You will?"

"Definitely. Day after tomorrow, your Uncle Spence and I will come over here and pick you up. We can get hamburgers for supper."

"Can we get hot dogs, instead?" Katie's insecurity began to subside somewhat, her interest growing.

"Sure."

"And go to the park for a picnic and then roller-skating?" Katie added, her cheeks dimpling in a small smile, her eyes beginning to sparkle.

Rachel laughed, holding up her hand. "I'm afraid we won't have time for all that on the first visit."

Katie's features clustered in a look of mild disappointment but she conceded the point. "All right."

"We'll probably be by no later than six o'clock," Rachel continued, looking from Katie to Mary Edwards.

When it came time for Rachel to leave, Katie followed her to the door. "Miss Rachel?"

Rachel looked down into the child's wistful, worried eyes. "Yes, honey?"

"Do you promise to come back?"

It was the question Katie asked her at the end of every visit. Rachel had never gotten used to hearing it. The worry and hurt in the little girl's eyes brought a lump to her throat. She reached out a hand to smooth Katie's hair. "I promise," she said, but she could see the vague doubt shrouding Katie's eyes. "I'll see you the day after tomorrow."

The child's haunted look followed Rachel after she'd left. She'd seen it so many times before, in so many little faces. She hoped that someday, for Katie, at least, it would be gone. And at this point, that was largely up to Spence Garrett.

Chapter Four

It was a quarter to seven that evening when Rachel pulled into the shaded driveway of her 1930s-era, red-brick duplex. The neighborhood was a peaceful one in an older part of River Plains. She had chosen it for its charm and because the rent was unbelievably reasonable. Her elderly landlady had a kind heart and no financial worries, and enjoyed renting to people who lived quietly as she did. Rachel met that requirement, and her downstairs neighbor was a chemistry major at River Plains University who never seemed to see the light of day. The cheaper rent enabled Rachel to lease additional office space downtown with another social worker in private practice.

Rachel carried a sack of groceries up the concrete steps to the screened-in porch of her front door. She let the screen door bang shut behind her. The grocery sack slid to rest beside her feet as she fumbled with the keys to the inner door.

The locks were in a shabby state of repair. The dead bolt could be unlocked by almost any small key. Rachel reminded herself for the hundredth time to get the lock replaced. She would simply have to make the time to get it done. One of these days, she promised herself.

Inside, she faced the steep, narrow stairway leading up to the second floor that comprised her apartment. The wooden steps creaked in complaint of her every footstep. "I know just how you feel," she confided to the stairwell, lugging herself and the groceries along.

The door at the top opened into the kitchen. Her large, orange, tiger-striped cat slipped out to rub against her ankles. Rachel gingerly sidestepped him to set the groceries on the kitchen counter.

She knelt to ruffle the fur on his head. "How was your day, Simon? Pretty good, I would think. You don't have to fool with arrogant judges or much of anything else, do you?"

She straightened and moved to a cabinet to get a can of his food. "No, all you have to worry about is where to sleep and when to eat. You've got it made, bud."

Simon meowed as she opened the can of food and spooned it into his bowl. That taken care of, Rachel put the groceries away and headed for her bedroom to change her clothes.

With daylight saving time in effect, sunlight still streamed in through the long windows in the living room, casting golden pools of light onto the polished hardwood floor. As threadbare as it was, the apartment still held an air of elegance with its high ceilings, fine woodwork and its original ornate fixtures, including a chandelier in the dining room. The plumbing was sometimes

unreliable and there was no air conditioning for the
summer months. But, furnished with the collection of
antiques she'd painstakingly acquired over the years from
estate auctions, garage sales and flea markets, it was
home.

Rachel changed into a pair of white drawstring shorts,
a sweatshirt, socks and well-worn sneakers. She needed
the therapy of a walk tonight. It always helped her to
clear her mind, and she felt restless.

The change of seasons from winter to spring had left
the early-evening air still briskly cool, perfect for exer-
cising. Rachel stretched her legs into a long stride, letting her arms swing at her sides in motion with her pace,
working the tension out of her body. By the time she had
covered five blocks' distance, she had to admit to herself
that the cause of her restlessness was Spence Garrett. His
face, his eyes, his smile, seemed to intrude into her every
thought.

Of all people.

There was no reason for this...this interest she held in
him. And there was every reason in the world for caution. She didn't need another Hugh Mitchell in her life.

Rachel always felt a renewed sense of foolishness when
she thought of her years with Hugh. *Gullible* and *naive*
were the two words that could best describe her then.
Hugh had been ambitious, decidedly handsome and financially struggling. He'd charmed his way into her life.
He'd loved her, he said, because of her exquisite sensi-
tivity, caring and understanding. He'd talked often of law
school, but money was tight. So she'd helped him fi-
nance his tuition and his living expenses. She'd helped
him through the ups and downs and stresses of law
school.

Looking back, Rachel realized that Hugh's need for her help was probably what had brought them together. Oh, she hadn't seen it at the time. He'd made her feel needed and loved. That is, until he didn't need her anymore.

The change had been subtle, beginning around the time Hugh took the position at the law firm. He'd gradually shut her out. Then at the firm's New Year's party, Rachel had watched him find excuses to avoid her, watched him seeking out Sandra Brinkley. A month later, Hugh had married Sandra, securing his position with River Plains's elite. Which is what he'd really wanted all along. And he didn't need Rachel for that.

Rachel had long spent her tears over him. Now she only felt angry with herself for letting herself be duped. Mostly she felt grateful he was out of her life.

So what was it about Spence Garrett? So he was a good-looking, sexy man. So what? She'd been around a lot of good-looking, sexy men, but they didn't have this effect on her. Rachel lengthened her stride, trying to work off the annoying tension that tingled through every fiber of her being. Spence Garrett was imperious and arrogant and he was a part of a life she no longer belonged to, nor had any desire to return to.

Perspiration dampened her forehead and the neck of her sweatshirt, cooling her skin. She pressed forward vigorously over the sidewalk. Maybe it was because she'd been celibate for nearly two years. Maybe it was because he needed her help. Oh, that was just great. Just what she needed. Another man who needed her help.

"How can you be such an idiot?" she snapped at herself. There was no place in her life for such feelings, not under these circumstances and certainly not with a man like the judge.

Maybe it was the stress of changing jobs. Maybe it was just him. Maybe it didn't matter. It would pass.

An hour and a half later, after a warm shower and dinner, Rachel stretched out on top of the blue floral comforter on her bed, Simon curled up beside her. She tried to lose herself in the latest bestseller.

The evening breeze fluttered the curtains over the open window and ruffled through the pages of her book, stealing away the chapter she was reading. But she didn't really notice or care. Her mind was on the judge with the entrancing smile and brilliant blue eyes, a man she would never find in a thousand novels, a man a thousand times more compelling because he was real.

The next morning, Rachel arrived at work thirty minutes early. She wanted to have time to relax and prepare for her interview with Spence.

She pulled open the curtains behind her desk. Pink and pale gold wisps of clouds streaked the blueing sky. Concrete crisscrossings of highway bridged the view of the Arkansas River from her downtown office building. The river stretched and curled like a wide, lazy banner through the green, rolling plains that edged the city. Oil wells dotted the landscape across the river, some pumping slowly up and down like black iron seesaws, others dormant and spent.

What was it she'd heard about Spence's family and oil? Something to the effect that Frank Garrett could have owned his own oil company had he so chosen. She'd also heard the scuttlebutt that Spence could subsist very comfortably on family money alone.

Anticipation filled her chest. If she were completely honest, she would have to admit to a twinge of nervousness at the prospect of this interview with Spence.

"Good morning."

Rachel started at the sound of Spence's resonant voice behind her. She pivoted to see him standing in the doorway. Her hand fluttered to her throat and she took a steadying breath. "You startled me. I didn't hear you come in." She wondered how long he had been standing there.

"I didn't mean to scare you. The entrance was unlocked so I came on in." He sounded mildly contrite, but the teasing glint in his eyes contradicted him.

"No, that's all right. I just didn't expect you so soon."

"If I'm too early, I can wait in the lobby," he offered with a glance toward the door.

"No, we can start now, if you want. Have a seat," Rachel replied equably. She couldn't help but return the easy smile crinkling the corners of Spence's eyes.

"Thanks," he said, moving into the office.

"Would you like a cup of coffee before we begin?"

"If you're already planning to get some." He sat in the same chair as he had the morning of their first meeting. He stretched his legs out in front of him and crossed them casually at the ankles.

Rachel realized this was the first time she had seen him without a jacket, with nothing to conceal the angular lines of his build. His navy-blue polo shirt defined a solid, broad chest, and tapered to a trim girth. Tan trousers emphasized strong thighs and very sexy hips. He was an undeniably great-looking man.

So what? You're his caseworker, for crying out loud. Go get the damned coffee. "Do you take anything with it?" she asked politely.

"No, thanks."

Rachel excused herself. *Better get it together, Moran.* She thought she'd convinced herself the night before. He was going to have to prove himself, for Katie's sake. And she wasn't going to let him sway her with his charm. But the way he looked at her, the blue of his eyes deeper with a smoky warmth she didn't remember from their previous meetings . . . the way his smile seemed to wrap itself around her . . . Ignoring him was going to be harder than she thought.

Spence watched Rachel's departure. He smiled to himself, thinking of the alluring picture she'd made standing at an angle in front of the window, lost in thought, completely unaware of him.

It had been impossible for him not to notice the appealing curve of her hips outlined by white slacks. Or the swell of her breasts beneath her loose-fitting jade sweater. Or the way her slender waist looked as if he could easily span it with both hands and touch at his fingertips.

Her dark brown hair was nearly black and had the rich, silken look of hair a man could tangle his fingers in. And he liked her smile. It made her sparkle with a warmth that stirred him. But it was the spark of sensuality that fairly crackled between them in her unguarded moments that interested him the most. He could tell it still annoyed her. He wondered if she was involved with anyone.

He looked at the framed diplomas and certificates hanging on the wall behind her desk. A bachelor's degree in psychology from the University of Arkansas, a master's degree in social work from the University of Oklahoma, her Oklahoma license, her national certification—all solid, impressive credentials.

Smart and sexy. A powerful combination in a woman.

Spence rubbed a hand across his face and chuckled at himself. If anyone had predicted he would ever be assigned a welfare social worker, much less one so attractive to him, he would have laughed in his face.

In his courtroom, she was always very professional, very composed and always prepared. That impressed him. He wasn't otherwise impressed with social workers, therapists and the like. He knew some of the attorneys deliberately tried to ruffle her at times, but they were never successful. She never lingered at the courthouse or got involved with the legal professionals in the community. He wondered if Hugh Mitchell was the reason for that.

He wasn't sure what to think of Rachel. He'd wondered about her since he'd first met her. Idle curiosity, he supposed. She had certainly never encouraged him to get to know her. But she ran hot and cold, one minute warm, gentle, alluring, and the next minute cool, tough, reserved.

His mood sobered. And he needed her. As much as he wanted to keep her out of his family's private business, he needed her help with the most terrifying decision he had ever made in his life. He didn't like having to rely on a social worker for help. But for the first time he could remember, he didn't know where else to begin.

Rachel came back with two cups of coffee. "I hope you don't mind instant, Judge Garrett," she said, handing him a cup.

"Not at all." He took the cup from her and watched her sit down across from him. "Rachel, I think we can drop the formalities, considering I'm here to open up my life for your investigation."

Rachel looked at him for a moment, trying to decide if he was making fun of her. Not that it mattered. But if he didn't care, then fine. She simply wasn't going to be the one to set a casual mood. "Okay, Spence," she replied, her tone pleasant but neutral. She pulled the clipboard with her interview outline from her desk. "First off, I'll need to get some basic information from you."

Spence didn't seem the least put off by her practiced neutrality. He answered her questions readily. His full name was John Spencer Garrett. Despite herself, Rachel liked the way it sounded, strong and gentle all at once. His birth date told her he was thirty-six years old. He was probably one of the youngest judges she'd ever worked with.

His address was in a rural area outside River Plains. "I'll probably need a map to find my way to your home," Rachel commented, writing down the information.

"Sure. I'd enjoy having you to my home." His tone was unmistakably suggestive.

Rachel glanced up at him and lifted an eyebrow. How quickly he assumed she would be interested in something personal between them. She felt like asking him if he was always this conceited when it came to women. "It's a routine part of the adoptive study," she told him, her tone benign.

Spence just smiled at her reply.

Conceited and a smart aleck. "How long have you been associate district judge?" she asked smoothly, returning his smile. She wasn't going to let him sidetrack the interview.

"A year and a half. Two years this coming autumn."

She remembered now the circle's celebration of Spence's election. A bash held at Arnold Brinkley's very large, very elegant home in the very expensive Osage Hills area of the city. She'd gone, at Hugh's beckoning.

Thinking along the same lines, Spence added, "I remember seeing you at the election party. Did you vote for me or did you just come with your date?"

"I'm surprised you would remember. There were a lot of people there that night," she said, ignoring the teasing light in his eyes. She remembered. As always, their eyes had met in brief acknowledgment of each other, leaving her with that sense of physical connection.

Spence remembered, all right. She'd congratulated him in her polite way and moved on in the crowd. She'd worn a sleek red dress that showed fit, sexy, feminine curves. But it wasn't her dress that made him remember her. A lot of the women had worn sexy cocktail dresses. It was that physical tension between them that set her apart, and the fact that she didn't play it up with him. And the fact that Hugh never really talked about her to his colleagues. It had made Rachel something of a mystery to Spence.

"I have a good memory," he simply said.

"Do you enjoy your work?"

"Very much. And you?"

"For the most part," Rachel replied, not looking up from her notes.

"But there are problems with any job," Spence supplied for her.

Rachel looked at him. This interview wasn't to talk about her. It was to talk about him. And he was adept at avoiding that. "Sure there are. In fact, I think there are some similarities between your work as a judge and mine as a social worker."

Spence looked skeptical. "How do you figure that?"

"We both gather information to get to the truth of a problem. You have the law for your guideline, I have principles of social work for mine. Any mistake in judgment could be devastating to someone's life." Rachel was surprised to see an appreciative light flicker in Spence's eyes.

"Have you ever made such an error in judgment?" he asked in faint challenge.

"No, I haven't. Have you?"

"I've never had a decision overturned."

"But were you right?"

Spence's eyes narrowed in thought. "Within the law, yes. My decisions have to be based on concrete, provable facts, not on intuition or what 'feels' best."

"You don't believe in intuition?"

"I'm not saying I don't believe in it. But I think it can sometimes come from prejudice or insufficient evidence instead of the truth." He took a swallow of coffee, his expression unrevealing.

"That's an interesting theory." He clearly realized she had intuitive doubts about him, about his family, and he was trying to make a point. *Show me there's no reason to worry, Garrett,* she told him silently. "I imagine your work demands long hours," she continued, refocusing the conversation.

Spence set his cup on an end table and leaned back into the chair, letting his elbows rest on the arms. "Yes, it can."

"How do you plan to coordinate working full-time with providing daycare for Katie when she's not in school?"

"I want to avoid using a day-care center. I want someone who can give Katie the kind of attention her mother would have given her instead of allowing her to get lost in a group of twenty other children."

"You're planning to hire a nanny?"

"I thought that would be the most practical. My hours are sometimes unpredictable."

Rachel thought of some of the single mothers and fathers she worked with and of their struggle to balance working with the needs of their children. They struggled to simply get by. Yet she felt much more certain of their motives than his.

"Is there a problem with that?" Spence's voice cut into her thoughts.

Realizing her silence was ill-placed, Rachel gave him a quick smile. "No, not at all. I think it's fortunate you have the financial resources to provide that kind of care."

"I agree."

"How do you feel about becoming a ready-made father?"

"It scares the hell out of me."

His blunt honesty surprised Rachel, and unexpectedly touched her heart. "I can understand that. You haven't had much time to prepare for a child. Most expectant fathers have at least nine months to adjust to the notion," she said softly, a smile in her voice.

Spence chuckled. "I don't know the first thing about it." He shook his head in self-wonderment and his voice grew a bit rougher. "I wonder what kind of father figure I'll make, what kind of mistakes I'll make.... I don't even have the experience of having simply been an uncle."

A shadow of pain dimmed the gray flecks in his eyes. Rachel shifted forward, listening.

Spence cleared his throat, thinking of lost chances, lost hopes. "Like you said yesterday, loving her will be the best thing I can do for her."

His voice tightened with an emotion Rachel couldn't quite identify. Guilt, maybe? "Spence, loving her may or may not be as automatic as you would want it to be," she observed gently.

Spence frowned, then shook his head. "Katie is Julia's daughter, my niece." He hesitated, uncertain how to put his feelings into words. "That fact alone makes her a part of me."

Rachel sensed something in him that made her believe he was truly capable of loving a child he had never met. Maybe he needed someone to love....

"What's your next question?" he asked abruptly, ready to get on with it.

Rachel moved on, respecting his need for distance from his sadness over Julia. She hoped he wouldn't consider her next questions too intrusive. "You mentioned your mother has some health problems. How is she doing?"

Was that hesitation in his eyes? She couldn't really tell. But he answered her question smoothly. "As well as can be expected. She has some problems with arthritis. I didn't think she'd have the stamina to manage a five-year-old. That's one reason I decided to adopt Katie. But I do want Katie to spend time with her grandmother, get to know her."

"I agree. That will give Katie a stronger sense of family," Rachel said. She paused, then said, "You mentioned you were divorced. Could you tell me a little about what happened?"

Spence settled back into his chair and told her about Diane, his college years, his work. He skirted any specifics concerning the problems between his sister and parents. There were so many questions Rachel wanted to ask, but she didn't, not just yet. A comfortable aura was beginning to settle around them and she didn't want to break its fragile web.

She detected only a ghost of bitterness in his feelings about his wife. And she wondered if she just imagined in him the longing to love someone again. The same longings that pulled at her from deep within, feelings she hadn't acknowledged in years....

Rachel lowered her eyes, making herself concentrate on the interview instead of such incongruous thoughts. "How do you see your life-style changing with the addition of a five-year-old?"

"For one thing, my time will be more restricted." Spence's lips twitched in enigmatic self-amusement. "I'll have less personal time, but I don't mind that."

"Do you plan to remarry in the near future?"

At Spence's quizzical expression, Rachel wished she'd been a little more discreet in the asking. "Any change in the prospective household has to be considered. Something as significant as marriage would be another stress for Katie to deal with, and we simply want to help her adjust as well as possible."

"I don't mind your question, Rachel. This is all new to me. I've never adopted a child before. And to answer your question, I have been seeing a woman on a fairly regular basis, but we don't have any plans for marriage."

Rachel felt an absurd stab of disappointment. Of course he was seeing someone. When had he ever not been? And what difference did it make? It was irrelevant to her personally. "How do you think adopting Katie will affect your personal relationships?"

"That's partly what I meant when I said my time will be more restricted. And..." Spence paused, searching for the appropriate words, a half smile playing at his lips. "Discretion will be extremely important."

It took a second for the meaning of his words to sink in. Rachel watched his eyes drop to linger on her lips for a fraction of a moment, feeling her skin grow warm at the touch of his candidly sexual gaze. He looked back up into her eyes with unsettling directness.

An image of Spence kissing her, an urgent, demanding kiss, flashed into her mind, sending a flush through her body, making her achingly aware of his sexuality, and worse, her own.

It wasn't as though a man had never discussed his relationships with her before. "I know that's an issue all single parents are faced with," Rachel replied coolly.

Spence's smile deepened. "I didn't mean to embarrass you, Rachel."

I'll bet. "You didn't," she lied. Convincingly, she thought.

"I'm not going to pretend to take a vow of celibacy simply because I plan to adopt my niece."

"And I wouldn't expect you to. But I appreciate your being honest about it."

"I intended to be."

"What are your thoughts on schooling for Katie?" Rachel ignored the teasing twinkle in Spence's eyes at her change of topic.

But he seemed to consider her question with as much seriousness as he had all the others. "I think a private school. She'd get the personal attention she needed, and a good education."

Katie wouldn't lack for anything material with Spence, Rachel thought. It was emotional nurturance and a safe home that concerned her the most.

Rachel skimmed her outline. "I think I have most of the information I need for now."

"What else will you need?"

"A statement of your financial status, a medical examination report and six personal references," she listed. "Also, we'll need to run a background check on you," she added, thumbing through her notes.

Spence suddenly began to laugh, a rich resonant sound that pulled a cautious smile from Rachel.

"What's so funny?" she asked with faint suspicion.

He shook his head, still chuckling. "You don't cut any slack, do you?"

"I beg your pardon?"

"I'm a judge, Rachel. I wouldn't be allowed to practice law in any form if I had a criminal record of any kind."

"We do background checks on everyone, without exception. Even on judges," she retorted mildly, but she felt a smile tugging at her lips as she considered how it must sound from his perspective.

He rubbed a hand across his face to stifle another wave of chuckles, then grinned at her. "You play strictly by the rules, don't you?"

"I guess you could say I don't take any chances where children are concerned."

Spence looked at her with that disturbing intensity that made her feel weak inside. "I'm thankful Katie has you," he said, his voice suddenly very gentle.

Rachel swallowed, her throat unexpectedly dry. "Thank you. She's very special to me."

"I realize that."

She stood, feeling suddenly awkward, hugging the clipboard to her chest like armor. "I'll be supervising your visits outside Katie's foster home until you get comfortable with each other. Unless you have any questions for me, I think we're finished for this morning."

Spence got to his feet, looking distracted himself. "I'll be here tomorrow, no later than five-thirty." He turned abruptly and left her office.

Rachel dropped the clipboard onto the desk. She sighed and massaged her temples with her fingertips. She could not keep letting Spence get to her. It was all a game to him, she knew. A game with high stakes, though. The welfare of a little girl.

Within the secluded chambers of the Adams County Courthouse in downtown River Plains, Spence pulled on the black robe that was the hallmark of his judicial position. But his thoughts were on the woman to whom he was cautiously opening his life, and on the little girl who would change it. As long as he could balance the family's privacy with what Rachel needed to know, he felt sure he could make the adoption work. Jacqueline would just have to swallow some of her snobbish pride, and cut back on her drinking.

And there was Victoria. Somehow, he didn't think she would be too pleased with his decision, but it didn't really matter now. In fact, he hadn't thought much about Victoria at all in the past week. He felt a twinge of surprise at that realization.

This morning with Rachel, he had wondered what it would be like to hold her, to touch her, to kiss her. Even now, those thoughts sent a thread of desire through him. Spence took a deep breath.

What in the hell's wrong with you, Garrett? She's not even your type. That's what he'd told himself all along. But he was beginning to wonder just what his type was.

Maybe he was just losing his mind. This had to be about the most difficult circumstance he'd ever faced. He knew she didn't trust him, and he wasn't sure how much he could trust her.

Making such an impulsive decision had been unlike him, but he had no regrets. He owed it to Julia, to his niece, to himself. His family's problems had guided Katie's destiny and he would accept responsibility for it now.

Spence checked the afternoon docket. With any luck, he would be finished by six o'clock. He had an important meeting to keep with an interior decorator, one with a knack for designing little girls' rooms.

Chapter Five

"Court is recessed until nine o'clock tomorrow morning." Judge Spencer Garrett brought down his gavel.

"All rise," the bailiff intoned.

The sound of movement in unison rustled through the courtroom as spectators and participants arose and Spence strode out. Beneath his robe he wore blue jeans and a blue striped oxford cloth shirt. Only the pressed collar and cuffs of his shirt and the polished black tips of his shoes were visible. He had dressed in anticipation of his meeting with Katie and had decided the more casual the better.

In the privacy of his chambers, Spence took off his robe and sat down at his desk to change shoes. He didn't want to be late. He'd cut proceedings short as it was, considering his reputation for hearing cases late into the night. The Department of Human Services was about five blocks from the courthouse, but he had planned a stop at the florist's before the shop closed.

He had to admit to himself he was actually a little nervous about meeting Katie. No, he was more than a little nervous.

What did you say to a five-year-old child who had lost both her parents? What if she didn't even like him? His palms dampened as he mulled over the possibilities. Thank God, Rachel would be there, he thought. She would make their meeting easier, more comfortable.

He finished tying the laces of his tennis shoes and thrust the pair of dress shoes into the athletic bag he'd brought with him. Still, the doubts intruded. Was he really doing the right thing? Could he really handle the responsibility of raising a child—alone?

This was ludicrous. He had never felt incapable of anything in his life. Yet, facing his niece intimidated the hell out of him. He would need a lot of time to get to know her. And time couldn't be tighter with the beginning of jury docket and his working toward a state supreme court appointment.

He'd been plagued by these questions all weekend, but he always came full circle, back to his original decision. There was no one else for Katie. Except for himself... and a very stubborn, very insightful, welfare social worker.

A myriad of emotions constricted his chest—anger, sadness, guilt. He was angry with Julia for rejecting his efforts to help. But he knew in some ways he had allowed her to drift away as much as she had chosen to leave. He regretted not intervening sooner. Maybe things would have been different. But he hadn't.

Now he was about to come face-to-face with the reality of a small child who desperately needed the security of a home. And when he thought of it, maybe he needed her as much as she needed him.

Rachel waited inside the foyer of her office building, watching the traffic through the glass doors. The office was nearly empty and the silence felt peaceful after a harried day. She slipped her hands into the pockets of her flax linen trousers and leaned against the metal press bar of the door. The long-sleeved, indigo cotton sweater she wore would be warm enough for the cool evening air, but not too warm. She watched the passing cars, waiting for the one that would bring Spence.

Let's see how the judge does in unfamiliar territory. Rachel wondered again if he really knew what he was getting himself into. She sincerely doubted it.

This meeting was a critical point for both Spence and Katie. For Rachel, spending time with them together would help her learn about Spence. And her curiosity about the man was growing. Professional curiosity, of course.

A slow-moving, nondescript gray sedan nearing the office caught Rachel's eye. She tensed in anticipation. Her anticipation faded when she realized the driver was a dark-haired plumpish man she didn't recognize. For an instant, the man seemed to look her way, but before she could see his face clearly, the car accelerated and sped down the hill. Unease prickled the back of Rachel's neck.

Before she could give it another thought, a sleek black sports car slowed at the entrance to the parking lot. A flash of sunlight danced off the polished chrome as the car turned in toward her. It had that understated look of affluence, unpretentious but unquestionably rich. And she knew who the driver must be.

Rachel stepped out of the building into the sun, the wind gusting around her. Spence climbed out of the car to wait for her. Rachel couldn't help but smile at the contrast he made against the car. He looked so boyishly casual standing there with both hands thrust in his jeans pockets, the wind tousling his blond hair.

"Hello," she said, lifting a hand to smooth a stray wisp of hair into the French braid at the back of her neck.

"Hello." He returned her smile.

A twinge of unaccountable shyness seized her. She looked away, nodding toward the employee parking lot. "My car's over there."

"Why don't we take mine?" Spence suggested. "So I can show you how safe a driver I am," he added with a grin.

"Good point." She returned his grin, the shyness lifting.

Spence rounded the front of the car to open the passenger-side door for her.

"Thank you," Rachel said, getting in. How nice to be treated so courteously, she thought. It made her feel very...feminine. And that felt very nice.

She couldn't resist running a hand over the supple, cream-colored leather upholstery. The masculine scent of the car, the leather and musk, made her think of the man with her.

Spence slid in behind the steering wheel. Rachel was suddenly very aware of the intimacy of the car, even as spacious as it was. Warmth tingled through her. She focused her attention out the windshield, hating this edge of excitement he made her feel...and being drawn to it all the same.

Spence fastened his seat belt. "How do we get there?"

His question brought Rachel's attention around. She relaxed. Business. She gave him the directions to Katie's foster home.

"Where would you suggest we take her for dinner?" he asked, turning the key in the ignition.

"The Pixie Dog."

"The Pixie Dog?" he echoed. He put the car into gear and pulled out into traffic. "I'm afraid I'll need directions for that, too," he admitted with a chuckle.

"Not your usual hot spot, I suppose. Katie loves hot dogs."

The strong lines of his jaw eased into a broad grin. "Just like her mother."

"Really?" That he spoke so easily of Julia surprised Rachel.

Spence nodded. "And she loved picnics, kites, stray puppies...stray animals of any kind. She couldn't stand to see any creature suffer. And she loved dancing. And gymnastics. She was really quite good at it...." His voice trailed off. "In some ways, you remind me of her," he said unexpectedly.

"Me? In what way?" Rachel now sounded as surprised as she felt.

"Your protectiveness of helpless creatures, the children who have no one else to care for them."

The husky softness of his tone touched her like a caress. The compliment pleased her more than she expected, more than it should. Why should it matter what he thought of her? This was her job. What was important was that he'd opened the subject of Julia. And she wanted to steer the topic away from herself. "What was Julia like?"

She held her breath for a few seconds of silence that stretched between them. Spence slowed the car to make a turn, then accelerated to the speed limit.

He took a breath, then let it out. "I think I knew the child Julia better than the young woman she grew up to be. I was in junior high school when she was born. By the time she was old enough to really take places and do things with, I was already in college."

He paused, thinking. "I remember when I would come home on holidays and semester breaks. She would follow me around, so excited to have her big brother home.... She was a beautiful little girl." Again the silence. "Then one day, during all those years apart, the little girl disappeared. She became an angry, bitter teenager...and I didn't know her anymore." His words faded into thought. A muscle tensed in his cheek.

Rachel sensed his pain, the chances lost during Julia's lifetime, chances lost forever. "What happened?" The question slipped out, her voice soft and tentative.

"I'm not sure."

She believed him. At least she believed that he didn't know exactly how it happened, that he had his own unanswered questions. "What would you have done differently if you'd had the chance?"

"Maybe made time for her." Irritation edged his words. He flexed his fingers around the steering wheel. "It's pointless to speculate, don't you think?"

It was more a statement than a question. Rachel shrugged. "Maybe. Maybe not. I guess I'm thinking it wasn't really your fault."

"Of course it wasn't all my fault. But that doesn't change the fact I wasn't there when she needed me."

His tone was sharper than he'd intended, but if Rachel noticed, she was undaunted. "Do you think Julia would have allowed you to help her?"

Spence took his eyes from the road long enough to give her a surprised look. "Why do you ask?"

"Just an impression. Sometimes angry people reject help from those closest to them."

Spence rubbed the back of his neck, feeling suddenly very uncomfortable, not wanting *her* coming in so close. "Rachel, you're a very bright woman, but you don't have to play counselor with me." He couldn't keep the hint of defensive sarcasm from his tone. He rarely discussed his personal problems outside the family. He wasn't sure he wanted to discuss them now. "What happened in the past is over. Talking about it doesn't change anything."

"Sometimes the past can help us understand what we need now. Maybe you're just not ready to talk about it."

"The past is completely irrelevant. What's important is Katie and what she needs." His tone told her to back off, to not breach this invisible line of privacy he so guarded.

"Spence, I'm your caseworker. That means I'm going to sometimes ask questions that may be difficult to answer, whether you like it or not. What and how you choose to answer is up to you," she replied with equal bluntness.

He didn't answer that.

She granted him his silence.

They made the rest of the drive with minimal conversation, except for Rachel's occasional directions.

At the Edwards' home, Spence parked the car along the curb in front of the house.

Rachel looked at him. "Ready?"

Spence took a deep breath and expelled it with his answer of yes, already opening his door and swinging both legs out.

Rachel fumbled with her seat belt. Before she could get out of the car, Spence was already there, extending a hand to help her. He grasped her hand, pulling her to stand with him. He even sort of smiled at her. A grim smile. *My, my,* she thought. *I do believe the judge is unsure of himself.* Apparently their disagreement was in a moment of cease-fire.

The front door to the house swung open. Mary and Louis Edwards stepped out onto the porch, Katie behind them. The little girl, dressed in blue jeans and a hooded pink sweatshirt, clutched a knapsack with her beloved bear poking out from the top.

Katie came down the steps to meet Rachel. At the sight of the tall man behind her caseworker, she hesitated, uncertainty clouding her eyes.

Rachel held her hand out. "Hi, Katie."

Katie didn't reply, but grasped Rachel's outstretched hand. In shyness, she hung back next to Rachel's legs, watching Spence from her stronghold.

Rachel knelt and gave her an encouraging smile. "Katie, this is your Uncle Spence."

Spence hunkered down, but didn't try to make any physical contact with his niece. The little girl's large blue eyes, Julia's eyes, were rounded in apprehension. A surge of emotion constricted his chest, and for a moment he wasn't sure he could speak. "Hello, Katie," he said, the words miraculously emerging.

Katie peered up from behind Rachel. "Hello," she replied politely, but she shied away from his smile and dropped her gaze to watch the toe of her tennis shoe scrape a crack in the sidewalk.

Spence gave the teddy bear's ear a tug. "Who's this?"

"Bitsy," Katie answered, switching toes.

"That sounds like a good name for a teddy bear." He smiled at her and asked, "What do you say we go get some hot dogs?"

It was then that Katie ventured a glance at him, her expression one of curiosity. She looked to Rachel and nodded in affirmation.

Rachel hugged her. "I think it will be fun."

Katie shrugged. "Okay, Miss Rachel." She didn't sound sure.

Rachel looked up at Spence and smiled encouragement to him as he straightened to stand. His returning smile looked almost... grateful.

She introduced Spence to Katie's foster parents, who had discreetly stayed on the porch.

Louis Edwards came down the stairs to shake Spence's hand. "Judge Garrett," he greeted him with a nod. "It's a real pleasure to meet you. It's a rare time Mary and I meet a family member of one of our foster kids. In Katie's case, it's a little different. If there's anything we can do to help, just let us know."

Rachel watched Spence's expression relax. Her heart felt warmed as it always did around the Edwardses, with their solid sense of values and family.

"We'll be a couple of hours. We'll have her back before dark," Rachel told them.

Spence buckled Katie into the front seat next to him at Rachel's instructions. The little girl looked at him directly for the first time and asked him, "How did you know I like hot dogs?"

Spence gave her an easy grin. "Rachel, uh, Miss Rachel told me." He paused, his expression growing tender.

"And I remember your mother liked hot dogs, too, when she was your age."

Katie continued to stare at him inquisitively, as though she saw something familiar in his eyes, something that made her want to be closer to him.

From her seat in the back of the car, Rachel saw the sheen of moisture in the corner of Spence's eye as he looked down at Katie. And she saw the need in both their expressions, the need to find out how they belonged together. She couldn't miss the uncertainty, either.

Spence cleared his throat and started the car.

Katie, with the unfettered curiosity of childhood, tugged open the console lid between her and her uncle. "You have a phone in your car!" she informed Spence, her eyes wide with fascination, her shyness lifting. She inspected it. "It isn't plugged in. How does it work?"

Rachel listened to Spence try to explain his cellular phone in a five-year-old's language. He moved on to questions about kindergarten and summertime fun. He did pretty well, Rachel thought. It was a beginning.

Spence detoured into the parking lot of a general merchandise store. "Hold on for about ten minutes. I'll be right back," he told them with a secretive glint in his eyes. He returned shortly with an elongated object wrapped in a brown paper sack.

Katie eyed it quizzically. "What is it?"

"A surprise for after we eat," Spence replied, smiling down at the little girl's upturned face.

The drive-in restaurant was easy to spot with its huge brown bun and red wiener canopying the parking stalls. They ordered their food, and in minutes, an attendant whizzed out on roller skates with their order.

Spence pocketed his change and looked back at Rachel with a dubious expression on his face. "This place is incredible."

"Get used to it," she warned with a laugh. She accepted the soft drink he handed to her, and the extra cup of water-no-ice he had ordered.

He answered with a good-natured grunt and backed the car out of the stall.

Their final destination was a park in the heart of the city. Spence pulled a wicker picnic basket from the trunk and carried it to a graffiti-marred concrete picnic table. He covered the table with a red-and-white-checked cloth.

Rachel watched him spread blankets on the concrete benches. "You certainly know how to come prepared," she commented. She set out their food.

Spence looked at Rachel and his niece with a mischievous twinkle in his eyes. "This is a very special occasion," he replied. He returned to the trunk of the car and pulled out three, long-stemmed pink roses wrapped in green tissue paper. He put them in the cup of water-no-ice in the middle of the table.

Katie exclaimed with delight at the picnic setting, complete with the cup of roses. A mild wind fluttered the tablecloth.

"They're beautiful," Rachel murmured, sitting across from Katie.

Spence sat next to his niece and her stuffed bear. "It seemed appropriate, considering I'm in the company of two beautiful ladies." He said it as if it were the most natural thing in the world to say.

What a line, Rachel thought. It was, of course, just that. This was a man who was obviously resorting to what he knew best—taking women out—in a situation he wasn't comfortable with.

But when Spence looked from Katie to Rachel, his eyes held a warmth that surprised her. Rachel had the sudden sensation that he'd meant what he said. A blush threatened to rise to her cheeks. She turned her attention to helping Katie with her hot dog, annoyed with herself. Since when was she so vulnerable to flattery? After all, that's all it was. But even with this rational perspective, she found it very difficult to fight the warm feeling his comment evoked.

In the wake of intermittent, playful conversation, the awkward moment faded for Rachel. If Spence had been unsure of himself with Katie earlier, he showed little sign of it now, she thought. His manner was gentle and kind and easy, and he had Katie smiling and giggling more than Rachel had ever seen her do before. And Rachel found herself laughing right along with them.

With the last of their supper gone, Rachel and Katie cleared the table and disposed of the trash. Spence went back to his car to retrieve the temporarily forgotten brown paper package.

He handed it to Katie. Katie could hardly sit still from excitement. But she tore the package open with surprising care for a five-year-old. She held her present up for Rachel and Spence to see. "A kite." She inspected it a moment, turning it over in her hands. "I think. How do you make it work?" she asked, looking at her uncle.

"I'll help you," Spence said. He showed her how to set up the frame.

He handed the kite back to Katie. She was plainly impressed with the gift, a rainbow of colors and streamers.

Rachel prompted her. "What do you say when someone gives you something, Katie?"

"Thank you...Uncle Spence," she said in her girlish voice, looking suddenly shy again.

Spence grinned. "You're welcome. Let's go fly this thing before the sun drops much lower and it gets too cool." He turned to Rachel. "Ready?"

Rachel smiled, but shook her head. "You two go on ahead," she said. "This is your time together. My job is to watch you two have fun." She waved them off.

Rachel rested her forearms on the picnic table. What she'd said was true. It was her job to observe them together. She watched Spence kneel to Katie's level, coaching her on the how-to's of kite-flying. Then he was up, and they were running together across the grassy lawn of the park, coaxing the kite into the sky. The setting sun limned them in warm light against the dropping temperature. The kite twirled and dipped in the wind. Katie's childish squeals of excitement and Spence's deep, calm voice carried across the park to where Rachel sat.

They looked as though they belonged together, Rachel thought, watching them from afar. She felt a painful twinge of longing. To be part of a family, to have a family of her own...those dreams now seemed much more difficult to realize than she'd once thought. Katie needed that sense of security in family from Spence. Rachel envied him the opportunity. It was only a matter of time before she would be out of their lives forever. But then, there was still much she didn't know, much that could swing the balance...maybe.

Rachel let her eyes drift back to the roses he'd brought, the petals pastel fragile, the scent faintly ambrosial. A simple touch that seemed suddenly so much like him— understated, gentle but strong. Or was he simply adept at charming women to get what he wanted? Thought and emotion waged a small battle in her heart. *Who are you, really, Spence Garrett?* she wondered in silence.

Spence and Katie reeled in the kite and walked back toward the picnic table. They looked windblown and breathless. Rachel smiled at the picture the two of them made.

Katie tugged at her uncle's hand, her wistful face smudged with dirt. "Just one more time, please?"

Spence smoothed her blown-about blond hair from her face. "I think you've about worn me out. Let's ask Miss Rachel if we can get together again soon."

Katie persisted. "And maybe ride horses? I love ponies. Or maybe we can go roller-skating?"

"Miss Rachel?" Spence asked.

They both looked at Rachel with expectant, hopeful faces. She smiled. They were irresistible. "It's up to your Uncle Spence."

"Then why don't we talk with Mrs. Edwards about visiting you at your foster home this week?"

Katie bobbed her head in affirmation.

Rachel agreed. "Sounds good to me. I guess we need to be getting on, before it gets dark."

"And back in time for your bedtime," Spence said to Katie, taking the roses from their cup and wrapping them in the tissue paper. He turned to Katie, handing the roses to her. She tugged at him to bend down a listening ear. Spence listened and nodded.

Katie looked at Rachel. "Would you like one?" She held out the roses.

Rachel glanced up from packing the tablecloth. "You don't have to, honey. Your Uncle Spence is giving them to you."

Spence took Rachel's hand and closed her fingers around the tissue-cushioned stem of one of the roses. "We want you to have this," he interjected firmly. Then he took the wicker basket in one hand, and reached for Katie's hand with the other.

"Thank you," Rachel murmured, lifting the rose to her nostrils. Spence, beyond the attorney, beyond the judge, was proving to be different from what she'd anticipated. Could it be that he was, in fact, being sincere?

On the front porch of the Edwards' home, Rachel and Spence discussed arrangements for him to visit Katie.

Katie held up Bitsy to Spence as she prepared to go inside with her foster parents.

Spence took the bear, not knowing what else to do. He gave Rachel a questioning glance.

Katie pushed the bear into his chest. "You have to hug her," she explained.

Rachel nodded at Spence, crossing her arms over her chest in a symbolic hug.

"Oh, I see," Spence replied, realizing what was expected of him. He gave the bear a tight hug, then placed it back in Katie's outstretched hands.

Katie hugged the bear, then stood stock-still, staring at her uncle. "Will you come back?" She whispered the question, her blue eyes wide with worry, her lower lip trembling with a threat of tears.

Spence felt his throat tighten. He had never seen such sadness in the innocent eyes of a child. He had to clear his throat before he dared speak. "I will, Katie. I will." And he realized the promise he was making to the child, the commitment. He hoped to God he'd never let her down.

Katie simply stared at him, then lifted her hand in goodbye before darting into the house.

On the way back to her office, Rachel looked at Spence while he drove. "It's hard to leave her," she said, guessing at his feelings.

Spence nodded, quiet for a few seconds. "There's so much of Julia in her...." His voice was husky. "It's the sadness in her eyes I can't—" He didn't finish, breaking the sentence off with a mute shake of his head.

"I know," Rachel said, her voice quiet.

"Why did she want me to hug her bear?" he asked, remembering the little girl's insistence.

"The bear is very special to her. I gave it to her the day I told her about her mom and dad...something to hold on to when she felt sad, even though it couldn't make the sadness go away. I hugged the bear and gave it to her. I think the hug meant a lot more to her than I realized at first, because when we got to her foster home, she had Mary and Louis hug the bear, and now you. It's as though as long as she has this teddy bear filled with all those hugs from all of us...she can hang on." Rachel fell silent, remembering. "She's never let the bear out of her sight."

Spence listened to her in silence. He wondered how much sadness a human being could bear. Especially a vulnerable child. And he wondered how much he could bear. Images of Katie's sad eyes, of bewildered children, of Rachel's gentle ministrations filled his mind.

When they arrived at the Department of Human Services, where Rachel had left her car, Spence braked to a halt. For a short moment, their eyes met.

Rachel had the distinct sensation she was seeing a part of Spence she hadn't seen before. A tenderness, a curiosity in his eyes...a curiosity about her.

She looked away. It was all part of the game, she thought. Or just the natural progression for someone in his situation, to be curious about the person he had to rely on—not a comfortable position for him, she knew.

But she understood it. So why did it make her feel self-conscious?

Spence had the distinct impression he was seeing Rachel for the first time—as a woman with the ability to touch his heart. That realization surprised him. He looked away. She was an attractive, sexy woman. That was all. So why didn't it seem that simple?

Rachel broke the moment. "If you want to take Katie out again next week, let me know. You can arrange visits at the house with Mary and Louis." Her tone, all business, dissipated the tenuous mood between them.

Spence nodded, looking through the windshield in front of him. He cleared his throat. "I'll call you."

Rachel walked to her car. The engine of Spence's car hummed behind her until she was safely in the driver's seat; then it faded away. *He just needs you right now, Moran. That's why he looks at you the way he does. And that kind of need is transient. In another week, the study will be over. And you and Spence will go back to your separate worlds and everything will be back to normal.*

Right?

Chapter Six

"Hello, darling." The woman's voice purred with studied sensuality, but there was also the faintest edge of displeasure.

"Hello, Victoria," Spence replied from his end of the telephone. He kicked off his shoes and stretched out on top of his bed. It was Friday, nine-thirty at night, only half an hour since he'd adjourned court at the end of a tiring damages suit. All he wanted to do was relax.

"I've missed you." Again that hint of displeasure.

"You know how time-consuming jury docket is, Victoria." Spence felt surprised at the complete detachment he felt. Only a few weeks ago, he'd met her at her town house, shared drinks, relaxed under the touch of her hands. It seemed a lifetime ago.

"Haven't you missed me?"

Spence could almost see Victoria's lower lip curving into a pout, cajoling him, trying to make him feel guilty.

Before, he'd usually let it work. And he realized he didn't miss her. An image of Rachel came into his mind.

"Victoria, I'm really tired—"

"Why don't you come over tonight? I'm lonely and I thought you might want some company, too," she interrupted, her tone childishly petulant. How had he ever found it attractive?

Spence tried to think of what he wanted to say to her. He hadn't yet told her about Katie. "Victoria... I've made some decisions you need to know about." He hated telling her over the phone, but it was something that needed to be done. And Victoria clearly wasn't going to be put off tonight.

"What do you mean?" Her tone cooled.

"I'm going to adopt my niece. She'll be living with me... probably in a month's time."

The line was silent for a few seconds. "It's difficult for me to imagine you with a child," she said with a strained laugh.

No kids, no commitments—the understanding that was the basis for their relationship. He understood her surprise. "I'm going through with it."

"Do you really *want* the responsibility of a child?" The brittleness of her tone told him it was she who didn't relish the thought of a child intruding into their relationship.

"Yes." Her question was one he'd asked himself over and over.

"Really, darling. Do you think this is a good idea? Isn't there someone else who could take her? Your mother?"

Spence rubbed the back of his neck. "Victoria, this isn't open to discussion. I've made my decision and it's final." Impatience seeped into his tone.

There was a long pause. "Adopting a child is hardly what I expected from you."

"And I can't pretend that things aren't different. It wouldn't be fair to you." *And I can't pretend there isn't another woman in my thoughts.* "Things... our relationship has been changing over the past few months, as it is.... I don't think this is going to work out between us."

"Whatever you say," Victoria snapped, no longer bothering to hide her displeasure or her anger. "I'm not going to wait around for you forever, Spence. I have my life to consider even if you don't."

Her farewell was the sound of the dial tone in his ear. In a way, he didn't blame her. The abruptness of his decision on Katie had to come as something of a shock to her. But the dissolution of their relationship had been brewing for some months, a casualty of their changing needs, needs carrying them further and further apart. He knew she was resilient. He knew the choices he'd made were the right ones. The only ones.

And now there was Rachel, complicating an already complicated situation and, at the same time, easing it. She touched something in him that made him feel alive, that pulled him to her. It was something that he resisted... that they *both* resisted. Something more than sexual attraction....

Enough of women. Spence pushed himself off the bed and walked into the dressing room, unbuttoning his shirt. He changed out of his suit trousers in favor of jeans and a sweatshirt.

Downstairs, he lounged on the sofa with a book on child development that was touted to be the best in the field. He picked up reading where he'd left off the previous evening. "Little girls often imitate their mothers, dressing up as their mothers do, emulating their actions.'' Who would Katie have as a role model? he wondered.

Rachel. The answering thought popped into his head like a preconditioned response.

He snapped the book shut and tossed it on the cocktail table. What in the hell was he doing? What in the hell was he thinking? He didn't know the first thing about children. And he hadn't been successful at marriage. He rubbed the back of his neck.

The vibrancy between Rachel and him existed. Naturally. Relentlessly. It plagued him. But where it fitted into his life at this point, he didn't know. Certainly not marriage. He enjoyed being single. And he enjoyed being around Rachel, too, and yes, he needed her help with Katie. But that's all it added up to, right? The answers weren't really there.

On the following Tuesday morning, Mary Edwards telephoned Rachel. Oh, yes, Judge Garrett had been out to visit Katie over the weekend; he'd spent Sunday brunch with them after church; they'd had a delightful visit. And he'd come out Monday evening after court for a quick visit.

"Oh, Rachel, I think Judge Garrett is such a nice man. So polite and courteous. Such a gentleman. I couldn't be happier for Katie," Mary told her effusively.

Rachel had never known Mary to be effusive about anyone. Mary made Spence sound like manna from heaven. Irritation grated at Rachel. Was she the only one who approached Spence Garrett with an ounce of caution?

"Mary, what does Louis think about him?" Rachel asked, trying not to sound peevish. *Let's get a male point of view. That's a surefire way to cut through the pull of Spence's charm,* she thought.

"They're both Texas Rangers fans...."

Geez. What does having a baseball team in common have to do with anything?

"And Judge Garrett has season tickets. We talked about going to Dallas for a game, maybe make a weekend of it...."

Rachel gave up. "Mary," she said, rubbing her forehead and trying to be patient, "that sounds fine."

"Rachel, dear, are you feeling all right today? You don't sound quite like yourself."

"I'm fine, really. I'm just a little tired." *I'm just a little out of my mind.* "I'm glad it's going so well. Has Judge Garrett made any further plans to her?"

"Not yet. He talked about taking her to meet her grandmother, but he said he needed to talk to you first. He promised Katie he'd call her. And they've talked about roller-skating and horseback riding. I think Katie's going to keep the judge a very busy man if he isn't careful."

Rachel laughed. "He'll learn. I'll call you back when I find out what we're going to do."

She hung up the phone and leaned back in her chair. *What are you going to do?*

Stay objective. Spence Garrett was shaping up to be a great parent for Katie. A week ago, she wouldn't have believed it. But in the span of just a few days, he'd revealed facets of his character she hadn't seen before—an honesty of emotion, a vulnerability, a tenderness—facets that pulled at her.

She couldn't allow that. She couldn't allow anything to cloud her judgment, her objectivity.

She wanted to be absolutely certain, for Katie's sake, that whatever had driven Julia from the Garrett family was not still somehow a threat to the little girl.

But there wasn't much time left. And to be fair to Spence, it looked as if there was no reason for Katie not to live with him. Rachel suspected the problems lay with his mother. And if this were so, it didn't warrant keeping Katie from Spence. Katie needed as normal a life as possible. It seemed Spence could provide this. Soon, Rachel would be able to make her decision.

And that would put an end to this...this foolishness she felt when she was around him.

"Spence, Peggy and I were sorry to hear about your sister.... We didn't realize last February..." Over the telephone line, Harry Rubin's voice was raspy deep with sympathy.

Spence tilted back in his chair at the courthouse and pinched the bridge of his nose while he considered how he wanted to handle this. "Thanks, Harry. I'm okay. You been needing a tennis partner?"

"Yeah. I wanted to make sure you haven't given up the sport. What about this weekend at the club?"

Spence enjoyed tennis, but his friend Harry was a tennis addict. Spence hadn't played the past couple of weeks, not since Katie. He made up his mind. "Yeah, this weekend, Saturday morning. But I want to bring someone."

"Victoria? Sure."

"No, not Victoria."

"You two have a fight, or something?"

"We're not seeing each other anymore."

"Should I be sorry to hear that, Garrett?"

"No. It's for the best."

"So, is there some new woman in your life?"

Spence smiled to himself. *Two of them.* "You might say that. I want to bring Katie, my niece, Julia's daughter. She's five years old."

Harry's end of the line was quiet for a thoughtful moment. "Okay by me. You know, Hillary's only a year older. Peggy could bring her, the kids could play together. Maybe we can give them a tennis lesson."

Harry was a good friend. For a contract attorney with one of the larger brokerage firms in River Plains, he had a solid sense of family and never put them second. Spence appreciated Harry's unspoken support in a difficult situation. "That sounds great. And I'll probably be bringing someone else."

"Yeah?"

"My social worker."

Dead silence traveled over the telephone wires between them. Then Harry said, "Are you kidding me?"

"No, I'm not. I'm planning to adopt my niece. I have a social worker assigned to me to do this 'home study.' So right now, where I go with Katie, she goes."

"Is she one of those salt-of-the-earth, ex-flower-children social workers? Man, they're tough. I encountered one of those when I was in law school. She all but told me I was a corrupt, useless human being, the scum of the earth, because I wanted to devote my life to protecting the financial interests of impersonal corporations."

Spence chuckled. "No, she's nothing like that. But she's pretty tough, in her own way. Plays by the rules. You may know her. Rachel Moran?"

"Can't place the name."

"She used to go with Hugh Mitchell."

"Mitchell. Vaguely. Attractive woman, if I remember correctly. Didn't know she was a social worker. Mitchell never did say much about her. Bring her along, Saturday morning, eight o'clock sharp."

Now all Spence had to do was convince Rachel. He dialed the number for the Department of Human Services.

She came on the line. "Rachel Moran." Her voice was soft and clear and gentle, but professional, as always.

"Do you work on Saturday mornings?" Spence asked without preamble.

She paused. "Why do you ask, Spence?" She sounded the smallest bit wary, he thought.

"I have a tennis game scheduled for Saturday morning with a friend of mine. His little girl will be there. I want to take Katie to meet them."

"Well, I think I can arrange to go with you Saturday. As long as I'm through by eleven o'clock." She thought of her private-practice appointments, beginning at eleven-thirty that particular Saturday. "Where will you be playing?" The caution eased from her tone.

"The country club at eight in the morning."

"Why don't I meet you at the Edwardses' around seven-thirty, then."

She sounded more reserved than usual, but at least she had agreed to go. "I'll be there."

From the stone-terraced tier overlooking the tennis courts, shaded by leafing walnut trees and striped café umbrellas, Rachel watched Harry Rubin and Spence give Hillary and Katie a tennis lesson.

Harry's height didn't quite match Spence's. His hair was dark and thinning on top, but he had a healthy physique. Hillary's coloring matched her father's.

Spence knelt behind Katie, helping her find the right grip with which to hold the tennis racket. They looked as if they belonged together as much as Harry and Hillary. The giggles of both little girls rang clear as the melody of morning sparrows up to where Rachel sat with Peggy Rubin.

Peggy freshened her cup of coffee, then nodded to Rachel, lifting the carafe. "Would you like some more?"

"Hmm, no thanks."

Peggy retied the arms of the sweater she'd draped over her shoulders against the cool of the morning air. Her auburn hair lay cropped close to her head, stylishly short. She looked at Rachel with friendly curiosity. "Katie's a very sweet little girl."

"She really is," Rachel agreed with a smile, sipping at her coffee.

"We were so sorry to hear about Julia. We never had the opportunity to meet her." Peggy looked back down to the green-topped tennis courts. "We think the world of Spence. He's a good man. I think he'll do well with Katie." Peggy spoke with the loyal protectiveness of a friend, but her voice was kind.

Spence was fortunate to have such friends, Rachel thought. "How long have you known him?" she asked, rearranging her linen napkin on the lap of her khaki slacks.

"A good ten years, I think. Harry and Spence were in the same class at Harvard. Harry and I'd only been married a couple of months. I was a law-school widow for a while." She laughed at the memory with a shake of her head.

Rachel was prompted to remember the years of lonely nights Hugh had spent hour upon hour at the law-school library, studying, trying to keep up. She knew what Peggy was talking about.

"I cooked, they studied. But we'd go out on weekends, sometimes, Harry and I, Spence and Diane when they were still together...."

Rachel was no longer curious about Spence's ex-wife. He'd been brief but succinct in his recounting of his marriage. But what about the "woman friend" he was seeing? Considering the nearly palpable attraction she felt radiating between them too often for comfort, and the amount of time he now spent with Katie, it seemed doubtful that Spence was giving this other woman much thought. She suspected Peggy would be much too discreet to volunteer any information about her, and of course, she wouldn't ask. She admired the woman's loyalty. In fact, Peggy was someone Rachel wouldn't mind having for a friend.

"Now it seems we're all so busy with our lives, we don't get to see much of each other," Peggy continued.

"Do you work outside the home, too?" Rachel asked, genuinely interested, and fully aware that Peggy would probably never have to work.

"I do interior decorating part-time, for my sanity, I think," she said, laughing. "I love the kids and Harry, but I need the creative outlet."

Time flowed by. The six of them ate a light breakfast after the tennis lesson and a quick set played by Spence and Harry.

Spence pulled his chair in close to Rachel's to accommodate all of them at the same table. His leg pressed against hers, making her acutely aware of hard, muscled strength. He simply took up more space than there was to be taken. Rachel could have sworn he was doing it on purpose, to be closer to her. To annoy her, she was beginning to suspect. She would have shifted another half inch away if she could.

Spence tilted his head, lowering it until his lips were just inches from her ear. "How am I doing?"

The question could have meant any number of things at the moment. If she turned her head to answer him, they'd probably bump noses, he was so close. "Fine. Katie seems comfortable," Rachel murmured, turning just enough to check his expression.

He smiled. "Good."

On the drive back to the foster home, Rachel tried to enforce the emotional distance she kept promising herself. Katie busily chattered with Spence, making it easier for Rachel to be, or at least to appear, detached.

Once they were at the Edwardses', Mary and Louis tried to convince Rachel to stay. She was aware of Spence watching for her response.

Rachel shook her head, softening her refusal with a smile. "Thanks, but I need to get going. I have an appointment I have to keep."

Rachel felt Spence's eyes on her. She hated the feeling he could read through her every expression. Of course, he couldn't. She turned to him. "What about next week?"

"I don't know what kind of time frame is best for Katie, but I'd like her to meet her grandmother Monday evening."

"I think it's time for that."

"And I thought I might have Katie to dinner Wednesday or Thursday night at my house. You're invited," he said, his smile warming his voice, "naturally, since you are our social worker and probably plan to be there, anyway."

Rachel felt her detachment slipping out of her control, shoved aside by an unreasoning sweep of pleasure at his smile and the warmth in his voice. "That'll probably do. I'll need to check my schedule for next week to be sure. I'm supposed to see your home at some point, as it is."

"See if I can keep house? Do my own laundry? Cook?"

"And make sure there are no monsters in the basement."

He chuckled. "I think I can manage that."

The easiness of the conversation was almost too relaxed. Rachel took a breath. "Oh, and I wanted to let you know I got your references, medical records and financial statement in the mail yesterday morning. You're very prompt."

"You're welcome."

"How are you doing on your search for a nanny?"

"Not very well," he admitted. "I've interviewed several women, but I'm not confident any of them can do the job the way I want it done."

Exacting, precise. He could be difficult to work for, Rachel thought. It was going to take just the right person. "You know, I think I know someone who might be interested."

"I'm certainly open to suggestions."

"Mrs. Bea Millican. Her husband died a few years ago. She and her husband were two of our best foster parents. I could give her a call, if you want."

"That would help." Again that smile that always seemed to wrap itself around her.

Rachel tried to ignore it. "We don't have much else left to complete on the study. I think the only thing holding you back will be getting a suitable nanny hired," she said.

Spence's expression turned quizzical. "I didn't think you'd cut me loose so easily."

She smiled. "Spence, you know from court we really don't want to keep kids in foster care any longer than necessary. Yes, there are a few things to finish up first. But if Katie's to live with you, we want to make the transition as soon as we can reasonably manage, all things considered. And, I have to say, you've been doing a pretty good job so far."

He grinned and shook his head. "Coming from you, that certainly means something."

"Have I been so hard on you?" she asked, returning his grin in spite of herself.

His expression softened. "I think you've been doing what you have to do."

He was doing it again, drawing her in. Rachel looked away. *Do what you have to do.* She needed to go.

They set a time for Monday. Rachel left the Edwardses', grumbling at herself. *You're going to have to do better than this.*

Sunday evening, Spence waited in the den of his mother's home. Through the bay window, lightning illuminated the western horizon in a collage of bursting lights. The rumble of thunder vibrated the windowpanes. An upsurge of wind flung a patter of raindrops against the glass, the first of spring's thundershowers.

Jacqueline moved carefully into the room. "Spencer." She smiled. In her hand she carried a half-empty crystal tumbler of what he knew must be gin and tonic. From the unnatural flush to her cheeks and her unsteady gait, he was certain it wasn't her first drink of the evening.

She bumped against the sofa, spilling some of her drink on the brocade upholstery. "Oh dear, how clumsy of me," she murmured.

Oh, hell, Spence thought. He crossed the room to steady her. He took her drink from her hand and put it on the coffee table while she sat down. Then he sat in the armchair across the coffee table from her.

Jacqueline dabbed at the wet patch on the sofa with a napkin. She looked up at her son, her blue eyes brightening in anticipation. "So, she's coming tomorrow?"

"Yes."

Jacqueline clasped her hands and continued. "What time? We could have a family dinner. It's been so, so long..."

"Mother," he interjected, trying to think of what he wanted to say. Yes, he'd come to talk about Katie, but Jacqueline was inadvertently forcing an issue he wasn't sure he knew how to confront. "Before we talk about this, tell me something. How much are you drinking these days?"

She seemed to bristle. "I'm an adult, Spencer."

"How much?"

"I don't think that's any of your business," she told him, indignation raising her voice a half-octave. But at the pointed look Spence gave her, she backed down. "But if you must know, it helps my pain and helps me to get to sleep if I have a drink. There's no harm in it."

He doubted it was as harmless as she made it sound. But as she'd said, she was an adult. She wasn't out on the streets in a car driving from bar to bar. And at this point, how much right did he have to demand she stop drinking? Katie would be living with him, not her. "I hope not." He let the subject drop.

Jacqueline waved away his concern. "Tomorrow we can have a family dinner—"

"Mother," Spence interrupted her as gently as he knew how, "Rachel Moran will be coming with us."

A frown creased her forehead. "What on earth for?"

"To help Katie feel more comfortable with the meeting—"

"I'm her grandmother," she burst out, clearly offended. A flicker of anger brightened her eyes. "I hardly need a welfare worker to supervise the introduction of my own granddaughter."

"Katie's had to face a lot of difficult adjustments," he continued, trying to explain what he himself had had to reconcile. "Rachel is the only constant person Katie has had in her life since Julia and Sam died."

"*We* will become Katie's constants," Jacqueline insisted, the pitch of her voice rising with her frustration. "And I don't see how we can possibly do that with that welfare worker's continuous interference, her nosing into our family's private matters. Who does she think she is?" This last statement she seemed to make more to herself than to Spence. She reached for her drink and took a long sip, her hand trembling slightly.

"Coming without Rachel isn't an option, Mother. Not for this first visit. And quite frankly, I can't see how it will interfere at all."

"This is a family matter."

"It's our family matters that have put us in this situation."

Jacqueline stared at her son. "What do you mean by that?" she asked, her tone defensive. She took another sip.

"Just what I said." All those years past, all that had happened, had brought them to this point. He knew some of it. He wanted to know it all, finally. "The night Julia left home—"

"I don't want to discuss it," his mother interjected.

"The night she left was a culmination of years of struggle," he said, ignoring her objection. "What was going on in this family, Mother?"

"You can't change the past, Spencer," she said, her voice tight with emotion. "Talking about it won't help."

"I want to understand it."

"What does it matter now, Spencer? Julia is dead. Frank is dead. If he hadn't gotten so angry with Julia that night, maybe he wouldn't have had a heart attack."

Spence had heard this before, but he suddenly saw or heard it from a different perspective. "Julia got the blame for a lot of problems, Mother. Why? Haven't you ever asked yourself why?"

His mother's lips trembled, making him feel guilty for bringing up the subject. That's how it had always worked, hadn't it? She'd make him feel guilty so he'd drop it? But he wouldn't let it go, not anymore.

Jacqueline pressed two fingers to her lips. "I know why," she whispered.

"Then tell me."

She stared at him. "I loved your father, you know."

Spence nodded, confused by her disjointed answers. Where was she headed with this? "I know."

"He had an affair, anyway."

"What?" Spence stared back, his mind frozen in disbelief.

"He had an affair," she repeated, the shadow of pain and betrayal lingering in her eyes.

Spence wanted her to be wrong about this so much it nearly hurt. "How do you know? Are you sure?"

"Oh, I knew. He admitted it."

Spence had never suspected. But then, problems had rarely been discussed openly in the family. They were "dealt with" quietly. And what good had come of doing things that way? He rubbed the back of his neck. "When did this happen?" He hated asking but he had to.

His mother was quiet for a few seconds. "I was pregnant with Julia. He didn't want me to be pregnant any more than I did. My God, I was forty-four years old, too old to be having a baby, with you nearly grown." She took a breath. It came out in a sort of sob. "Sometimes I think he hated looking at me." Her words were beginning to take on a slur.

Spence felt sick at heart, visualizing the unfolding history he'd never realized existed. He didn't know what to say. He remembered his father as a family man, even though his business often took him out of town. What had happened all those years ago?

"He told me it lasted only a few months, that she didn't really mean anything to him. I don't know. She was young and beautiful. She was a gold digger. That's all she was, really. She tried to steal him from me but she couldn't do it...." Her words faded into a moment of silence.

She sighed. "I loved Julia. But deep down in my heart, I think I always resented her." She stared at her son, in her eyes the reflection of the terrible sadness she felt. And the guilt. She finished her drink.

He'd asked and she'd answered. Probably with the most truthfulness he could recall. He had the fleeting wish he could talk with his father, with Julia. But, of course, stealing back even a second of time was impossible.

"And I'm still angry with Julia." Jacqueline trembled. "She was so stubborn, so difficult. If only she hadn't met that boy in Kansas."

"That boy" had been Sam West.

"If only she had been different..."

Different? Spence suspected she'd wanted Julia to be more like herself. Another source of conflict. Another reason to blame. "She was different, Mother. She was Julia, and right or wrong, her stubbornness was a part of who she was. Her choices stemmed from who she was."

His mother looked away, avoiding his blunt summation. "Can't you see now why I don't want a welfare worker involved in our business? These are private matters."

"Rachel is coming with us tomorrow night. It's not open to discussion."

Jacqueline didn't answer him. She looked very tired. Spence knew it was time to end the conversation.

"We'll be here tomorrow evening."

Her lips thinned into a disapproving line, but she nodded in acquiescence. Her eyelids drooped from the sedating effect of the alcohol.

Spence drove home. The brunt of the thunderstorm had bypassed River Plains, leaving only scattered droplets of rain behind. The wet asphalt road gleamed like black ice in the headlights, sliced by broken flashes of yellow. The air was heavy and sticky with humidity. Spence edged the car faster, ready to be home.

Katie, Katie, he thought. What kind of broken legacy had his family handed down to the poor kid? A grandmother who blamed the child's mother for the disintegration of her marriage and the death of her grandfather; who blamed Julia for being Julia.

And an uncle who didn't have the first clue about raising kids.

Thank God for Rachel. For the first time, he wondered, really wondered, what he'd do without her.

Chapter Seven

The Garrett family home reminded Rachel of an antebellum Southern manor. The redbrick house was flanked by half an acre of green lawn, landscaped with artistic precision with various specimen trees and shrubs, lush from the previous evening's rain. Neighboring homes rose on either side with equal elegance.

Katie held on to Rachel's hand on one side, Spence's hand on the other, and they walked up to the massive door.

They had decided against dinner and were limiting this to a short visit. Because, as Spence had confirmed, surprise raising his eyebrows and his voice, "You're agreeing with my mother about this?"

Rachel had laughed. "See, I'm not so nosy. Some things are family. It won't be long before I'm out of your lives, anyway. She can have her family dinner later, without me around."

Spence had given her a thoughtful frown she didn't quite understand, but the conversation had ended there.

The front door opened and swung wide at the hand of a rotund, middle-aged, black-haired woman who gave them a welcoming smile. "Well, well. I was just on my way out."

Spence greeted the woman. "Hello, Louise. This is my niece Katie, and Rachel Moran." He looked at Katie. "Louise helps your grandmother during the day." He released Katie's hand, letting her go in before him.

Rachel felt his hand at the small of her back, guiding her into the foyer. The gesture was very gentlemanly, very courteous, but her skin warmed at his touch, even through the fabric of her dark blue challis dress.

In fact, he'd seemed particularly attentive to her tonight, seeming more... possessive. And his attentiveness was almost seductive. Not sexual. Seductive... catching her sensibilities through the way he looked at her, the way he spoke to her. It was almost addictive, something she could get used to. Rachel felt a warm shiver run through her. *What a stupid thought. A dangerous thought.* She stepped away from him, moving into the wide hall, Katie still clinging to her hand. Tension prickled the back of her neck.

From the hallway, Rachel could see into the living room, giving her impressions of pale blues and creams, and brocade-upholstered furniture in dark, contrasting shades. At the bay window was an ebony baby grand topped by a collection of photographs. A carved marble fireplace mantel was inlaid with mosaic tiles. It was a bit austere for her tastes.

A woman who looked to be in her sixties stepped forward, supported by a polished, hardwood cane. She wore a khaki pantsuit, casual but impeccably, expensively tailored. Her silver hair was styled in neat curls, her makeup applied with care.

The woman's blue eyes connected with Rachel's dark ones for an instant with no hint of acknowledgment, immediately swinging away to Spence behind her. "Spencer," she greeted him, moving past Rachel to receive his kiss.

"Mother," he replied. He moved closer to Rachel. "This is Rachel Moran. Jacqueline Garrett."

"Mrs. Garrett." Rachel smiled.

Jacqueline eyed Rachel with reserve. "Miss Moran."

Spence put his hands on Katie's shoulders. "And this is Katie."

Jacqueline brightened, her eyes becoming misty as she looked down at the child. "Katie. It's so nice to meet you," she said softly, her voice brimming with emotion.

And so the evening went. Rachel sat with them as unobtrusively as possible. She had to give Jacqueline Garrett credit for trying...sort of. She was attentive to her granddaughter. But the chilled atmosphere didn't ease over the evening. Jacqueline didn't seem to realize Rachel's participation really was quite minor, as an observer only.

From the terrace she watched Jacqueline try to keep up with the energy of her five-year-old grandchild, pointing out the hummingbirds in the flowers, the old swing set behind the garage from years long gone. She promised to have it taken back out and set up for use, or if it didn't work, she'd buy a new one. Spence stayed with his mother and niece.

Rachel found her thoughts wandering from her task to the man...to how handsome he looked in the jeans and pressed white linen shirt he wore. She was learning he was a very compassionate and kind man. A very compelling man. So different from what she'd expected....

Within an hour, fatigue showed in Jacqueline's face and in her movements. Her hands trembled at times.

Spence looked at Rachel. "I think it's about time to be going. It's getting late."

Jacqueline gave him a shaky smile, admitting, "My bedtime comes much earlier these days. And with a good hour of sunlight left."

Katie bobbed her head in understanding. "My bedtime comes pretty soon, too."

Jacqueline smiled down at her, touching the child's blond head with her hand. "We'll have you here again soon," she said, ignoring Rachel.

Rachel could see that Jacqueline Garrett could be a very cool, forbidding woman. How far did it go, she wondered. Enough to drive Julia away? Or was there another reason for Julia's departure? In any event, tonight Jacqueline had behaved appropriately with Katie, acting very much the grandmother.

They returned to the house, where Jacqueline excused herself. "You'll forgive me if I don't see you out. Louise has already left for the night. Spencer, please lock the door for me. Good night." She left them then, retiring to her bedroom.

Rachel turned to Spence, concerned. "Will she be all right here, alone? She doesn't look like she feels well."

"She insists. She's very stubborn about her privacy in her home." But he wondered about her shakiness, about her hurry to retire to her bedroom.

Rachel gave him a sympathetic glance. It worried him, she could see that very clearly. "And you respect her wishes."

"As long as she can manage." Spence turned his head. "Where's Katie?"

Rachel looked behind him and nodded. "Over at the piano."

Katie had wandered to the baby grand with its cluster of family photographs. Spence walked over to look with her.

Katie stood very still, staring with wide, haunted eyes at a silver-framed portrait of Julia. She lifted her hand and touched the glass-covered picture. "Mommy."

It was a whisper, but Spence heard it, and he felt his throat constrict, his chest burn with a sudden emotion he couldn't name.

Rachel heard it, and she thought her heart would break. Katie didn't have any pictures of her parents.

But Katie simply stared in silence, stroking her mother's image with her fingertips.

Spence squatted beside her and put an arm around her. He lifted his other hand and touched Julia's picture with his fingers, next to Katie's. Julia's face blurred from the moisture in his eyes.

"Mommy..." The word ended on a whimper, as though Katie were calling to her and she knew there would never be an answer. Her blue eyes brimmed with tears and her body trembled. A round, fat tear rolled down her cheek, leaving a wet trail, followed by another and another until her little shoulders shook from the force of her sobbing. She pulled the photograph from the piano and hugged it to her chest.

Spence looked up at Rachel with a feeling that bordered on panic, his eyes questioning and worried. *What should I do?*

Rachel blinked back tears and nodded encouragement to him. She mouthed her answer to his unspoken question. *She needs you.* No one else would do. She made no move to join them.

Spence held Katie, a sharp edge of the picture frame between them digging into his chest. He stroked her hair in an effort to soothe her.

Katie balled a fist and rubbed at her eyes, but the tears wouldn't stop. "I m-miss my mommy," she stuttered, hiccuping convulsively, her small body racked with grief.

Again, Spence looked to Rachel in desperation, but she'd bowed her head. He saw a tear slip from the tip of her eyelashes.

"I want my mommy and daddy," Katie whimpered, her voice muffled against Spence's neck.

Spence squeezed his eyes shut but he couldn't stop a tear from sliding down his face. "I know, honey. I miss your mommy, too." His words were a bare whisper with the pain of understanding, the ache in his heart. He gathered Katie more closely to him and rocked her in his arms.

Spence held Katie until her sobs quieted to an occasional hiccup. He pulled a handkerchief from his jeans pocket and gently dried the tearstains from her face and helped her blow her red, runny nose. Then he picked her up and held her balanced on his hip. Katie clutched the picture of Julia. "I think we're ready to go home now," he said, turning to Rachel, his voice deeper than usual. He looked at the photograph. "I'll explain to Mother tomorrow about the picture. We have plenty more."

Rachel moved over to them then. She smoothed Katie's hair back into her ponytail. The child's eyelids drooped with exhaustion. Rachel's eyes connected with Spence's in silent understanding.

For a moment, time seemed to stand still between them. *So this is who you are,* Rachel thought. The energy that had always existed between them seemed to wrap itself around her like a warm cocoon.

In that unguarded moment, Spence saw a tenderness, a warmth, an understanding in Rachel's dark eyes that touched him. It was as though she could see into his heart, and in doing so, he could see into hers, establishing an unbreakable connection between them.

Rachel looked away, feeling suddenly self-conscious, wondering what was happening between them and knowing, all the same. "We'd better get going," she murmured.

By the time they'd arrived at the Edwardses', Katie was asleep. Spence left the photograph of Julia with Mary and Louis, explaining what had happened.

As before, Spence had picked Rachel up at the welfare department right after work. Now he drove her back across town to her car.

Rachel glanced over at him, sensing some uncertainty in his mood. "You did well with Katie, you know," she said.

"I wasn't sure how to take care of her when she started to cry," he admitted.

"You were wonderful with her. She needed you. I think you gave her something no one else could give her. A sense of her own family. It needed to happen just the way it happened."

"I had to hear that to be certain," he replied, glancing over at her.

"Oh, I'd have jumped in if it had been necessary. But you didn't really need me. Neither one of you did."

His sideways glance implied that he disagreed, but he didn't argue the point.

Rachel looked at the smudges on Spence's shirt where Katie had pressed against it. "I guess you've discovered white isn't the color of choice for dealing with five-year-olds," she commented with a smile, wanting to lighten the mood of the conversation.

"What?"

"Your shirt."

Spence gave his shirt a brief look and grinned. "I guess so. Something else I need to get used to, right?"

"Right."

They rode in a few minutes of silence. Then Spence said, "You're very good at what you do."

"Thank you." The compliment pleased her more than it should. His approval shouldn't matter—but it did. Rachel tried to ignore it.

"Why did you get into this line of work?"

Rachel shrugged. "Because helping children and their families is important to me."

"You seem to have an intimate knowledge of these children's pain."

His insight startled her. And she was surprised to hear herself answering his implied question. "I do, in some ways. I lost both my parents in a car accident. I was seven years old at the time."

"I'm sorry," Spence said softly, and his glance was sympathetic.

"It was a long time ago, Spence." Rachel felt uncomfortable talking about herself, her past, with him. There was no reason to talk about her. She tried to think of another topic.

"Were you left alone?"

Rachel was very still for a moment. Old memories. She didn't want to talk about this but there was no graceful way out. "Not exactly. I had an older brother."

"Hmm." Spence nodded with interest. "What does he do now?"

Rachel intertwined her fingers in her lap. "He die
some years later."

Spence's mouth twisted in apology. "I'm sorry, Ra
chel."

"It's okay, Spence. That was a long time ago, too." I
was true. She'd come to terms with David's death ove
the years. But she wondered what Spence would think i
he knew how much David's death had to do with her de
cision to do this kind of work. For a moment, sh
thought of sharing it with him. It seemed like the natu
ral thing to do. But the more she told him about herseli
the more blurred the already fuzzy boundaries of thei
relationship became.

She changed the topic back to Spence. "What doe
your woman friend think about Katie?" She'd almos
forgotten the woman's existence for what little Spenc
had mentioned her.

Spence gave her a glance. "Victoria? It doesn't ma
ter. We're not seeing each other anymore."

"Oh. I'm sorry." But she wasn't, not really, except t
the extent that Spence may have been hurt.

"I'm not. We didn't want the same things out of lif
And I wasn't in love with her." His tone was very ma
ter-of-fact. The brief glance he gave her held curiosity, a
though he wanted to ask her something. About Hug
maybe?

She was relieved when he began to discuss more ca
sual topics. But nothing seemed casual between the
anymore.

The return drive passed so rapidly, Rachel was su
prised when they pulled into the office parking lot. Sl
felt relief . . . and disappointment.

Spence braked to a halt next to her car. Rachel thanked him and was opening her door when she felt his fingers close around her arm, holding her back.

"Rachel, wait a minute, please."

She turned to him in question.

The wind had died down to a soft breeze and it swirled into the car, carrying with it the sweetness of spring, casting a strand of her hair into her face. Before she could reach up to brush it back into place, his hand was already there, smoothing her hair from her cheek with a gentle touch of his fingers, leaving a heated trail on her skin.

Rachel couldn't move. Spence's eyes held her transfixed with an openness of expression that spoke of immeasurable tenderness, of desire....

I could fall in love with a man like you, she thought, and she nearly shivered with the realization.

Spence's eyes darkened, silently beckoning her.

Rachel's cheek burned with the caress of his fingers. Her body ached with the knowledge this man wanted to kiss her, to hold her in his arms, to make love to her...and she wanted him to.

Spence brushed the curve of her lips with his thumb, feeling the warm rush of her breath at his touch. Beneath his fingertips, her skin felt like satin on a sultry summer's night.

This can't be happening. "I have to go." Rachel's voice caught hoarsely in her throat.

It was an excuse, and he knew it. "Why?" he asked, his voice husky as he leaned closer.

"I can't..." Her eyes were drawn to the sensual lines of his mouth. "It's wrong...it isn't ethical." Her skin flamed with wanting. She swallowed and looked away.

Spence let his hand fall from her face, letting her go, for now. He said nothing more, but he watched her practically run the few feet to her car, like a skittish deer that had spied the hunter. Wrong? Unethical? Nothing had ever seemed more right to him.

Rachel was aware Spence didn't immediately drive away, but she couldn't look back at him. She just couldn't.

Finally, out of the corner of her eye, she saw his car pull out of the parking lot into traffic, and then it was gone. Rachel sat motionless in her car for a few minutes, stunned.

What had just happened here? But she knew. She knew that she'd crossed a line, emotionally, that she'd been powerless to stop it. And with a man whose relationship with her was solely professional, and now, based on his need for her help and support. She knew she'd lost her ability to be objective.

Needing her help made her very attractive to him, she knew. But when her job was done, how would he feel about her? He'd return to his world, and she to hers.

If only they'd gotten to know each other under different circumstances... Whom was she kidding? The circumstances of their lives didn't involve each other personally, only professionally. To men like Spence, everything was a game to win. Yes, he needed her right now, but that kind of need didn't make for a relationship that could endure the passage of time, or real-life circumstances.

Somehow she would have to put an end to these impossible thoughts, impossible fantasies, impossible desires....

* * *

"Rachel, so tell me, how's it been going with the judge?" Leslie asked.

In the past weeks, Rachel and Leslie had barely had time to say hello to each other. Now, Tuesday noon, they sat across from each other in the Amaryllis for lunch. The decor was a profusion of color. Reds and blues, greens and yellows painted the floral wall coverings and the furnishings like a vibrant Victorian garden.

"How's it been going?" Rachel repeated, her chest constricted with guilt and an ache that wouldn't ease.

"Yeah. What's he like to work with?"

"He's been great."

Leslie's eyebrows raised in surprise. "Really?"

"Yes, really." Rachel gave a strained laugh.

"Who would have thought?" Leslie murmured, eyeing her friend. "How are you? You don't look too good today."

"Thanks."

"You know what I mean. If I weren't your friend and didn't know you so well, I probably wouldn't even notice. You look . . . kind of stressed."

Rachel rearranged her napkin. "I'm okay. Really. And he's been great, just very confusing."

"Confusing? Judge Garrett?"

"He hasn't been what I expected."

Rachel saw the puzzlement in Leslie's expression. Rachel knew she had a reputation for being quick and decisive in her assessments. She suspected her vagueness today surprised Leslie.

Rachel squeezed a lemon wedge over her glass of iced tea and stirred it mindlessly. "It's like I've been walking this tightrope with him and unless I keep my vision straight ahead, I'll fall." She gave a short laugh, a laugh that held no amusement whatsoever, and shook her head in disbelief. She'd already slipped dangerously.

Leslie frowned. "Rachel, what are you talking about?"

Rachel felt foolish, even though Leslie was the one person she knew she could trust with whatever troubled her. She sucked in her breath and decided to start with the easy part. The part that, taken alone, without the complication of her heart, she could manage. "This is going to sound crazy, Les, but I'm terribly attracted to him. It was there the first day, this...this sexual tension." She watched Leslie for her reaction. "So, are you shocked?"

"Shocked?" Leslie repeated, shifting forward to rest her forearms on the table. "No. He's a handsome man. Intimidating, but handsome. I don't see how it's necessarily a problem, though, depending on what you do with it."

"I don't want to do anything with it."

"Then what's the problem?"

Rachel stalled. "The irony of it."

"This isn't like you, Rachel. You're not making any sense."

"I'm his caseworker, for heaven's sake."

Their waiter arrived with their order, providing Rachel with a short respite from the conversation. She poked at her salad with her fork.

Leslie gave her a reproachful glance. "You know, it's not a sin to be attracted to him, even if he is your case. You knew him before this."

"Not very well. And I don't get attracted to the relatives of my kids."

"You haven't been attracted to anyone in almost two years and now all of a sudden you feel something for

Judge Garrett? I think either you've been too long without a man or there's something to it."

Rachel didn't tell Leslie the attraction between them had existed all along. It was her heart that hadn't been involved, until now.... "You're right. He's a hunk and I'm starved for sex."

"Not your style. I was kidding, anyway. But I have to say, Rachel, Judge Garrett is about the last guy I would have picked to hook your interest."

Rachel had to smile in spite of the mess she'd set herself up for. "He's really a very kind man."

Leslie became very still. Her face took on that knowing look that always irritated Rachel, because she was so often right. Leslie's expression softened with realization. "You care about him, don't you? That's the problem?"

"I don't know what I feel," Rachel hedged, but she felt an incriminating blush rise from her neck. This was the hard part, the part she didn't want to face.

"How is he with Katie?"

"Wonderful."

From Leslie's sudden quiet, Rachel knew she couldn't fool her friend about her feelings for Spence Garrett, whatever they might be.

"So wait and see what happens after you finish the study," Leslie suggested.

"There's nothing to wait for. Personal involvement with clients is unethical," Rachel replied with a shrug.

"Yes and no. You certainly wouldn't want to pursue anything with him while you're his caseworker. But you know, it's not like he's in therapy with you, or anything. You're about done with the study, he'll get Katie and probably be out of the welfare system by the end of next week."

"He has to get a full-time day sitter first. I think he's been talking with Bea Millican, but they haven't settled on a start date yet. And, client past or present, it doesn't matter," Rachel argued.

"Some might agree with you. Some might not. But what I really want to know is, who are you trying to convince, me or you?"

"Me, of course," Rachel retorted dryly.

"You have become a difficult person, Moran."

"Sorry." Rachel sighed. "It's just that I don't understand it myself. Everything about it is wrong—the fact that he's a client, that he needs my help, that he's been resistant to telling me much about the problems his sister Julia had with their parents.... What it tells me is that I had better be very careful."

"Or else what?"

Rachel picked restively at her food. "Or I might miss something." She shook her head. "I've lost my objectivity."

"Come on, Rachel. I think it's all more basic than that. I think you're afraid of getting hurt again."

"It isn't that simple. There's a child involved. You know that. And let's face it, the caseworker-client relationship won't work in real life. It's one-sided, based on me-helping-you. I don't need that in my love life ever again."

"How can you know for sure if you don't give it a chance? Maybe there's more to it."

"Oh, Les, I've known Spence Garrett for almost two years. If anything, we've clashed. I didn't even like him." Rachel hesitated and amended her statement. "Or, at least, I didn't like what he seemed to be at times. Now he needs me. It's in his best interest for us to get along."

"Of course. But that doesn't make it insincere on his part," Leslie observed. She closed her mouth abruptly, a look of consternation crossing her face. "I can't believe I'm sitting here defending the man who raked me over the coals in court last month. I'm not sure he deserves my help."

Rachel couldn't help but laugh. It was either that or cry. But crying wouldn't change the decision she was faced with. "I'm Katie and Spence's caseworker. I have to base my actions and decisions from that point of reference."

"You're right," Leslie conceded. "You're their caseworker. That's your first and foremost concern. So, where does that leave you?"

"At transferring the case, stat."

"What?" This time, Leslie did look shocked.

"I have to get off the case."

"Oh, Rachel. Is it really necessary to go that far?"

Rachel looked away. Even in remembrance, her skin felt the warmth from his touch. "Yes."

"But I know you really wanted to see Katie through to a good home placement."

Misery settled over Rachel. In voicing her decision, it became all the more real to her. She met her friend's perplexed gaze head-on. "I already have regrets about this case, Les. I don't want to jeopardize the integrity of the placement in any way. I don't want any more regrets than I already have."

Leslie looked doubtful, but she didn't press for anything more. "I'm sorry," she said, her eyes filling with sympathy. "What are you going to tell the boss?"

"I'm going to give him my month's notice today." Before Leslie could protest, Rachel went on, "It's only a month earlier than I'd originally planned. Once I transfer Katie's case, there's really no reason for me to stay on. My other cases can be transferred with a minimum of interference to the kids. I have a month's leave saved, and my private practice can support me. It's what I've been working toward. It's time for me to leave.''

Her friend sat back in her chair, trying to assimilate Rachel's decisions. ''Well, do what you have to do...and if you need to talk, you know where you can find me.''

Rachel gave her a smile. ''Thanks.'' But she knew talking couldn't really help beyond this point.

Leslie was right about one thing: Rachel *was* afraid of getting hurt. Or worse, losing her license over a foolish love affair. But she was also afraid of making a mistake, the kind of mistake her own childhood social worker had made: falling victim to the ''halo effect,'' which could blind you to people's faults simply because they were otherwise upstanding pillars of the community. Prestigious, wealthy families like Rachel's old foster family, the Lyonses. Rachel had survived. Her brother David hadn't.

Deep in her heart, Rachel believed she could trust Spence to take care of Katie. But that didn't change the fact she couldn't stay their caseworker.

Now, how was she going to tell Katie?

How was she going to tell Spence?

Chapter Eight

Spence wondered if something wasn't quite right. Rachel had sounded strained when she'd called, telling him, "I'd like to talk with you. Today, if possible."

He'd taken her call during a short recess. "I don't know exactly when I'll be through with this case, Rachel. The best I can do is suggest you come by the courthouse when you get off work and see where we stand."

A pause. "All right."

He'd finished at six o'clock. He hung his robe on the walnut coatrack in one corner of his chambers. Outside the doorway, footsteps echoed and faded in the marble halls, the hollow sounds of the courthouse emptying at the close of day.

Where was she?

He wanted to see her... he needed to see her. He wondered why he hadn't realized how lovely she was all along. He thought of all the time he'd wasted.

He thought of the night before last.

He thought of the rosy flush to her ivory skin, her lips parted with breathlessness, inviting him, her dark eyes reflecting the desire in his own. He'd wanted to bury his face in her neck, to drink in the fragrance of roses and jasmine that seemed so uniquely Rachel.

He would have kissed her that night in his car if she'd lingered a tempting moment longer. But she hadn't lingered. A devout sense of ethics, and a measure of apprehension he didn't quite understand, had sent her running from him. He understood her professional restrictions... to a point. But patience wasn't one of his best virtues, and he wasn't sure he'd let her off so easily the next time....

"Spence?" Her voice was soft and tentative in the quiet of the halls.

He looked up from his desk to see Rachel standing in the doorway. She wore a very tailored coatdress, deep violet in color, that was very businesslike and, on her, very sexy.

He smiled. "Come in."

Rachel walked through the door. The chambers smelled of wood polish and books. The walls of burnished teakwood seemed to glow with the yellow lamplight from Spence's massive desk. The desk chair and other armchairs were upholstered in rich maroon leather. The east wall behind the desk was a floor-to-ceiling built-in bookcase filled with bulky law books. Sloping rays of sunlight slipped through the west windows. On the adjacent wall hung framed black-and-white photographs of landscapes. Rachel wondered if Spence had taken the pictures. But that was personal, and not the reason she was here. She glanced back at him.

He moved to the coatrack and lifted a navy sports coat from a hook. "Let's talk somewhere else, okay? I'm ready to get out of here."

She hesitated.

He pulled on the coat. "They'll be locking this place up in about ten minutes."

"Don't you have a key?" Rachel asked.

"Yes, I have a key. That wasn't the point."

His look of mild exasperation pulled an involuntary smile from her. Then her smile faded. How was she going to say what she had to say? "I won't keep you long."

Spence leaned against the edge of his desk, his arms folded across his chest. "What did you need to tell me?"

"I've requested your case be transferred to another caseworker," she told him, plunging in without any preliminaries.

He lifted his head appraisingly, a muscle twitching in his jaw. "Why?"

What could she say? *I'm afraid I might fall in love with you? I'm afraid you wouldn't want me after you didn't need me anymore? I'm afraid this is all just a game with you?* She didn't want to look at him, but she kept eye contact with him through sheer force of will. "I'm going to be leaving the welfare department in a month. You and Katie will need another worker, as it is, so I thought it would be best to ease into the transition as soon as possible—"

"How soon?"

"Your case has already been reassigned to another worker. I talked with Paul Burris yesterday afternoon, and we both feel Sue Sheehan would be the most helpful to you. She's an adoption specialist." Rachel studied him. His expression was opaque, impossible to read. She couldn't begin to guess how he felt about her decision.

Maybe it didn't matter to him. Maybe he was relieved. Maybe this was painful and difficult only for her.

"Yesterday?" he asked, his eyebrows lifting.

Rachel swallowed and nodded. "I can introduce you to her tomorrow, if that's convenient for you. And I'll be there for Katie to meet her."

"And?"

And? What more did he want? "And you and Katie can get on with your lives."

"And where do you fit into this?"

He issued his questions with such deceptive calm she still couldn't read him. "I don't. Not anymore."

Spence's voice was so quiet, she didn't realize how angry he really was at first. "That's a bunch of garbage, Rachel."

A blush of embarrassment threatened to redden her cheeks but she fought it down with a careful breath. "What do you mean?"

"You know damn well what I mean."

Rachel could see the granite look of anger in his eyes, hear it in his voice. An answering anger welled up in her chest. He was running a line of questioning on her like a prosecuting attorney, trying to force her to show all, bare all, for his judgment, and she didn't like it. "No, I don't know. You tell me," she replied with quiet calm, folding her arms across her chest.

He measured her words, his eyes shadowing, his lips pressing into a thin line. Then he said, "Maybe I've misjudged you." He paused, studying her face, his anger evident. "Maybe you really would just drop Katie."

His statement stung. Rachel's anger bled into the threat of tears. How could he say that? But then, what had she expected him to think? *Look him in the eye,* she ordered herself, using the trick she'd learned long ago to dry up her tears. "The last thing I want to do is hurt Katie. I'll try to make this as easy on her as possible. But Spence, all of my relationships with foster children and their families are time-limited."

"I don't want someone new walking into this situation, Rachel. I don't think Katie needs to adjust to someone else. We were doing just fine with you."

Her shoulders slumped. She couldn't have agreed with him more. They *had* done just fine with her, until her feelings evolved into something more than professional concern. "I'll consult with Sue on the case as necessary to make this transition as smooth as I can. But sooner or later, you're going to have to get on with a normal life together without a social worker. Without me." Her voice was thick with emotion. But the words sounded unconvincing, even to her. She felt heartsick.

"Rachel, believe me, I want nothing more than to get the welfare department out of my life."

"Then we agree on this."

"We haven't agreed on anything," he replied, opening his arms in a gesture of exasperation.

"What do you want from me?" The question tumbled out, surprising her, scaring her.

Spence watched the conflicting emotions cross her face and strode over to where she stood by the door, making her take an instinctive step backward. He shut the door and turned to her, thrusting his hands into his trouser pockets. His steel blue eyes pierced hers pointedly. "The truth."

"What are you talking about?" she asked. But, of course, she knew. Her stomach felt hollow.

"I don't believe you. I think you're making excuses." He took his hands out of his pockets and stepped closer, close enough that she could see the glitter of anger in his eyes, smell the faint scent of his spicy cologne, feel the tension crackling in the air between them. He stopped inches away, resting one hand on the wall above her head, the other at his waist.

Rachel couldn't find her voice. She could barely breathe. His gaze held her very still.

His voice was gritty and dangerously calm. "A few days ago, we were talking about what we were going to do with Katie next week. Today, you tell me you're quitting your job in a month and that you had Paul Burris transfer the case to another worker. Now, you tell me, Ms. Moran, what's *really* going on?"

He was so close she could feel the warm, feathery touch of his breath over her skin. She swallowed, her throat dry. Her heart thrummed in her chest. "I..." She didn't know what to say.

"You what?" His voice was husky.

"I didn't have any other choice," she whispered helplessly.

"You *do* have a choice, dammit."

They stared at each other, their gazes tangled.

Nothing had been voiced, nothing had actually happened, but they both knew something had kindled between them. And now Rachel was trying to end it.

Silence fell between them. Time flowed to a halt.

Spence said, "This is about the other evening." It was a statement of fact, not a question. The anger in his eyes faded into awareness.

Rachel wanted to tell him no. She wanted to tell him she felt nothing. But she couldn't pretend it wasn't true, not without being a hypocrite. "Yes," she answered, her voice hoarse. "I requested the transfer because of the other evening."

His expression gentled. "Nothing happened between us, Rachel."

"Like nothing's happening right now?" she whispered in return.

"If you're asking whether I'm thinking about kissing you, yes, I am. Is that so wrong?"

His blunt admission silenced her. He met her confused gaze with one of questioning. *Is it so wrong?* The sudden need to touch her nearly overwhelmed him. He stepped closer and cradled her face in his hands.

"Is this really so wrong, Rachel?" he muttered.

Rachel closed her eyes, leaning into his touch. She couldn't stop it. It was too late. It had been too late since the moment they'd met. She felt the light touch of his lips on hers, tentative, tender. She felt the warm rush of his breath over her cheek. It sent a shimmer of sensual warmth through her.

It wasn't enough. She opened her eyes, seeking relief from him, letting her hands slide up to curl around his neck. She threaded her fingers into the silky blond hair at the nape of his neck.

He kissed her again, this time with the urgency of need, his restraint weakening. Her mouth was warm and giving. He tasted the faint traces of mint on her tongue, and the sweetness that was hers alone. He slid his arms around her, pressing his hands against her back, pressing her closer to him, savoring the touch and taste of her.

He broke the kiss with a soft groan, needing to breathe, and he pressed his face into her neck, drinking in the fragrance of her.

With the broken kiss, reason penetrated Rachel's consciousness. *My God, what am I doing?* She pressed her hands against his chest and tried to step out of his arms. "Spence," she whispered, trying to catch her breath.

"Don't, Rachel," he muttered into her hair. He kissed her neck, her cheek, her mouth, every touch wonderful...

"I can't do this." She stepped away from him. A threat of tears burned at the back of her eyes. She lifted a hand to rub her temple in distraction.

"Rachel..."

She felt his hand on her arm. He pulled her around to face him. His eyes were knowing. He wasn't going to let her off so easily.

"Spence, I can't...I can't let this happen."

"But it is happening, Rachel."

"You don't understand."

"Make me understand."

"I am—I was—your social worker. Katie's social worker. It isn't right—" She tried to move out of his grasp, but he held her in front of him, holding her upper arms.

"I understand about your professional ethics, Rachel. But you're not our caseworker anymore. You just told me you transferred the case to someone else yesterday. There's nothing standing between us."

"Yes, there is." The words came out in a hoarse whisper. "Transferring the case doesn't change anything."

"Why not?"

"Because what we have won't work in real life."

Spence released her arms. "What are you talking about? What could be more real than this?"

"We've known each other a couple of years, Spence. Up until now, would you have given me a second thought if I hadn't become your caseworker?"

"That's an impossible question, Rachel. I've never had the chance to get to know you until now."

"Exactly my point. And what we have is based on how I can help you."

"So what?"

"So the idea of raising Katie alone scares the hell out of you. With me here, with my help, it's not so scary. But that won't work in real life."

"How do you know if you don't give it a chance?" he reasoned. But he couldn't argue with some of what she said. He *did* need her help, badly. An inkling of panic was trying to worm its way into his consciousness. He'd never really thought about what it would be like to raise Katie without Rachel's help.

"Eventually, you'll become comfortable taking care of Katie by yourself. And you'll probably find I'm not so attractive to you once you realize you can take care of her without me, once you don't need me."

Spence ducked his head. Damn, how she could make him so mad in a heartbeat. "You think you have this all figured out. That's how you see everything, isn't it, Rachel?"

"What do you mean?" Rachel asked, her heart tumbling at the anger in his eyes.

"Right and wrong, black and white, with no in-between. What are you afraid of, Rachel? That you might make a mistake?"

"Where kids are concerned, yes, you're damned right I'm afraid of making a mistake."

"I'm not talking about your children or your work. I'm talking about *you*."

She didn't want to hear this. "We're not teenagers, Spence. There's a lot at stake here. Mainly a five-year-old kid who has to forge a life with you. There's no room in this scenario for a—a ..." She couldn't think of what to call whatever it was they had. A frivolous sexual attraction? But for her, nothing about it seemed frivolous.

"For us to get to know each other better?" Spence supplied quietly.

"You make it sound so simple," she replied in an equally quiet voice. "But it isn't. You need to get to know Katie. And she needs to get to know you. That's what's most important. And you need a worker who can be objective. I can't do that."

He listened, his eyes narrowing in thought. "Why are you so adamant about this?"

She didn't answer immediately.

He prompted her. "What are you afraid could happen?"

What could happen? "I don't know. Nothing, anything," she hedged.

"Come on, Rachel, you have your reasons."

He was pushing her. Why was she so adamant? Her own brother had died at the hands of a family as prominent as Spence's family. She pushed back with the last question she wanted to ask him, the one question that might finally kill this insane attraction. "What really happened between Julia and your parents?"

The answering silence roared in her ears.

Spence rubbed the back of his neck restively, and looked away from her for several seconds of very private thought. Then he said, "If you're worried about Katie moving into the same situation that drove Julia away, don't be." His muscles felt rigid with tension. He hated talking about this. Of course, he'd set himself up for her question. If he had thought it would do any good to talk about it, he might have. But not now. Not with his emotions so raw.

Oh, Spence, Rachel thought. "It wasn't you I was worried about," she told him softly.

He moved to stand in front of the windows. A rumble of thunder vibrated from the horizon heralding another spring rainstorm. Clouds shaded the sunset, casting early shadows into the room.

He shook his head. "Let's just leave this alone, Rachel. All of it. Just leave it alone." He looked back at her. For the life of him, he couldn't believe how important it seemed to keep Rachel in his life. He couldn't remember when he'd ever felt this strongly about any woman. That should be enough to warn him he needed some distance. And she was pushing him away. "I'll have to unlock the doors to let you out."

So that was it. Rachel had to compress her lips to keep them from trembling. This was what she'd wanted, wasn't it? Yet she hated this feeling that she'd failed. Failed Katie, failed Spence, by not being the one to see them through the next weeks with impartial guidance.

There seemed nothing else to be said between them. Spence walked her to a side door opening onto one of the main streets circling the courthouse.

The air outside was as oppressively humid and heavy as her mood.

"Good night," he said, then turned and walked away toward his car.

Rachel watched him. Maybe in time, when he became secure with Katie, he would see that she was right. A few raindrops splattered around her, prompting her to hurry to the shelter of her car. From the look of the turbulent clouds rolling in from the northwest, it was going to be a stormy night. She already missed Katie and Spence.

Rachel initiated the transition to Sue Sheehan on Thursday in a joint visit with Spence and Katie. Katie behaved irascibly, refusing to speak to Sue except in monosyllables. Sue's patience was inexhaustible. Spence was polite but distant, Sue's presence unwittingly providing a buffer between him and Rachel. Every minute of the meeting was an exercise in discipline for Rachel, an exercise in keeping her emotions contained. Letting go of cases was a part of the job. But she felt as green as a beginner, letting go of Spence and Katie, letting Sue be the caseworker to check for monsters in the basement and see the placement through to the end.

All weekend long, the weather alternated between cold downpours peppered with hail and lazy drizzles. The sun never once appeared, which suited Rachel's mood just fine.

Saturday morning, she stayed busy with private clients. That afternoon, she reviewed a contract to do social work consultation on retainer with one of River Plains's medical centers beginning in June. That work would supplement her part-time private practice very nicely. Sunday, she focused on a grant proposal she needed to finish writing. She had a deadline to meet in a month's time, but she wanted to be prepared well in advance for the other project board members to have ample opportunity to review it. So much for the weekend.

Rachel had also scheduled Monday off from work, knowing she'd need the extra hours to complete the grant application. She arose early Monday morning. At seven-fifteen, she stepped into the bathroom, ready to shower. She shook the two bottles of shampoo on the shower shelf. "No shampoo," she muttered. She looked at the crumpled tube of toothpaste. Out of that, too. She grumbled at herself. She was bad about letting her shopping go when she had weekend work deadlines. And when she was trying to stay too busy to dwell on what bothered her. So, it was time for a trip to the twenty-four-hour drugstore. She pulled on a pair of jeans and a shirt.

Outside, the clouds were beginning to break up, letting orange, radiant rays of sunlight streak upward from the eastern horizon. It was the time she usually left for work. The air was cool and damp. Within forty-five minutes, she was driving back to her apartment.

From half a block's distance, she could see a plain gray sedan parked at the curb in front of her apartment. Why did it seem familiar? A stodgy man in a dark suit walked down the steps of her porch. She couldn't see him clearly but her mouth went dry with the apprehension that gripped her chest. She was almost certain she remembered him and that car from drive-bys around the welfare department. There had been several occasions since the first time she'd spotted him in the office parking lot.

Who is this guy?

The man looked up, freezing in midstride for an almost imperceptible moment, then hastened the last few feet to the gray sedan. With a squeal of tires against pavement and a cloud of black exhaust, the car careened around the street corner and out of sight.

He was running from *her*. Rachel's heart skipped with the sudden flow of adrenaline at the realization that this man was acting very guilty, very suspicious, and that he was a complete stranger to her. He'd been following her. Why?

Rachel parked her car and walked to the porch on rubbery legs. Simon picked his way through damp grass around the corner of the house, his tail straight up in the air, waggling the tip to and fro for her attention.

"Oh, no," she whispered. She never let her pet out unattended. She picked the cat up, cradling him in her arms. "He was inside, wasn't he?" she murmured to her cat, feeling sick with the realization.

She walked slowly up the steps to the door. She tried the doorknob. It was unlocked. She closed her eyes and expelled the breath she'd been unconsciously holding. Why, why hadn't she gotten that lock fixed? She climbed the stairs, her heart thumping, afraid of what she might find.

At first glance, everything seemed in place. With that moment of relief, Rachel took an easier breath. On taking a second look, she realized some of the personal papers on her writing desk in the living room had been rifled through. A sense of violation sickened her. She wanted to sit down in the middle of the floor and cry.

She hugged Simon, pressing her cheek against his fur. "Oh, kitty. What is going on?" she whispered. She didn't have anything anyone could possibly want.

She let the cat slip from her arms to the floor. She picked up the telephone and dialed the police department.

The dispatcher's voice was sympathetic. "I'm sorry, miss, but most of the officers are tied up with some flooding and accidents this morning. It may be later this afternoon before anyone can get by to take your statement."

"Okay, thank you." *What now?* she wondered, hanging up the phone.

Get a locksmith and get that lock changed. After making those arrangements, Rachel went into her living room and flopped into the blue-print, wing-back chair angled toward the windows. Outside, a sparrow perched on a sycamore branch, pecking industriously at the bark. She watched its endeavors. For that moment, she envied the bird's uncomplicated existence. Too much was happening all at once.

She simply sat in the chair, staring out the window for a few minutes, then she reached for the telephone and dialed again. "Jean? This is Rachel. I need to talk with Paul, if he's free." She tapped her foot with impatience while she waited on hold.

Paul Burris came on the line. She told him about the break-in. "I don't know if this has anything to do with work or not. I think I've seen this guy drive around the office a couple of times, but I didn't think anything about it until now."

"Be very careful, Rachel. I know of cases where social workers have gotten hurt. Can you think of anyone who might be harboring a grudge against you?"

She couldn't think, period. "I don't know. I don't think so. He could be anyone."

"Did you get his license plate number?"

"No, it all happened so fast." She felt wrung-out.

"I understand. When you come in tomorrow, we'll go over your cases to look for possibilities."

"Paul, I can't think of anyone who even remotely resembles this guy. Maybe it doesn't have anything to do with work."

"You can't be too careful, Rachel."

"I know. You're right. Thanks. I'll be here at home today, so call me if you need anything."

She replaced the receiver. She sat, trying to decide what to do next. Take a bath? Put on comfortable clothes? Move out of town tomorrow? Or better yet, move out of town today. With a groan, she shoved herself out of the chair. *You can't run from any of this, so you'd better figure out how to deal with it, quick.*

Depression threatened to settle over her. She tried to relax in the tub, but she was too keyed-up to relax. She towel-dried her hair. The sun-warmed breeze would do the rest. Wanting absolute comfort, she pulled on a pair of faded denim cutoffs and a white, cropped T-shirt.

She opened the windows to let fresh, rain-washed air in. The sunshine seemed strange after so many days of clouds and storms. She knew the day would be hot and muggy later.

She sat at the kitchen table working on the final draft of the grant proposal. It was for an after-school peer-support program for teenagers, a project for which she'd volunteered time and energy to support. The program would need this grant to continue. That impetus kept her focused on the project.

The hours passed slowly from morning into afternoon. The locksmith came to install the new dead bolt. Rachel continued her work. Simon jumped up on the table and stepped on each page of the proposal outline in turn. Rachel scooped him up. "Oh, you," she scolded him mildly. "This is important, you little turkey."

She lost her concentration. It had been a constant battle, keeping her mind on her work and off Spence Garrett, off the stranger who had broken into her apartment, off waiting for the police. But she was nearly through with the application as it was. She pushed back from the kitchen table, ran her fingers through her hair and stood, stretching her limbs, stiff from sitting for so long.

Her gaze fell on one of the few photographs she had of her own parents. She thought of Spence, remembered him holding Katie, drying the little girl's tears while she clutched the photograph of Julia. She thought of the looks of warm understanding they'd shared, of the sense of connection she'd felt with him. Still felt.

Stop it. Do something, anything. Anything to not think about Spence and Katie.

Finally, she sat down to proofread the final draft of the proposal. She sat in front of the old, bronze oscillating fan to stay cool. She tried to read but she couldn't concentrate. The humid, summery temperature was sedating. Her eyelids drooped, the binder slid from her fingers and she drifted to sleep.

The sound of knocking on the door downstairs infiltrated Rachel's subconscious, startling her awake. *The police,* she thought. *Finally.* With the recollection of this morning's incident, adrenaline spurted through her and propelled her to her feet. She looked at her watch. Six o'clock. She'd napped for four hours. She half ran to the stairwell.

"I'm coming," she called as she skipped down the stairs, the wooden risers creaking with each barefooted step.

She flipped the inside dead bolt and pulled at the door. It stuck, swollen against the doorjamb by the humidity and rain. She gave the doorknob an extra tug to get it open and nearly knocked herself down when the door swung free. "Oh, excuse me," she said with a laugh, regaining her balance. "The door sticks when—"

She didn't finish her sentence, her words arrested as she looked up into Spence's blue eyes through the locked screen door.

Chapter Nine

She looked at him for a speechless moment, stunned that he'd come to her home unannounced.

"I would have called but I didn't think you'd agree to see me." There was no hint of apology in his tone. He looked as though he'd come straight from the courthouse, in long sleeves, his blue cotton shirt pressed, a tie knotted at his neck. His hands were thrust into the pockets of his brown trousers.

Spence looked at Rachel's visage of tomboyish femininity, all shapely, slender limbs and curves, her dark hair silky and tousled around her face. Her skin tinted pink against ivory under his lingering gaze.

She moved partially behind the door. "How did you get my address?" She'd given him her phone number, which was unlisted, but not her home address.

"You have a parking ticket you haven't paid," he said, not looking the least apologetic.

"One of the perks of being a judge?" she asked dryly, but her heart thudded so heavily she was afraid he could hear it.

Spence didn't answer that. He looked away from her as if trying to get up the courage to explain his presence.

Rachel's heart melted a little at his almost boyish awkwardness. "Why did you come?" she asked in a soft voice.

"I want to talk with you about last week."

Rachel twisted the doorknob in slight nervousness. What was there left to discuss? "Spence, I..." Her parry failed her. If he wanted to talk, they'd talk. "All right," she conceded.

"May I come in?" he asked.

She nodded and unlocked the screen door, pushing it open to let him in. She led the way up the stairs, her knees weak with a cascade of emotion.

Her apartment was sultry warm. Rachel paused in the kitchen. "Would you like a glass of iced tea?" she asked, needing something to wet her parched throat. At his nod, she tilted her head toward the living room. "Make yourself comfortable."

"Thanks."

In the living room, Spence didn't sit down. He wasn't sure he should be there at all, but at this point he didn't care. He watched Rachel move round in the kitchen. Her legs were slender and finely toned, her bared waist graceful curves disappearing into frayed denim shorts. Her T-shirt silhouetted her breasts. She looked healthy and fit. And sexy.

Restlessly, he loosened his tie and freed the top button of his shirt. *This has to stop,* he reminded himself. He unbuttoned his shirtsleeves and rolled them up to get some relief from the warmth, from both the sun-heated spring air and his involuntary reaction to Rachel.

He distracted himself from the effect she had on him by looking around the room. Two Manet prints, framed in black, hung over the fireplace mantel. The sofa was an early-American piece, upholstered in cream-colored fabric, scattered with plump throw pillows. Many of the furnishings were antiques, rich in craftsmanship and comfort.

His vision trailed down a hallway to an open door. Through it, he glimpsed the flutter of ivory lace curtains and the edge of an Aubusson-style rug in light blues, pinks and ivories. A delicately flowered comforter lay in quilted folds at the foot of a brass bed. Everything was so distinctly personal, so distinctly a reflection of Rachel.

Rachel brought in two glasses of iced tea. She handed him one, then sat on the sofa, pulling her legs under her, her eyes troubled and uncertain.

Spence sat in the wing-back chair. He took a drink of the cold tea, then set the glass on the coffee table. "I don't intend to cause you any problems at your job, Rachel. And I'm not going to apologize for kissing you."

He regarded her with a meaningful gaze. The tension was still there between them. Rachel could feel it. In a burning flashback, she visualized the moment he'd pulled her to him, the moment his lips had touched hers.

She set her glass on the coffee table and got up from the sofa. Nervously, she wiped her hands on her cutoffs. "No, it was my job, my responsibility to set limits. I didn't do that." She paced to stand in front of the fan at an open window.

"You tried all along, Rachel. I wouldn't let you."

"I'm a big girl, Spence. I can take care of myself. You couldn't have gotten near me if I—" She cut herself off in midsentence.

"If you hadn't wanted me to?" he finished for her.

She ignored his words, ignored the knowing glint in his eyes. She looked away in a moment of exasperation. She looked back at him. "Why are you here, Spence?" she asked, a hint of uncharacteristic sharpness in her tone.

"To make a proposition."

"What kind of proposition?" Her eyebrows drew together in an inquisitive frown.

"I want you to help me with Katie for a few more weeks, until she gets moved in and settled—"

"Oh, Spence—"

"Just hear me out first, Rachel. That's all I'm asking."

"All right," she murmured, startled by the intensity in his voice.

"I've talked to Sue Sheehan about it, the fact that you know quite a bit about Katie's nightmares, the fact that Katie has a bond with you already. She didn't have any problem with your still being involved as a friend. It wouldn't interfere with her work as our caseworker. In fact, she said you knew much more than she does about the kind of nightmares Katie has."

"I'm not the only person who can help you with Katie. I don't think it's a good idea." Perspiration dampened Rachel's skin. She turned toward the fan, pushing her hair away from her face, closing her eyes briefly against the gentle force of the air. The motor of the fan whirred, pushing its breeze back and forth.

"Rachel, there won't be a repeat of the other night. Besides, what happened between us was just that. Between us. Private. No one else has to know."

"*I* would know." She combed her fingers up into her hair and pressed her palms against the sides of her head. "I can't believe I let it happen," she whispered, more to herself than to him. She dropped her hands in despondency.

"What happened to make you so distrusting of what's happened between us?"

"Spence, personal involvement with clients is unethical. You're a judge, you know that."

"I'm not your client. And all you were to me was a welfare caseworker for a couple of weeks. I think you're too damned stubborn about your rules and regulations for your own good," he said, clearly frustrated with her.

Rachel's eyes flashed with a spark of anger. "I don't have to justify my professional ethics to you. And yes, you're right. I'm stubborn when it comes to rules and regulations. Peoples' lives depend on it. Being involved with you would be a mistake. Can't you understand that?"

"I'm not asking you to be involved with me. I'm asking you to help me with Katie."

They stared at each other, each silently asking something of the other. Why did they always end up at odds?

Rachel looked away. She knew the answer. She was afraid. And so was he. For different reasons; maybe the same reasons. . . .

Spence studied her, his expression growing thoughtful. "I don't think it's as simple as ethics, Rachel. Who hurt you?"

She compressed her lips. perturbed by his insistent questioning. She didn't want to talk about herself, about the past, all the hurts. But she wanted him to leave her alone. "Okay. I was in love once, with a man who loved me for as long as he needed me. When he didn't need me anymore, he dropped me. Just like that." She folded her arms across her chest.

"Hugh Mitchell?" The man was a true bastard if he'd hurt her to this extent.

There were no secrets in small circles. "Yes, Hugh Mitchell."

"Do you still love him?"

"No," she replied with complete honesty. "But I'm not going to put myself into a one-sided relationship like that again. Not with you, not with anyone." She delivered the words with assertive calm but her heart ached with the effort of saying every syllable.

"Not everyone who asks for your help is a complete bastard, Rachel," Spence snapped, losing his patience with her.

Her heart sank. "Oh, Spence, I didn't mean for it to sound like that." Regret tore through her. Tears came to her eyes.

A shadow flickered over Spence's face as the finality of her statement took hold. But his eyes glittered blue-gray like winter ice. "Mary Edwards told me Katie has had nightmares every night since she found out you were turning her case over to Sue. Katie needs you." He wanted to tell her he needed her...but he couldn't. Too much of her past, of his past, stood between them. "Do it for Katie. That's the ethical thing to do."

His argument was compelling. And if she'd been in his place, she'd be right here, arguing the very same position. "All right," she answered, her voice so quiet, Spence had to tilt his head to catch the sound.

"All right?" he repeated, to be certain he'd heard correctly.

"Yes. I'll help you with Katie for a while longer." Maybe she was crazy, but it felt like the right thing to do.

"Good. Then can you come out with us tomorrow night to Red Oak Farms? I've scheduled a riding lesson for Katie. I think it'll do her good for you to be there. And we can talk."

Rachel listened, and realized something. For a man who originally hadn't wanted to talk to her about much of anything personal, he was now soliciting the time to talk. For the first time in days, a genuine smile welled up inside her and touched her lips. "All right. I'll meet you at the Edwardses'."

"Six-thirty," he said.

She listened to the echo of his footsteps in the stairwell. He was gone. She sank into the cushions of the sofa. Borrowed time. That's all she had with them. It didn't really change anything. She leaned forward, hanging her head in despair. She stared at his glass of iced tea. The melting ice had diluted its hue from a rich brown to a pale golden honey. A rivulet of condensation slipped slowly down the side of the glass like a teardrop. But Rachel hurt too much to cry. She loved them both. Which meant, she suddenly realized, that she loved him.

An hour later, the police arrived, apologetic about the delay. They told Rachel what she already knew. There was little they could do with the skimpy information she had to offer them. The officers advised her to be cautious and to call if she saw the stranger again.

Rachel locked the inside dead bolt and hooked the chain behind the police, her hands shaking. She stared at the door. Even with the new lock, it wasn't enough. She brought a chair down and lodged it against the doorknob.

She was afraid to sleep in her bed that night, afraid she might not hear if an intruder tried to break in. So she curled up on the sofa under a light sheet. She was exhausted but sleep eluded her. Her eyelids flew open at every creak, groan and clank of the old apartment. Her ears strained to discern whether the sounds belonged or not. She hugged the wooden softball bat from her college years. She'd never felt more alone, or so lonely.

Spence rolled over, kicking away the covers, and lay on his back, staring up into the darkness. With a groan, he sat upright in bed and held his head between his hands. What in the hell had he gotten himself into? He didn't know the first thing about raising a child. And it had never really occurred to him that Rachel wouldn't be with him every step of the way. Was that why he wanted her so badly it hurt? Because he wasn't sure he could handle a five-year-old child? Was Rachel right? Were his fears the basis for his attraction to her?

The faint, ghostly memory of the sweet taste of her kiss came back to haunt him. He could have wrapped himself around her forever. It was only a few nights ago, but it seemed an eternity.

Maybe she was right. Maybe his feelings for her would just go away once he knew what he was doing with Katie. But he couldn't imagine the feelings he harbored for her deep within his soul simply disappearing. It would be like having a part of his heart cut out.

But she'd given him only a few more weeks. After that, there would be no choice. He'd have to find those answers for himself. Without her.

Rachel swiped some straw from the legs of her jeans, then leaned her arms atop the whitewashed fence surrounding the sandy riding ring. The fabric of her pink oxford cloth shirt protected her arms from the rough-hewn edges of the fence boards.

The air carried the scents of greening pastures and horses to her nostrils. The late-afternoon sun slanted its rays over the riding ring. In the center of the ring, the instructor, a wiry, gray-haired woman, adjusted the length of the stirrup leathers on the child-size English riding saddle to fit Katie's legs.

Spence stood at the pony's head. His blue jeans were faded and worn to an outline of his long legs and the contours of his build. The chambray shirt he wore fitted with the same ease over his broad shoulders down to where it tucked in at his waist.

Rachel watched him when she was sure he wasn't looking. She liked watching his movements, the way he tilted his head to listen to the instructor, the way he let the pony nuzzle the palm of his hand, the way his smile brought joy to Katie's face.

Rachel kept her focus on Katie when Rachel turned and walked over to the fence to stand a few feet from her. He leaned his back against the inside of the fence, watching his niece.

The bay pony moved out at a sedate walk around the ring. From the middle, the instructor held a lunge line in one hand, the end clipped to the pony's bridle. She held a long, thin lunging whip in her other hand. Katie's eyes sparkled with the excitement of her first riding lesson, but she turned her head to listen carefully to the instructor's guidance.

Rachel tried to concentrate on Katie. Spence was quiet, reserved, impassive. She knew he was only responding to her behavior, to the distance she'd established between them on the way to the stables. She'd been the one to make absolutely certain Katie was the center of attention. Spence had only followed suit. Now she sensed him waiting for her to set the pace.

Guilt pricked at her conscience. He deserved more than this from her, even under these circumstances. There were issues they needed to discuss. If only when her eyes met his, she didn't get that melting sensation inside. Where was the balance she needed so badly?

Snatches of the instructor's voice carried across the ring. "Keep your heels down...your elbows into your sides...very nice, very nice."

Try again, she told herself. "Katie looks good, doesn't she?" That sounded benign enough.

Spence nodded, keeping his focus on the ring. "She does." He folded his arms across his chest.

The peaceful sounds of creaking leather, of hoofbeats plodding in sand still damp from earlier rains, and the songs of barn swallows filled the moment of silence between them.

Rachel edged a glance at him. "How do you think things are going between you and Katie?"

Spence's chest rose and fell with a deep breath. He thought for a few seconds. "I think she's more relaxed with me. It's those nightmares that sound pretty frightening. I understand she wakes up screaming and there's no comforting her." His concern was evident.

Rachel nodded. "She has what's called a sleep-terror disorder. I think it's actually more terrifying for the parents than the child because the child doesn't remember anything the next morning. She may have some fragmentary recollection of the dream and its terror right after it happens, but the memory doesn't last."

"Why can't she remember them?"

"That's the nature of the disorder. Unfortunately, the condition isn't clearly understood."

"I thought you also said she has some dreams she remembers the next day."

Rachel nodded again. "Sometimes she has REM sleep nightmares—those are regular nightmares that occur during rapid eye movement sleep. She does remember those, but she doesn't have them very often and they're less intense to deal with."

"Do you think she has these nightmares because of the accident?"

"Possibly. But they could have begun before the accident. We don't really know. Stress and fatigue generally make them worse."

"The stress of losing you?" Spence said, raising an eyebrow in question.

She looked straight back at him. "Yes, the change in my relationship with her has to be stressful."

"So, what will help?"

"What we're doing with her now, and time."

"Are you sure?"

Rachel smiled at his doubt, knowing he was more worried about his ability to help than hers. "Spence, we took her to a neurologist, ran EEGs, the works, to make sure she doesn't have epilepsy or some other medical problem, and the tests showed she was fine…physically. What Katie needs is to bond with an adult who loves her and who will be stable in her life. That's you."

She could practically feel the anxiety radiate through him as he considered the magnitude of the responsibility he'd accepted. Her heart nearly melted at the expression on his face as he watched Katie in the riding ring. He held Katie with his eyes as if he were a new father holding a tiny baby in his arms, worried to death he might do something wrong.

"Spence, kids aren't as fragile as we sometimes think they are. They can be very resilient when given half a chance and a whole lot of love. Katie's going to be fine. Give it time."

Spence expelled his breath, and with it, some of the anxiety. He turned to fully face Rachel. "What would I do without you, Rachel Moran?" he said without thinking.

A smile touched his lips and deepened the blue of his eyes. It was the smile that always seemed to reach deep within her and connect with her soul. It was happening again. Rachel felt herself falling into the heaven of his gaze. She forced herself to look away, to break the magic. "You'd do fine," she replied in her matter-of-fact voice.

Spence bit back his response. He'd wanted to ask her how in the hell she thought she knew what he did and didn't need. But a deal was a deal. He'd asked her for her help with no strings attached, no personal involvement other than her spending time with Katie.

The instructor had removed the lunge line and now Katie rode the pony around the ring on her own, at an easy walk. She brought the pony to a halt at the fence where Spence and Rachel stood.

Katie leaned forward and hugged the pony's neck. "Isn't Christopher Robin pretty?"

Rachel patted the pony's dished forehead and smoothed its long, black forelock down the center. "He's a lovely pony," she agreed with a smile.

"Uncle Spence, do you like him?"

"Absolutely."

Katie was a grimy but satisfied little girl on the return drive to her foster home. Her eyes sparkled with life. Rachel knew it wasn't really the pony; it was the sharing of time and laughter with her uncle, the sense of family, the sense of belonging. Something Rachel didn't have in her own life.

And so their visits went. Rachel spent time with Spence and Katie together a couple of times a week for the next two weeks. Sue Sheehan took Katie on the visits to Spence's home. Other evenings, Rachel would meet them at the foster home for dinner or a trip to the park. But she spent less and less time with them, trying to wean Katie from her.

Spence still needed her, though, to help come up with answers to Katie's sometimes-difficult questions.

"What do I tell her when she asks me if I'm going to die like Julia and Sam?" he asked once, opening his arms in a gesture conveying he was at a complete loss for an answer.

As always, Rachel couldn't help but smile at his openness. "What do you tell her now?"

"I hug her and tell her we all hope to live for a long, long time."

"That's probably enough for now. You're trying to be as reassuring as you can without being untruthful."

"I can't wait until she asks me where babies come from."

"Yeah? Well, get ready, because it could happen any time."

Spence looked startled. "I was thinking years from now... when she's a lot older."

Rachel just smiled.

Spence shook his head ruefully.

They both sensed those moments when they felt drawn closer and closer together. But neither openly acknowledged them. Rachel knew it was the stress of the circumstances. Spence had his doubts. The moments would disintegrate into awkwardness, then into friction between them. And at the end of each visit, they parted ways without lingering.

It was now mid-May; Rachel faced her last two weeks with the Department of Human Services. She let her pen drum over the desk calendar. She looked forward to her last day only halfheartedly. Her work, and soon just her private practice, was all she had. It used to be enough....

The phone intercom buzzed.

"Judge Garrett, line two."

"Thanks, Jean." Rachel let her fingers rest on the phone for a few seconds. She still had to gather her wits about her every time she talked to him. "This is Rachel."

"I've hired Mrs. Millican. She'll start next week." His voice was controlled and neutral, the tone she'd come to expect from him.

This was it, then. "I think you'll be very satisfied with her," Rachel told him. She felt numb.

"I wouldn't have hired her if I thought otherwise," he replied unnecessarily. It was one of those rare moments he couldn't contain his displeasure with her.

She ignored it. "When do you want Sue and me to move Katie over with you?"

"Anytime in the next few days. I'll be taking two weeks' vacation beginning tomorrow. I want to be as available to Katie as I can these first few weeks."

"We can probably move her tomorrow. She's been expecting this and we need to finish the transition as soon as we can. I'll check with Sue and call you back."

"I'll be at the courthouse until five."

In the next couple of days... She couldn't believe it was all finally coming to an end.

* * *

Rachel and Sue Sheehan met Spence at the Edwardses' at ten o'clock the next morning. Katie's possessions consisted of a box of toys and books, a suitcase and her teddy bear.

She hugged her foster parents in silence, but tears glinted in her blue eyes. Mary Edwards knelt and spoke to her quietly. Rachel couldn't hear what was said, but a faint smile appeared on Katie's face, easing the tears.

Her bear tucked securely beneath her arm, Katie turned to Rachel, Sue and Spence. The morning sun haloed her golden head as she tilted her face upward. "I'm ready to go live with Uncle Spence," she said in a matter-of-fact voice.

Rachel glanced at Louis and Mary. The three of them had gone through this together innumerable times, but it was never an easy parting. Especially with a child like Katie.

Spence drove Katie to his home. Rachel and Sue followed behind in Sue's car. The winding gravel driveway dipped to a low water bridge, then curved uphill toward a cluster of hardwood trees obscuring the view of the house.

Rachel was dimly aware of stucco and natural wood and cactus plants surrounding her, but her attention focused on Katie, who had run ahead into the house to put her belongings away in her room.

Katie already seemed comfortable in her new home, Rachel thought. It was then she looked around the foyer. Slate paved the floor, and the rough-textured white walls seemed to glow with the warmth of the light. Down the hallway she could see the sweeping curve of a staircase in the same rough-textured white, with slate risers. Lovely simplicity, she thought.

Spence spoke briefly with Sue, then turned to Rachel. Something glimmered in his eyes. "Rachel, I want to thank you for all your help with Katie. I wish you the best in your private practice."

"Thank you," she murmured, gripping the strap of her shoulder bag. She couldn't act her part with the finesse he displayed.

Katie came up beside Rachel and tugged at her hand. "Miss Rachel, come and see my new room."

Katie's voice held an edge of desperation. Rachel realized she must have been listening to their conversation. Even though she'd tried to tell Katie she wouldn't be visiting much anymore, Katie had been resisting the change.

Rachel smiled for Katie's benefit. "Will you excuse us for a few minutes?" she asked Spence and Sue.

Katie's room was little-girl pink and cream and beautifully decorated. Professionally decorated. Katie busily showed her the array of toys and games, all arranged with meticulous care on the open shelving, ready to be rearranged by a five-year-old's hands. Clearly, all the toys and games had been selected with care. All were appropriate to Katie's age level, and many were educational.

The judge had done his homework well, she thought. Even the new clothes in Katie's closet were name-brand and the perfect size. On the nightstand next to Katie's bed sat a framed photograph of Katie with her mother and father. Rachel recognized it as an enlargement of the picture Spence had shown her at her office so many weeks ago. He'd thought of everything. . . .

Katie chattered excitedly as she showed Rachel this and that. Finally, Rachel put a hand on the child's shoulder to get her attention.

"Katie, I can't stay," she told her gently.

The activity stopped and Katie stared up at her with her bright blue eyes. "Why not?"

"Miss Sue will be helping you and your Uncle Spence from now on," she explained.

Tears brimmed in Katie's eyes and her lower lip trembled. She clenched her fists at her sides. "I don't want you to leave," she pleaded in her little-girl voice.

"Oh, Katie, I'll visit you sometimes." Rachel knew in her heart Spence would never deny that to Katie if that was what Katie needed. "It just won't be as often."

"When will you come back? Can't you come back tomorrow? Please, Miss Rachel, please?" Katie started to cry, the stress of all the changes catching up with her.

Spence's voice cut in behind them. "What's going on?"

Rachel reached down to soothe Katie, to stroke her hair, but Katie twisted away, silent tears rolling down her cheeks. She ran into her bathroom and shut the door behind her.

Rachel made herself look at Spence. "She's upset with me for leaving," she told him. Sue Sheehan stood in the doorway behind him.

His eyes were implacable.

Rachel continued. "I told her I'd come to visit her sometimes but not often. If it's okay with you, maybe I could drop by sometime when Mrs. Millican is here and visit with Katie. Maybe that would help this transition." *And I could see her when you're not here.*

A muscle twitched in his cheek. "Whatever is best for Katie," he replied in a terse voice.

Whatever you think is best for Katie, I'm willing to listen. The words of his April promise echoed in her memory. He was a man of his word.

Rachel swallowed back the emotion constricting her throat.

The bathroom door opened. Katie came out. She wouldn't look at Rachel, but she ran and wrapped her arms around her waist in a fierce hug. "I love you, Miss Rachel," she said, her voice muffled against Rachel's skirt.

Rachel knelt and hugged Katie back. "I love you, too, Katie. I'll miss you," she whispered.

"You promise to come back?"

"Yes, but it will probably be a few weeks."

"Okay. I'll miss you, too."

When Rachel left the room, left the house, she felt as though she'd left a part of her heart behind forever.

Spence sat up in bed, shocked awake by a child's shrill scream of terror. He rolled to his side and turned on the bedside lamp. The scream was followed by another and another, sounds of sheer panic. Apprehension billowed in his chest, propelling him out of bed and down the hall to Katie's bedroom.

He flipped on the light. He froze in shock. Katie was crouched on her bed, her eyes wide-open and filled with terror. Her pupils were dilated and perspiration beaded her hairline. She screamed in panic over and over, her little fingers picking at the blanket on her bed in agitation, her face flushed.

Spence was at her bedside in quick strides. "Katie, it's okay. It's okay." He tried to reassure her, but her wide, panic-filled blue eyes stared through him, unseeingly, as though he wasn't even there.

Oh, God. Spence tried to put his arms around her. She pushed at his arms frantically, her breathing coming in short rapid breaths. She still didn't know him. What was he going to do? *Rachel, Rachel, tell me what to do....*

"Katie, it's me. It's Uncle Spence. You're safe."

She didn't respond to his voice or his arms. Spence had never felt so helpless. He tried to think of what Rachel had told him.

Then her screams stopped. Katie's expression grew confused, and she looked at Spence. Her small shoulders heaved with a sob. She mumbled something unintelligible, her eyelids drooped and she pulled the bed covers over her, asleep again as abruptly as she'd awakened.

Spence sat on the edge of the small bed, drained. The whole episode had lasted less than five minutes, but it had ripped through his sensibilities, leaving him feeling powerless. His heartbeat quieted; he hadn't even realized how hard it had been pounding.

He rubbed a hand over his face, then slid it around to rub the back of his neck. He looked at his niece. Katie's features were in repose. Damp patches of tears smeared her cheeks. He pulled a tissue from a box on the nightstand and, with a careful touch, dried her cheeks.

The urge to call Rachel nearly overwhelmed him. But he didn't yield to it. He'd made it through this first time without her. And, he realized, this was just a part of what he had to face on his own.

He had the next two weeks off to devote to Katie, to help her become increasingly secure with him. He knew Katie missed Rachel. He did, too. Much more than he'd thought.

Chapter Ten

"Surprise!" The word rang out in a chorus of voices.

Rachel's mouth dropped open in amazement. "This doesn't look like an emergency staff meeting to me," she said in a joking voice. "You tricked me."

A banner stretched across one end of the room said, We'll Miss You, Rachel. The conference room was jammed with every staff person in her division. Beaming smiles and tears greeted her.

Leslie came up beside her and squeezed her arm. "We couldn't resist. Come on, you've got to see the cake."

On the table in the middle of the room lay a sheet cake with Good Luck, Rachel written in frosting on the top. Rachel dabbed away a tear from the corner of her eye. "I can't believe you all did this." She cut the cake and offered a piece to someone. "You guys will grab any excuse for a party," she said, laughing.

Paul came up to her. "Well, Moran, how does it feel to be on your last day here?"

"I'm not sure. I'll miss everyone."

Paul chuckled. "Good answer. By the way, if you have any more problems with The Shadow, be sure to give me a call."

Rachel grinned at his use of the nickname they'd given to her intruder. "I didn't know you knew we called him that," she said with a laugh. "I haven't seen him since the day he broke into my apartment. Maybe I scared him off."

"If you think of anything we missed in going over your files, let me know. But I think you're right. It didn't have anything to do with any of your cases, as far as I could see."

Sue Sheehan strolled over. "I like the theory he's a Peeping Tom on wheels."

Rachel smiled. "I haven't seen you in days, Sue. Is Paul keeping you snowed under with my old cases?"

"You bet."

Paul grinned at them. "I know when to make my exit," he retorted good-naturedly, and left them to talk with other staff.

"Speaking of cases, Katie West is doing better. She even says hello to me now," Sue said. She took a bite of cake.

"I'm glad to hear that," Rachel replied, trying to sound casual.

"Apparently, she had one episode of sleep terrors the first night she was at her uncle's, but none since."

"That's an improvement." Spence must be managing fairly well without her, she thought. She wasn't surprised. "Maybe I can get out to see her in a couple of weeks. How's Mrs. Millican working out?"

"Great. She's a sweet lady, the down-to-earth, mother-ly type. Oh, and Judge Garrett asked about you."

"He did?" Rachel tried to cover the crazy surge of pleasure she felt at hearing he'd asked at all.

Sue nodded. "Wanted to know how you were. That was about it." She sighed. "Boy, but he's good-looking. And he's fantastic with Katie. Surprised me, considering how formidable he can be in court."

It hurt more than Rachel had anticipated to hear about him, to think about him. She tried to keep her expression opaque. "He is very good with her," she agreed. "How's the grandmother doing? Have you talked much with her?"

Sue shrugged. "Not much. She seems real snooty to me. But she acts okay around Katie and the judge. I probably won't have much more to do with them at this point. The adoption's going through right on schedule."

Rachel nodded. Afraid that she wore her emotions on her shirtsleeves for all to see, she edged away as gra-ciously as she could. "Take care, Sue. Let me know if I can help in any way."

Sue nodded. "Thanks. You, too. Good luck in your new life."

By the end of the afternoon, Rachel had her personal items boxed and ready to take to her car. She sat on the edge of her empty desk. She took a last glance around the four walls of her last seven years. A hollowness filled the room. Its walls were now bare; the bookshelf held only black binders of departmental policy and procedure. It seemed so impersonal, as if she'd never been there at all.

She slid off the desk and walked out of the office for the last time. It was time to get on with her life.

The summer evening of early September shimmered with the radiant heat from the day's sun. Rachel's cotton dress was damp with perspiration when she returned from her private office at seven o'clock on Friday. *Next investment is an air conditioner,* she promised herself.

In her bedroom, she stepped out of the dress and let it drape over the back of the slipper chair. She rinsed off under a cool shower. The water streamed over her face, over her body, with cleansing therapy. She tried not to think about anything for those minutes in the shower. But she thought of Spence. She thought of him nearly every night, after work, when there was nothing else to distract her. She'd thought it would be easier. Since she was no longer with child welfare, her path didn't cross the courthouse grounds at all. She hadn't even seen Spence in passing in months. *Why do you do this to yourself?* she scolded herself. *Go work on the budget, read a book, anything.*

She toweled off and dusted her skin with a hyacinth-scented talc before pulling a tattered old T-shirt over lacy underwear. Friday evening stretched before her like all the weekends had the past couple of months.

She turned on the radio, tuning in a new-age jazz station, and settled on the sofa. She spread financial records and statements on the long coffee table. Simon draped his plump body over the arm of the sofa like a languid puddle of fur, watching her work.

She added and subtracted over and over on the calculator, double-checking her figures. "Well, what do you know," she murmured to herself in amazement and relief. She looked at her cat. "We're in the black!" she exclaimed, scooping him off his perch to hold him eye to eye.

In sublime ignorance, the cat stared her down with his slanted green eyes, then yawned widely.

"You're no fun," she said with a sigh. But who else really important was there for her to celebrate the success of her private practise with?

She let the cat slip to the floor. Who else? She looked at the mantel clock. It was only nine o'clock. She knew Leslie and her family were out of town on their end-of-summer vacation. Most of her other colleagues never spent a Friday evening at home.

At ten-thirty, Rachel was surprised when the telephone rang. Maybe her answering service was calling with an emergency. She picked up the receiver, tucking it under her chin while she sifted through her papers.

"Rachel, this is Spence."

Her heartbeat quickened at the sound of his voice, soft, deep, hesitant. "Yes." The word came out a hoarse syllable.

"I don't like bothering you at home this time of night, but Sue Sheehan suggested I call you."

"What's wrong?" she asked. A jump of worry for Katie strengthened her voice.

A second of silence passed at his end. "Katie's been having nightmares this week. Not the sleep terrors, those stopped a few months ago. The other kind, the kind she remembers. She dreams you've died and left her like Julia and Sam did. She had another one tonight. She won't stop crying. I can't convince her you're okay."

"I haven't been out to see her in about a month," Rachel murmured, feeling a pull of guilt.

"I know. That's why Sue suggested I call you." A pause. "Would you be willing to come over and talk to her? Show her you're all right?" His voice was husky.

"I'll come," she responded with no hesitation.

Again that pause, then Spence said, "Rachel, I wouldn't ask you to do this if Katie didn't need you."

The unspoken message played in Rachel's mind: *I wouldn't have called if I didn't need your help.* But she told him in a quiet voice, "Spence, I'm okay with it. I'll be leaving in a few minutes."

Rachel hung up and looked down at the T-shirt she wore. This would never do. She pulled it over the top of her head as she walked in quick strides to her bedroom. She pulled a casual cotton floral dress from the closet, shrugging into it, zipped up the back and slipped her bare feet into a pair of sandals, all in an economy of time and motion. The dress was airy and cool against the heated, humid night air, and against the rush of warmth that came to her skin in faint, nervous anticipation.

In thirty minutes, Rachel arrived at Spence's country home, her attention focused through the glass door into the lighted foyer. Spence appeared around the corner down the hallway. He strode toward her looking distracted but terribly handsome. He looked as though he'd dressed in haste, his shirt unbuttoned and untucked, exposing bare torso to the waistband of his jeans.

He held the door open for her. A rush of cool air swept over Rachel as she stepped past him into the air-conditioned foyer, but her skin warmed at the smile he gave her.

"Thanks for coming," he said.

"You're welcome. I just hope I can help," Rachel murmured, trying to ignore the pleasure she felt, trying to pretend it wasn't wonderful to see him again.

Spence closed the door behind them and turned to her. "She's in her room. Still awake." Tiny lines of concern radiated from the corners of his eyes.

He walked side by side with Rachel up the stairs to Katie's bedroom. Rachel could see the little girl curled up on her bed, her eyes open and red-rimmed, staring vacantly at the wall.

Spence knelt at the side of her bed and stroked her hair. Her pillow was wet from tears. "Katie, Miss Rachel's here to see you."

Katie pulled her head up and pushed herself up to sit. Red splotched her cheeks where tears had chapped her skin, but her blue eyes rounded in relief. "Miss Rachel."

Rachel sat on the edge of the bed. "I'm okay, Katie. I just haven't been able to come by much," she said in a gentle voice.

"But I had a bad dream. I thought you were killed like my mommy and daddy and you weren't coming back." Katie hiccupped with a stray sob.

Rachel put her arms around the little girl and hugged her close. "Katie, dreams aren't real. Sometimes our minds play tricks on us when we sleep and we wake up thinking something bad has happened. But it's not true. Your Uncle Spence knows when something's a bad dream and he can tell you when not to worry, too." She sat back to look at Katie.

Katie bobbed her head in understanding. Her little shoulders slumped with fatigue. She snuggled back under her bedclothes. Spence reached over and tucked the sheet around her. Rachel squeezed Katie's hand. "Good night, sleep tight."

Katie half smiled, but her forehead furrowed in a small frown. "Miss Rachel?"

"Yes?"

"I wish you could come to live with me and Uncle Spence." She spoke with all the hopeful innocence of a child.

Rachel exchanged a glance with Spence. He was no help at all. He returned her look with one of interested curiosity, with an intensity that made her feel self-conscious. It was as though he could read her mind and knew that it was a struggle for her to be here—that she was here because she loved them both. "Katie, it's not that simple...."

Katie opened her mouth to say more, but exhaustion caught up with her, making her eyelids droop with sleep. "Please come back soon," she murmured, pulling her bear in close with her.

"I will," Rachel whispered back.

"I love you, Miss Rachel."

"I love you, too, Katie," Rachel said softly.

Katie's eyelids fluttered closed and her breathing deepened with the peace of sleep.

Rachel carefully eased up from the bed. Spence stood, too, and turned off the bedside lamp. The glow from the seashell night-light illuminated the room like moonlight. They stood only inches apart. For an infinite second, their eyes met, and that circuit of warmth traveled between them.

Spence's eyes darkened with the impact of its power.

Rachel could hardly breathe. Would it never end? Would he always have this effect on her? Answerless questions. In an abrupt motion, she turned and walked out of the bedroom.

Spence followed her down to the foot of the staircase before he stopped her. "Rachel."

Knowing that she couldn't keep from running from him, that she didn't want to keep running, she turned back to face him.

He paused for a moment. "I know it was asking a lot for you to come here tonight. I wouldn't have called if there'd been any other way."

A prick of disappointment deflated her even more. *You can't have it both ways,* she told herself rationally. This would probably be the last time he did need her. If only she could forget about him, forget about the way he made her feel! "I'm glad I could help," she replied. She gave him a half smile, wanting to be as gracious as possible. She knew she should then say goodbye, turn away and walk to the door. But she didn't. Some contrary wishfulness rooted her to where she stood, allowing her a few more minutes with him.

Spence thought her smile looked strangely sad. He was surprised at her hesitancy. "I know it's late," he said, pausing, searching her face, "but you're welcome to stay awhile. I'd be interested in knowing what you're doing these days...."

Rachel's smile grew warmer. Her heart wanted this invitation...just a little more time. *You're a hopeless fool, Moran. But what's the harm in having just a little more time?* "Thank you. I'd like that."

Spence's returning smile was warm and irresistible. He moved to her side, showing her the way to the living room just past the staircase. "Make yourself comfortable. I'm going to have a cup of coffee. Can I get you one?"

"Yes, that sounds good. Thanks."

Rachel felt a little breathless. She knew why she'd lingered. She was just as curious about him as he was about her. What was the harm in that? But even left alone to explore on her own, she realized how surrounded by him she felt, how vulnerable to him. She nearly shivered.

She hadn't seen the house, really, except for Katie's room. Sue had made the home visit after she'd transferred the case. The living room fascinated Rachel. Polished oak flooring echoed her footsteps. An understated elegance intermingled with simplicity and comfort. A

sofa curved around a glass-topped granite cocktail table.
Massive bookshelves were built into the walls on both
sides of the fireplace. The music of the *Brandenberg
Concerto No. 5 in D Major* drifted in low volume from
unseen speakers. Wall sconces diffused the light into a
soft glow throughout the room.

Rachel skimmed over the array of books, a mixture of
classics, contemporary mysteries and nonfiction, including photography. A book on child development looked
new but well-thumbed-through. She smiled, feeling
wistful.

She crossed the room to the wall of picture windows
two stories in height. The lights of the cityscape flickered below, making her realize the house was built on one
of the bluffs edging the plains.

When Spence returned to the living room, Rachel
stood at the windows, her back to him, looking into the
darkness. The thin, enticingly slender straps of her dress
crisscrossed over the bare skin of her back, the bodice
tapering to her slender waist. The skirt blossomed over
her hips and fell gracefully to brush the curves of her
calves. Her bare arms and shoulders took on a silken
glow in the soft lighting of the room. He couldn't remember wanting anyone more than he wanted her.... He
stifled the thought.

The aroma of recently brewed coffee accompanied
Spence into the living room, and Rachel turned, accepting the ceramic mug. Their fingertips touched, their eyes
met, they looked away. She sat on the sofa, he in the
overstuffed chair perpendicular to hers. She noticed he'd
buttoned his shirt and tucked it in. He asked about her
work. No, he wasn't necessarily going to run for reelec-
tion as associate district judge since he'd been nomi-
nated for a state supreme court judgeship.... Yes,

photography was a hobby of his.... From moment to moment, their gazes would meet and connect in the way of two old, very good friends, as though nothing could be more natural, more comfortable...

Or more tempting, Rachel thought. Was it really so insane to want to be with him this much? Their conversation faded into silence. They were aware of only each other, and each knew it.

Yes, Rachel thought, it was insane. He'd called because he needed her help, and she couldn't ignore the implications of that. But she couldn't ignore the connectedness she felt with him when they were together.

She looked away, wondering what had gotten into her to linger when she should have simply left.

"Rachel," Spence began, sensing her struggle, "I would like for us to at least be friends—" *That sounds so damned corny,* he thought. And it was a lie. He wanted to be much more than just friends. But what else could he ask for?

"Friends?" Rachel repeated, that sadness touching her smile again.

"It's a place to begin," he said simply.

Maybe so, she thought. She met his gaze with resolute, determined consideration. Every time she was with him, she fell a little bit more in love. And she knew there were no certainties, no guarantees in a relationship, not really. "All right," she found herself saying. "A place to begin."

A glimmer of surprise showed in his eyes, as though he hadn't expected her to agree with him.

She felt awkward under the intentness of his gaze, feeling the familiar pull of tension between them. The pact seemed to be a moment of closure for the evening. To linger any longer...well, it was simply time to go, she told herself. "I suppose I'd better go now. It's getting late."

He looked distracted, but nodded, pushing up from the chair. But when she turned to move past him, he turned at the same time, as if intending to tell her something more, and they found themselves face-to-face.

Rachel wavered. Spence gripped her upper arms to steady her. Their gazes connected, and the knowledge that neither of them wanted to break the moment flowed between them. They both wanted this.

Spence looked down into her upturned face, at her eyes, sultry dark, her cheeks tinted crimson, her lips rosy and parted unconsciously, tempting him. He ached with the effort to control the need, the desire he felt for her. He wanted so much more than simple friendship from this woman. That he was holding her at all, so close, seemed a miracle.

Without really thinking, he pulled her closer, sliding his arms around her shoulders, lowering his head to brush her forehead with his lips. Without really realizing it, he muttered, "Don't be afraid of me, Rachel."

I already know the pain of not being with you, she thought. Her arms curved around him in natural response. *When the time comes to face it again, it will be no surprise, nothing unexpected.* In this moment, it seemed worth the risk. She pressed her cheek to his chest, feeling the thumping beat of his heart beneath the texture of his cotton shirt. She felt his breath warming her hair, heard the ragged edge to his breathing. A faint, spicy scent, sexy and masculine, drifted to her nostrils, reminding her of sandalwood. His chest was solid strength to steady her. She imagined the taste of his lips on hers. She raised her head and looked at him. "I'm not afraid of you," she told him in a hushed voice. She saw his eyes darken at her reply.

Time stopped.

He lowered his head and pressed his lips against hers, kissing her with the urgency of one long denied. He reveled in the sensual softness of her mouth against his, the taste of her tongue intertwining with his. He gathered her closer, trying to ease the aching need in his loins, but there was no relief.

Rachel was lost in the communion of his lips with hers, the taste of him, the feel of him. There was no thought, just insistent need.

His hands moved with increasing urgency over the bare skin of her back, to her rib cage, to the swell of her breasts. Rachel broke the kiss to catch her breath, her legs weakening beneath her.

Spence wrapped his arms around her. He rubbed his lips across her forehead, his breathing as rapid as hers. "I want all of you," he whispered, his voice uneven with need.

Rachel closed her eyes, wanting what he wanted, and knowing it wouldn't be tonight. "I thought you just wanted to be friends," she murmured in a seductive, mildly chastising tone. But she knew a platonic friendship was impossible.

And he looked mildly contrite. Only mildly. "Friends and lovers," he admitted. He dipped his head and kissed her again. When he raised his head to look at her, the regret at having to wait was evident. "Soon."

Rachel's expression grew somber. "This isn't a frivolous thing for me, Spence. I need time."

He looked at her a long moment. "I know. I'll try to go as slow as you want. But when I'm around you—" He grinned and looked away from her with a self-reproachful shake of his head.

"You just can't help yourself?" she finished teasingly for him.

"Something like that." He slipped an arm around her waist to distract her from noticing the sudden pensiveness that seized him. *I can't get you out of my system,* he thought. If he ever did, he knew she'd be hurt. She didn't deserve that. But the way he felt now, the way he'd felt for months, a lifetime couldn't give him enough of her. If what he felt wasn't love, then he didn't know what was. But he didn't want to make her a promise he couldn't keep. And she wasn't asking him to. "I'd better send you home," he told her.

At her car, he kissed her good-night.

"Just a friendly kiss," he murmured against her mouth.

She smiled under the touch of his lips. "Uh-huh."

They were suddenly spotlit by the headlights of a car coming up the driveway, startling them apart.

Spence squinted, trying to see into the car in the darkness. "I think that's Mrs. Millican." He shook his head with a half smile. "I called her, too. She didn't know I'd gotten you to come."

Rachel stayed long enough to give her regards to Mrs. Millican. Now, as she drove toward home, her heart struggled against doubt. He'd called her because he needed her help, she reminded herself for the umpteenth time. But she'd been his last resort, as it was. He'd even called Mrs. Millican.

And against all reason, her heart swelled with loving him, even still. If only... if only he grew to love her the way she loved him. Was that too much to wish for?

But she knew the risks. Simply loving him would have to be enough for now, for tonight, for tomorrow. It had to be.

Rachel inhaled a breath with wistful thinking. She glanced absently into the rearview mirror. A pair of headlights followed behind her. At first, she didn't think anything of it. But with each turn, through every intersection, the headlights stayed right behind her.

Apprehension tightened her chest. She strained to see if she could recognize the vehicle as it passed under streetlights. It had the boxy form of a Jeep-type vehicle, dark in color and completely unfamiliar to her. It was too dark to clearly see the driver. She had no doubt now that she was being followed.

Rachel had thought the threat of her intruder from last spring was over, but apparently she was wrong. Very wrong. "Oh, my God," she murmured to herself. Fear clutched at her throat. *What am I going to do?*

She was only a few blocks from home at this point. She pressed her foot down hard on the accelerator, widening the gap between her car and the other vehicle. The headlights behind her faded from sight.

Rachel kept an anxious eye on the rearview mirror, but nothing came into view. Her fingers ached from the tight grip she kept on the steering wheel. The fabric of her dress clung to her skin, damp with perspiration. With an inkling of relief, she took a deep breath, trying to settle the pounding of her heart.

Probably only a false alarm, she thought, feeling a little stupid. *I'm really losing it.*

She pulled into her driveway, parked, and turned off the headlights, leaving herself in darkness. *Dammit, why didn't I leave the porch light on?* she thought, feeling increasingly agitated. Her door was only twenty feet away, but tonight it might as well have been twenty miles.

Headlights swept the bushes lining her driveway in an illuminated path, then stopped right behind her, two balls of blinding white light.

A surge of adrenaline sent her heart slamming into her rib cage.

Oh, no. He'd followed her all the way home. Of course. He knew where she lived. How stupid could she be? She was afraid to move, afraid to stay. She slapped the car-door locks down.

Through the sideview mirror, she could see a car door open and a man step out. Rachel felt panic scream through every fiber of her being. She tasted the salt from the sweat of her fear on her lips. She pressed her hand down on the horn, breaking the quiet of the night. *Come on, wake up, Bob, if you're home. Please be home,* she prayed in a silent plea to her downstairs neighbor.

A tapping sound on Rachel's driver's-side window jerked her around, bringing her face-to-face with... *Spence* through the glass.

A light in the lower apartment snapped on. A second later, the porch lamp came on, spilling brightness across the lawn and into the driveway.

"Spence?" Rachel's panic crumpled into stark relief, then confusion, then anger.

"Rachel!" Spence barked her name, then looked up when Rachel's neighbor, Bob Turner, came barreling out his door, brandishing a baseball bat.

"Hey, you!" Bob yelled, holding the bat in front of him.

Spence straightened, immediately wary, lifting his hands to show he was not intent on violence.

Rachel fumbled with the door lock and nearly fell out of the car in her haste. "It's all right, Bob. I'm terribly sorry." She couldn't believe her mistake.

Behind her, Spence steadied her wobbly balance with his hands at her waist. "Rachel, what in the hell is going on?" he demanded.

Speechless with conflicting emotions, Rachel ignored him for the moment.

Bob walked around the front of the car, scratching his curly-haired dark head in sleepy confusion, and leaned against the bumper. He let the bat slide through his fingers to rest its tip on the pavement. "A case of mistaken identity, I presume?" He was barefoot and dressed only in boxer shorts.

Rachel's shoulders slumped in apology. "I'm really sorry, Bob. I didn't mean to get you out of bed for nothing." Embarrassment burned her face.

"That's all right," Bob replied with a shake of his head. "With all that went on last spring, it's better to be safe than sorry. What if you'd been right?" he finished, his expression sobering.

"Yeah," she murmured in halfhearted agreement. She touched a self-conscious hand to her temple. "Bob, this is Spence Garrett, a friend of mine. Spence, Bob Turner, my neighbor." She felt very contrite. "I didn't realize Spence was the one driving behind me."

The two men exchanged handshakes and nods.

Bob patted Rachel on her shoulder in his big-brotherly way. "Good night, girl," he said with a good-natured yawn. "You call me if you need any help. It's no trouble." He swung the bat onto his shoulder and walked back to his apartment.

Rachel spun around to face Spence. "What are you doing here? You scared me to death!"

Spence gave her a sardonic look. "For one thing, to make sure you got home safely. But I see now it was unnecessary, considering you seem to have the entire neighborhood on alert for your protection."

She glared at him in stubborn silence, folding her arms across her chest, and tried to back out of the range of his arms. She immediately bumped into her car.

Spence let his hands fall from her waist and stared at her in exasperation. "What are you so mad about?"

"I hate having the willies scared out of me," she snapped. She pivoted and ducked back into her car to get her purse. "I'm sorry if I embarrassed you," she said, getting back out and shutting the door with a shove of her hand, "but I didn't know you owned a Jeep or a Blazer or whatever that is." She tossed an unceremonious nod in the direction of his vehicle.

"It's a Bronco, and you didn't ask me for a list of my material assets, although I can't imagine why not. You asked for everything else."

She ignored that last comment and tried to walk around him.

He moved in front of her, grabbing her arm. "What did Bob Turner mean about last spring?"

"Nothing, really," she answered with an evasive shrug. "There was a prowler or something in the area three or four months ago and I'm still a little edgy about it." And she was still irritated with Spence for scaring her, unintentionally or not. Her heart continued pounding from residual terror and her knees felt wobbly.

"A 'prowler or something'?" Spence prompted, refusing to let go of her arm, incredulity spiking each word. "You acted like the devil himself was here to collect your soul."

"I overreacted, okay?"

"No, it's not okay."

"Look, Spence, all this happened last spring." She tried to shrug out of his grip. He had awfully strong hands for a judge. If he'd been an oil field worker, or something, she might have expected a grip like—

"Rachel, considering your neighbor almost beat the hell out of me with his baseball bat, I think I deserve to know why." He glared at her, a man at the end of his patience, his expression the epitome of exasperation.

She glared back, her lips a thin line of stubbornness, her eyes sparkling like angry black embers in the moonlight. Suddenly, the whole thing seemed so ridiculous to her. And that look on Spence's face... Rachel started to laugh. She didn't really know why. Laughter bubbled up inside her, so much it nearly hurt.

Spence released her, not knowing how to react.

Rachel pressed a hand to her stomach and leaned her hips against her car for support. "Oh, Spence. Poor Bob, coming to rescue me from you." Her laughter rippled over him.

A smile twitched at Spence's mouth. He rested his hands akimbo and shook his head at her. He put his hands around her waist. He felt laughter tremble through her, watched her wipe tears of merriment from the corners of her eyes. "You'll wish rescue if you're not careful," he warned, only half teasing, his voice suddenly husky.

Her merriment faded in the wake of his touch, her breath catching in her throat.

He stepped closer, looking down the length of her body, his trail of vision a seductive caress that brought a flush to her skin. He ran his hand slowly up from her

waist, over the soft floral bodice of her dress, between her
breasts, to the base of her throat. He touched her pulse,
watched the rise and fall of her breasts with each breath.
He looked into her eyes, asking a silent question.

Chapter Eleven

Rachel saw raw desire in Spence's eyes, felt it ripple over her. He wanted to make love to her, and she wanted him to, more than sanity could stop it.

Her silence, her dark eyes wide with sudden expectancy, her pulse throbbing at her throat drew Spence closer. He let his hands slide down to the fleshy curve of her hips and pulled her to him. She acquiesced, letting her body curve into his. He grazed her mouth with a kiss, then moved his lips to her ear. "Let me love all of you." His voice was a ragged whisper.

Her eyes struggled with want and dismay. "I'm not protected," she whispered in regret, her voice husky with need. "It's been a very long time."

Her admission pleased him. His feelings of possessiveness came as a surprise to him. Then a wicked sparkle came to his eyes. "I came prepared," he admitted, lowering his face to nuzzle her cheeks with his lips.

"You were that certain of yourself, were you?" she teased seductively.

He pulled back and grinned. "Not really. I was a Boy Scout."

"I should have known," she replied, her voice a lazy murmur, her hands drifting to his neck, pulling his face down to hers.

They made it as far as the bottom of the stairs before they had to kiss each other, touch each other again, giving each other just enough sustenance to get them up to the second floor of the duplex, into the living room. Amber light from a small table lamp mixed with moonlight through a window to cast a glow across the room.

He couldn't keep from kissing her. He sought her lips with his, her tongue with his tongue, demanding fulfillment.

Rachel threaded her fingers into his hair, pressing her mouth to his, meeting his demands with demands of her own. Every nerve ending in her body shimmered with the sensual heat between them. She felt dizzy, deliciously lost in the loving passion of this man.

She felt his arms go around her, felt his hands slide down to the curve of her hips, pulling up her dress, seeking more...

Quicksilver heat radiated through her. "Oh," she breathed, closing her eyes. The waiting seemed unbearable. She pressed her hand over the zipper of his jeans, against the hard outline of him, urging him to her.

Spence sucked in a breath at her exploring touch. His hands moved over the silk fabric covering her buttocks, pressing her hard against him. He expelled his breath in a heated rush.

"Rachel," he muttered, his voice raspy with desire, his need for release mounting like thirst after an eternity in the desert.

His fingers fumbled with the back of her dress until it came loose, falling to her waist. He slid his hands over the lacy white silk covering her breasts, feeling the soft swells and hardened peaks of each. Pushing the silk away, he ducked his head to kiss her bared skin. He heard her sharp intake of breath, felt her lean into the caress of his tongue.

He straightened and began unbuttoning his shirt, meeting her eyes intently with his.

Rachel returned his look, unwavering. They were past the need for words to communicate their wants. She slid her dress down over her hips, letting it fall to the floor at her feet. She stepped out of the pool of fabric, closer, helping him unbutton his shirt, then tugging his shirt-tails from the waistband of his jeans.

With a mutter of his intent, Spence covered her mouth with his. Putting his hands on her shoulders and nudging her legs with his, he walked her down the hall to her bedroom.

They tumbled onto her bed, their legs intertwining. Spence pulled away the silky underthings standing between his hands and Rachel's skin. He reveled in the sensual softness of her breasts, touching her, kissing her, tasting her. He was lost in this moment—in the touch of her, the taste of her—the moment he'd wanted since the day he'd met her. He slid his hand over the flat plane of her stomach, to her hipbones, then to touch the heated, dewy softness between her thighs, knowing she wanted this, knowing he couldn't hold back much longer.

Desire flowed through Rachel with liquid warmth, heightening with each touch, each caress of his hands, his lips, his tongue. She could hardly bear the intensity building between them. She wanted to touch him as he touched her. She ran her hands under his shirt, over the hard muscles of his chest, feeling the texture of his skin, its heat, the sprinkle of blond hair trailing to the waistband of his jeans.

A guttural sound came from the back of Spence's throat. He shifted, pulling off his shirt, then unzipping his jeans and shedding his remaining clothes.

Rachel pressed him against her. "Please," she whispered, seeking relief.

Moonlight filtered through the lace curtains at the bedroom windows. She could see the passion darkening his eyes. She helped him slide on their protection, stroking him with her fingers. At her touch, he trembled and rolled her over onto her back, holding her beneath him, hugging her close. "I can't stop, Rachel," he muttered.

Her eyes were bright with need, her lips swollen from his kisses. "I don't want you to stop," she whispered in return, her hands gripping the back of his shoulders.

He supported his weight with his forearms on either side of her head, tangling his fingers in her hair. *Beautiful, beautiful Rachel.* He wanted to share each moment of exquisite sensation with her, wanted her to feel what he felt. He watched her eyes close, her lips part with a sharp intake of air when his body merged with hers.

It was good, giving him a sense of wholeness he hadn't known he was missing....

It was good, filling an emptiness in her that perhaps had never been filled....

She opened herself to him, her hands sliding down to his hips, urging him into her. His skin felt hot to the touch, his muscles bunching and releasing beneath her fingers.

Their fragrances intermingled, flowers and spice, the scents sharper from body heat. Her fingers dug into his flesh, his fingers tangled in her hair. Finally... finally, cresting the passion, hot, sweet relief rippled through her, closing around him, granting them both complete, utter release.

They lay together, entangled with each other, breathless, spent. A fine sheen of perspiration glistened on his skin and hers.

Spence rolled over on his side, his face inches from hers, and propped himself up on an elbow to look at her.

Her lips were claret red, her cheeks rosy pink with the afterglow of their lovemaking. *Their lovemaking.* Erotic, intense, passionate sex as it had been, the driving force had come from... his heart. And he hadn't gotten her out of his system. Perhaps he never would.

Her eyelids fluttered open and her dark eyes met his. For a moment, he thought she could sense his thoughts. Would she believe in them? Did he? He knew he wanted the time with her to find out.

"You're a very beautiful woman." He traced the contours of her lips with a gentle fingertip, feeling them curve into a smile at his words. "Very sexy."

She stretched with the lazy satisfaction of a woman thoroughly loved, then wrapped her arms around him. "Thanks. I think you're pretty incredible yourself."

Their gazes met and held again. Rachel looked for his thoughts... his feelings for her. How deep did they go? How far beyond friendship? Did they reach into his heart? All she knew for certain was she loved him.

He leaned closer to give her a lingering kiss. Over her head, on the bedside table, the alarm clock told him it was nearly two in the morning.

He pulled back to look at her in apology. "Even though Mrs. Millican hinted it would be perfectly fine with her if I didn't show up for the rest of the night, I probably ought to get home before dawn."

Rachel smiled. "You take your parental duties very seriously."

He grinned back at her, then lowered his head to kiss a rosy nipple. He dragged his mouth away reluctantly. "I can't get enough of you," he muttered in a husky growl.

Another glance at the clock prompted him to sit up and swing his legs over the edge of the bed. He reached for his jeans and underwear, pulling them on.

Rachel rolled onto her side to watch him with complete fascination. "It's sexy watching a man get dressed."

Spence shook his head at the seductiveness of her voice, the sultry darkness of her gaze. "Don't tempt me."

She didn't look the least apologetic.

He buttoned his shirt. Concern shadowed his eyes. "I don't like leaving you here by yourself, with a 'prowler or something' hanging around," he said, lifting an eyebrow in reproval.

"I'll be fine, really. And don't forget, I have Bob to protect me. One scream and he'd be right here. You oughta know."

He gave her another dry glance at that comment, at the same time trying to stifle the definite pinch of jealousy he felt about Bob's readiness to be her protector. "You never did tell me exactly what happened."

Rachel hated to worry him at this point. "Spence, I haven't seen a hint of this guy since May. I thought I saw him drive by the office a couple of times last spring, and he broke into my apartment one morning. But he didn't take anything, just rifled through some of my stuff."

Spence frowned. "I still don't like it."

"Neither do I, but that's life."

Rachel got up from bed and put on a floral satin summer robe. From behind him, she slipped her arms around his waist, peering around to watch him in the oval mirror of her vanity dresser. "I'll be okay."

The reflection of their gazes met in the mirror. They looked at each other for a silent moment.

"I'll call you tomorrow," he said.

She closed her eyes. She couldn't believe he was suddenly such an intimate part of her life. For now, anyway....

At two-twenty, Rachel locked the dead bolt behind Spence.

A block away, from a parking place chosen to give a clear view of Rachel Moran's apartment, a man trained a pair of night-vision binoculars on the driveway of the duplex. He watched the Bronco pull away. He moved the binoculars to focus on the apartment windows and watched the lights go out.

Finally. He lowered the binoculars and angled his head, spitting his chaw of tobacco out the driver's-side window. He was tired and ready to go home and get some shut-eye. But in his profession, long nights awake in his car were the norm. It paid the bills.

He laid the binoculars on the seat next to his camera. He'd thought he was through with this job three months ago. Hell, he'd nearly bungled it. He'd been afraid she'd made him that morning, catching him coming out of her apartment, an embarrassment he couldn't afford. How could he have known she hadn't planned to go to work that day? But nothing ever came of it.

Then last week, he got another call to keep track of her a while longer. This time, he'd gotten what he needed.

That should just about wrap things up. He was tired of following her around. Go to work, go home, go to work, go home . . . She was unbelievably boring. Then, finally tonight she'd given him what he was paid to get.

With a flick of his hand, the car sputtered to life, and he called it a night.

Rachel drifted awake under the warming touch of morning. Sunlight filtered into her bedroom through the leaves of the sycamore tree outside the open window, making golden lattice patterns on the walls. She watched the pattern change, like a kaleidoscope, with the touch of a breeze.

She snuggled into her pillow, thinking of the man who'd shared her bed into the early-morning hours. She pulled the other pillow into her arms, hugging it to her body.

Sleep's haze evaporated and the memories of last night returned with breathless clarity. She recalled every touch, every kiss, every moment.

She could hardly believed any of it had happened. Last night, she'd taken a step off the edge of a cliff, but she wasn't falling, not yet—just sailing with the possibilities.

Sailing with her head in the clouds. A dose of reality washed over her. Friends and lovers . . . and a child's life to consider. It was one thing for Rachel to risk her own heart; it was quite another to get a child's hopes up for a real family, complete with a father *and* mother figure.

A sinking feeling pooled in her stomach. Amazing how lust could drive all reason away for those few stolen hours of passion. But she didn't regret it, not really. Last night was the inevitable conclusion of their meeting from the beginning. But she didn't want it to end. If only the thought of not having him in her life didn't hurt so much....

She wondered what Spence felt with the morning's light. Maybe he wouldn't call. But she knew he would.

She shivered, forcing herself out of bed. They definitely had to talk. Maybe a shower would clear her head.

She let the water stream over her body, then soaped her skin. In doing so, she remembered everywhere Spence had touched her. She closed her eyes, wanting him there with her. The water turned cool, taking the heat from her skin. Her breath came out in a wistful sigh and she rinsed off. There was no getting him out of her mind.

She was curled up on the sofa, dressed only in her robe, reading the Sunday-morning newspapers and sipping a cup of coffee, when the telephone rang.

"I waited two hours before I called. I couldn't wait any longer. I hope I didn't wake you." Spence's voice was soft and deep.

A ripple of pleasure traveled through her. "No, I've been up for a while, too." She hugged her knees to her chest, feeling like a teenager again.

At his end, Spence smiled at the warmth in her voice. "I told Miss Katie I talked with you last night. She wanted to be sure to invite you to go with us to the zoo this afternoon...and I would also like very much for you to come."

She melted a little at the soft urging in his voice. "I would love to come," she began.

"Great. We'll be by to pick you up at one this afternoon."

"Spence, I need to ask you about something first."

He paused, then asked, "What is it?"

"How we're going to handle our... friendship around Katie."

"Very discreetly." He drawled out the words.

"I mean it. This is important. I don't want Katie getting her hopes up that, that—" She fumbled for what she wanted to say.

"That we might get married or some such thing?" He said it with such nonchalance it hurt.

"Right. I don't want her to be disappointed—" To her dismay, her voice suddenly became hoarse, and she had to clear her throat. "Or hurt." She cleared her throat again. "Excuse me. I don't know why my throat's doing this." But she did know and she hated her transparency.

Spence sat on the edge of his bed, trying to decipher the emotions lacing Rachel's words. "I don't want her to be disappointed or hurt, either, Rachel," he said slowly, his voice gentle with his efforts to reassure. "And . . . I don't want to hurt you."

Rachel closed her eyes. "I know. I don't want to hurt you or Katie, either."

"Well, then, it sounds to me like we want the same thing."

She wasn't exactly sure how he meant that, but she didn't press the issue. She smiled into the phone.

"I think so." She hoped so.

At five minutes to one, Rachel heard two car doors shut outside. She looked out the window to see Spence and Katie strolling hand in hand up the sidewalk. Katie's long blond hair flowed behind her like a stream of sunlight, her face aglow with excitement.

Something's different, Rachel thought. Then she knew. Katie didn't have her teddy bear with her. She smiled to herself. *You've done well, Judge Garrett.*

Rachel had dressed for comfort in khaki shorts and a white camp shirt, ankle socks and walking shoes. She skipped down the stairs to meet Spence and Katie.

"Miss Rachel!" Katie ran up the stairs to the porch. "I've missed you!"

Rachel knelt to return Katie's hug. "I've missed you, too, honey. But I just saw you last night," she reminded her gently.

"I know," Katie said. She pointed behind Rachel. "Is that your kitty? Can I play with her?"

"She's a he. His name is Simon. But we need to ask your Uncle Spence if we have time."

"Sure we have time," Spence replied, stepping forward to give his niece's hair a tug.

Katie bounded up the stairs after Simon, who knew to run.

Rachel turned to Spence. "Poor cat. He's declawed, so he can't scratch her, that is if she can even get anywhere near him."

Spence chuckled, his eyes crinkling at the corners, the blue sparkling with warm emotion. He stepped closer and pulled her to him in a quick hug. He lowered his head and kissed her.

Rachel's breath left her, lost in the kiss.

He lifted his head to look down at her. "Good afternoon."

It was hopeless, she thought, looking into his handsome face, at the sexy sparkle of a smile in his eyes. How could she ever resist him? "Good afternoon, yourself," she said, her hands on the waistband of his blue jeans. He wore a cranberry cotton twill shirt that accentuated the angular lines of his chest and shoulders. Just hopeless.

"I'd have rather told you good morning from the other side of your bed, but—" He didn't finish his intimation, a teasing smile pulling at his mouth.

Rachel shook her head at him. "You're impossible." She took a step back. "Let's go up and see what Katie's doing. And have a cup of coffee?"

"Sounds good to me."

Katie was in the living room, down on her hands and knees trying to coax the cat out from underneath the sofa. Rachel brought two cups of coffee to the kitchen table where Spence sat.

She glanced over at Katie, then back to Spence. "You're doing a wonderful job with her."

"That's good to hear," he replied. "Sometimes I'm not so sure." His expression grew thoughtful. "I want to see you more often, Rachel, but the next few weeks are pretty heavily scheduled for me."

Disappointment struggled with reason within her. "I understand, Spence. You have obligations. And I do, too." She wanted to feel as grown-up about it as she sounded. She knew some distance would be good for them, give them both a chance to think over where this was headed. And there was always Katie to consider.

"In fact, I have a judicial conference to attend in Wyoming next week. I'll be flying out Tuesday morning."

Three days. "How long will you be gone?"

"A week. So I thought maybe we could meet for lunch Monday...just you and me."

Before Rachel could respond, Katie's voice piped up from the living room. "Miss Rachel can have dinner with us when Grandmother comes tonight, can't she? It's Mrs. Millican's day off."

Rachel watched Spence's face at Katie's request. He shot an apologetic glance at Rachel, then said, "Katie, I think Grandmother is looking forward to this being a family get-together tonight."

Katie's lower lip came up in the beginnings of a pout.

Rachel spoke up then. "Katie, honey, your Uncle Spence is right about that. Tonight is a family dinner. Maybe some other time we can have dinner, okay?"

Katie's eyes clouded. "I wish you could be in our family," she said in her little-girl voice.

Innocent words, but they struck close to Rachel's heart. "We're friends, Katie. Friends can love one another, even if they're not family," she explained carefully.

Katie seemed mollified—enough, anyway, to return her attention to playing with the cat.

Spence gave Rachel's face a searching glance, then he reached for her hand, giving it a quick, discreet squeeze. "Thanks for being so understanding about that," he said, his voice low.

"Little ears can hear a lot," she warned, her voice equally low. There was so much she wanted to ask him, about his mother and how she was doing, but now wasn't the right time.

"So what about lunch on Monday?" Spence asked again.

Rachel grinned at his persistence. "Twelve-thirty. But I'll only have thirty minutes," she warned.

"Obligations," Spence acknowledged with a regretful smile. "I'll pick you up at your office."

"I'll be expecting you." And looking very much forward to it. "I'll give you my new address." She didn't want to think about his being gone, just focus on the moment at hand. She looked at her watch. "If we want to go to the zoo, we'd probably better get going."

They departed a threesome.

Jacqueline Garrett watched her son answer the telephone. Judging from his glance at her, it was going to be a lengthy call. She knew he sometimes had to deal with pressing legal matters at home when they couldn't wait for regular business hours.

She slipped quietly out of the kitchen, which was spotlessly clean, once she'd finished with it after dinner. She climbed the stairs to the second floor and tapped on the half-open door to Katie's bedroom.

Katie looked up from the pages of the Dr. Seuss book she had open on the bed. Her cheeks dimpled in a smile. "You can come in, Grandmother."

Jacqueline smiled at her granddaughter. Oh, how she reminded her of young Julia. She came over to sit on the edge of the bed next to Katie. She watched the little girl peruse each page before turning to the next. "So," she said, clasping her hands in her lap, "you said you went to the zoo this afternoon. Did you have fun?"

Katie nodded, still focused on the colorful illustrations of the book.

"Did anyone else go with you and Uncle Spence?" Jacqueline asked very carefully, her voice even.

Katie turned a page and nodded. "Yup. Miss Rachel."

"Miss Rachel?" Jacqueline tried to keep the surge of anger she felt from seeping into her voice.

Katie nodded again. "I love Miss Rachel. She's my friend. And Uncle Spence's friend, too."

"I see. And you love Grandmother, too, don't you?" She couldn't quite keep the edge of jealousy out of her voice.

Katie looked up, a tiny frown of worry shadowing her gaze. "Yes," she said hesitantly, as though worried she'd done something she shouldn't have, but not knowing what.

Spence's resonant voice cut through the subtle tension suspended in the room. "What's going on?" He asked the question easily, walking through the doorway to kneel at the bedside.

Katie shrugged and looked at her book, turning another page.

Jacqueline's mouth thinned in irritation. "Just having a little conversation with my granddaughter."

"I see," Spence replied. He didn't miss the small look of worry in Katie's expression. Or the veil of irritability that had dropped over Jacqueline's mood. He wasn't sure what was going on, but he didn't like it.

Jacqueline eased up from the edge of the bed. "Well, I think it's time for me to be going. It's about Katie's bedtime." She bent to kiss Katie's cheek, saying "Good night, dear," then walked past Spence out of the room.

Spence smiled reassurance to Katie. "I'll be right back. I'm going to walk your grandmother to the door."

He caught up with his mother in the foyer. For just a moment, he was going to ask her what was bothering her, what she'd talked to Katie about. But he didn't want to risk an argument in Katie's earshot. All he said was "Good night."

A faint look of surprise crossed Jacqueline's fine features, but she left without further comment.

After Jacqueline's departure, Spence sat down with Katie. "Did you have a good time tonight?"

Katie shrugged. "Yeah."

"Is something bothering you, Katie?"

"I told Grandmother that I loved her but I think she was mad at me."

Damn. "You didn't do anything wrong, Katie. If your grandmother was...mad, or something, it wasn't because of anything you said or did." He was not going to have Katie feeling responsible for Jacqueline's problems.

Katie looked relieved. She wrapped her arms around his neck. "I love you, Uncle Spence," she mumbled into his shirt.

"I love you, too, Katie." He stroked her hair with a soothing hand. He forced cheerfulness into his tone. "Time for you to get to your bath, then bed."

Katie knew the routine.

He had to confront Jacqueline soon. He sighed in frustration. He wanted to talk to Rachel about it. But he didn't want to ask for her help any more than was absolutely necessary. That Rachel had come back to him seemed a miracle. But he knew she was afraid to trust him completely. And he couldn't in good conscience promise her a commitment, yet. Time in Wyoming would give him a chance to gain some perspective. But he suspected, deep in his heart, that he could never really let Rachel go....

Chapter Twelve

First thing Monday morning, Rachel called her answering service to check for messages. Three referrals and no problems over the weekend. *Good,* she thought in satisfaction. She called back the referrals and scheduled appointments for them.

She finished with her last appointment of the morning right before twelve-thirty. She called her answering service to intercept her calls for the next half hour, except for any emergencies, which would be routed through her pager.

She shivered in anticipation. She wanted every minute to count; she and Spence wouldn't be seeing each other for another week after today. It felt like forever.

Spence arrived, right on time, carrying a grocery sack in his arms.

Rachel came around her desk to help him.

Spence dropped a kiss on her lips. "I'd like to suggest a small change in our plans."

Rachel peeked into the sack. Roast beef sandwiches, turkey sandwiches, diet soda. "Hmm..."

"The idea of lunch in a public spot didn't appeal to me in the least. I was hoping you wouldn't mind if we..." He took the sack from her and put it on her desk. "Stayed here..." He moved closer, encircling her waist with both arms. "And locked the door..." He kissed her in a lingering kiss. "And had our own private lunch...." His breath grew ragged, his voice a rough whisper as he rubbed his lips over hers.

Rachel slid her hands up over the back of his suit jacket, over his shoulder blades, until her fingers entwined in his hair at the nape of his neck. "I think," she whispered, her eyes closing as he moved his lips down to the sensitive skin of her neck, "that's a wonderfully... wicked... idea."

He kissed her again, more deeply, more intimately, more urgently. He shrugged out of his suit jacket. She ached for his touch with an urgency that nearly made her reel, but...

"But," she murmured against his mouth, "I'd hate for my next client to find our associate district judge naked in my office."

"But it's lunchtime," he muttered in return, nuzzling at her ear.

"But it could happen...." She sighed with regret.

Spence groaned his reluctance, but let her go. "Are you always this rational?" he grumbled.

Rachel just smiled.

They made a picnic table of her desk. Rachel handed him a deli sandwich, saying, "This stuff looks great."

Spence looked around her office, seeing it for the first time, a few minutes earlier too preoccupied to notice anything but her. The carpeting was a regal evergreen. Her certificates and diplomas decorated the wall behind her desk. The shelves held books on psychology, social work, philosophy, diagnostics. The building itself was one of the older ones downtown, not far from the courthouse, housing several private offices and rich with architectural detail. She liked antiques, he remembered.

"This is nice, Rachel."

"Thank you."

"Do you rent?"

She nodded. "When I was part time, I shared this office with another woman in private practice. Now that we're both full time, we can both afford our own offices. She has hers down the hall. We cover for each other sometimes."

Spence looked at the prints of two of Monet's impressionist paintings, patches of color and images, both framed in gold-leaf wood. "*The Artist's Garden at Vetheuil* and *Bridge Over a Pool of Water.* Did you choose these prints for their serenity?"

She nodded. "And I really like Monet's works. When I was a kid, I always imagined I had a secret garden to escape to. I'd like to landscape a real garden one of these days."

Spence gave her a thoughtful look. *A garden to escape to. Escape from what?* The impression was fleeting, chased away by the smile she gave him, along with a diet soda.

They picnicked at her desk in easy silence.

Spence glanced past her. "Is that clock right?"

Rachel looked behind her. "Five to one. Yes, right on time," she confirmed, disappointment bringing down her shoulders a fraction.

His disappointment mirrored hers. He helped her clean up the remains of their picnic lunch. He pulled on his suit jacket. Rachel smoothed his tie for him, letting her fingers linger on his chest, feeling so reluctant to let him leave.

"I wish you weren't leaving," she said in a small voice. "I'm having trouble being a grown-up about this." She tried to laugh at herself.

Spence smiled and hugged her close. He kissed her hair. "I thought I was the only one who felt like that."

Rachel pressed her cheek against his chest, drawing sustenance from these last few minutes with him. Wonderful for now. But what would tomorrow bring?

Tuesday morning, Rachel looked at the clock. Ten-thirty. Spence's plane was airborne by now, carrying him to his judicial conference in Wyoming. She had enough to keep her busy, what with work and visits to Katie. She already missed Spence.

Three brisk knocks sounded on her office door, interrupting her train of thought. Her next appointment wasn't for another hour, and she didn't usually have drop-in visitors.

She opened the door to Jacqueline Garrett. Mrs. Garrett stood with her usual elegant bearing, dressed in a navy linen suit, her expression very cool, almost hard with distaste. For a small instant, she seemed to waver, but steadied herself with the balance of her cane.

A distinct prickle of tension sprang up between them. "Mrs. Garrett," Rachel began, automatically using her most quiet tone of voice. "Come in." She couldn't keep the surprise completely out of her voice, nor could she shake off the faint apprehension that shivered down her spine. She stepped aside to allow the other woman into the office.

Mrs. Garrett's perfume seemed oddly heavy, as though applied to distract from another scent. As the older woman moved into the room, Rachel caught a faint whiff of... alcohol? She couldn't be certain.

Mrs. Garrett sat in the chair Rachel indicated for her. She looked around the room, her expression unreadable, before returning her regard to Rachel. Her eyes swept her from head to toe in undisguised scrutiny.

"Mrs. Garrett, how may I help you?"

"Miss Moran, I don't intend to take up much of your time, but I have a family matter I need to discuss with you." Her smile seemed only a concession to polite discussion. Her words ended with a light slur.

"What kind of family matter?" Rachel wondered what, if anything, Spence had told his mother about her.

"About my son and granddaughter. I need your help."

"Then, how can I help you?" Rachel asked, sitting behind her desk. This lady was not easy to talk with.

Mrs. Garrett pursed her lips in speculation. "You can help me by disassociating yourself from them."

"I beg your pardon?" Rachel stifled a surge of outrage at such a ridiculous request.

"I want you to leave my family alone."

Rachel expelled a very careful breath. "Why?"

"I'm well aware that my son is a—" she paused, looking for the right word "—desirable catch. And you caught him at a very vulnerable time. I knew from the way he talked about you that very first week, he was completely taken in by you. I don't believe he had the objectivity to see what was really happening."

"And what is it you think was really happening?" Rachel asked. The woman talked about her son as if he were an impressionable boy who needed protection from predatory women, or in this case, Rachel.

"You think I don't know?"

"I don't know what you think. I need you to tell me." Rachel's voice was devoid of any emotion.

Mrs. Garrett studied her with overly bright eyes. "I know you came from a poor Arkansas farm family. That you and your brother were orphaned. You've more or less pulled yourself up by your bootstraps to overcome your background, but you don't make much money as a social worker. I know that your brother more or less killed himself with drugs—"

Rachel found her voice. "How dare you?" She quivered with outrage. "You know *nothing* about my life, nothing about my brother. If you have a point to make, then make it or get out of my office."

"The point is, you used my granddaughter to get to my son and his money. Like Sam West tried to use Julia. And that is the greatest miscarriage of professionalism I can imagine."

That was enough. The woman was irrational. Rachel got up from behind her desk. "Mrs. Garrett, I don't think we have anything left to discuss."

"Oh, but I think we do."

Rachel placed both hands on her desk for support. "I want you to leave now," she repeated, her voice steeled against anger and outrage.

Mrs. Garrett reached into her purse and pulled out a manila envelope. She leaned forward and slid it onto Rachel's desk.

Rachel stared back at her, not wanting to look at the contents for reasons she couldn't identify, but knowing she had to anyway. She picked up the envelope and pulled open the flap. She pulled out several black-and-white photographs—of herself and Spence. She was leaning against her car; he was smiling down at her, his hand touching her throat. It was from just a few nights ago.

Anger burned in Rachel's chest. And suddenly she felt frightened. "How did you get these?" She choked out the question. But she already had her suspicions.

"I hired a private investigator."

"How long—"

"How long has he been collecting his information? Since April, when I realized what you were doing."

"Why are you doing this?" Rachel couldn't comprehend the woman's actions.

"I told you. I want my family back. I know your type. You'd do anything for money, including take advantage of my family's tragedy. If you want to keep your social work license, get out of our lives. If not, I'll have no other choice than to make a complaint about you to your board." Mrs. Garrett's hands trembled with emotion. She pressed her lips into a thin line, as though she'd finished with a necessary but distasteful task.

Dead silence suspended in the air between them. It roared in Rachel's head. She sat down, slowly.

Mrs. Garrett stood and walked to the door. She paused, turning back. "I would advise you not to mention any of this to my son. It will only make everything more difficult for you." She exited, leaving the door wide-open behind her.

Rachel listened to the echo of the woman's footsteps fade into deafening silence. She forced herself up and went to the door, closing it. She turned around and let her body sag against its solid, wooden surface, feeling sick at heart.

My God, what just happened here? Her mind churned, trying to sort out the craziness. For the first time she could remember, she had no immediate idea what to do.

Rachel made herself breathe evenly, slowing her heartbeat and clearing her mind enough to think it through.

She knew Jacqueline Garrett had taken a number of truths, half truths and outright lies and organized them into a scenario that justified her desire to get Rachel out of the picture. Rachel knew Jacqueline had to feel very threatened by her to go to such an outrageous extreme. She had twisted her information just enough to make it sound believable, just enough to put doubts into people's minds.

And Rachel suspected that what she'd smelled had indeed been alcohol and that the woman had been drinking before arriving at Rachel's office. And she realized that this, most likely, was an example of the problem that had driven Julia from her home.

Katie. Rachel's temple throbbed. Tears formed a lump in her throat. She couldn't imagine that dear, sweet little girl being victimized by the jealous insecurities of her grandmother. It would be a travesty of everything she had worked for all these years. She could not, *would not* let that happen. Did Spence realize how out of control his mother really was?

Spence. She fought the urge to break down in tears. *I can't deal with this.* But she knew she had to deal with it. Friends and lovers. Hardly worth risking a child's well-being over. *I should never have fallen in love with him....* As if she'd had any choice.

And her job. Jacqueline Garrett could try to ruin her professionally.

She sat at her desk, her elbows propped on the ink blotter, her head between her hands. A private investigator. All those hours she'd spent in fear of the intruder in her apartment and all along he was a private investigator! All those wasted hours. She gave a sardonic laugh. He wasn't a lunatic, only a man who could ruin her life for a price.

She wanted to tear the photographs to shreds, destroy the destroyer, but she didn't. She jammed them back into the envelope and stuffed it into her purse.

In the private bathroom off her office, Rachel splashed cold water over her face. What was she going to do? She pressed her face into a towel. She suddenly realized the best action was no action, not just yet. But she didn't want to antagonize Mrs. Garrett further by seeing Katie, even though she hated to cancel their weekend plans. She needed to talk to Spence, but not over the telephone, not about something like this. She needed to talk to him face-to-face.

Rachel looked at the clock. It was nearly eleven. Her client would be here soon. And when the knock came on the door, Rachel presented the capable, professional demeanor expected of her, the capable professional she was.

It was only at the end of the day, in the privacy of her bedroom, that she let the facade fall.

Thursday evening, Rachel curled up on top of the comforter on her bed as she had the past two nights, since the conversation with Jacqueline Garrett. Rachel couldn't remember facing more painful choices than the ones she knew she would soon have to make... for everyone's sake. She felt that peculiar numbness that came after a shock wore off, when reality set in, and tears were spent, for the moment. She was even beyond the anger she'd felt toward Jacqueline Garrett.

The telephone on the bedside table rang at eight o'clock. Rachel sat up, plumped the pillows against the brass head of her bed and answered it on the fifth ring.

"Hello." Her voice was unusually deep and hoarse. She cleared her throat, hoping to sound more okay than she felt.

There was a brief pause at the end of the line, then she heard Spence's voice. "Hello, Rachel?" He sounded uncertain, as though maybe he had a wrong number.

"Yes. Spence, hi."

"You don't sound like yourself. Are you all right?"

His mellow timbre was both comforting and painful to hear. "I was taking a catnap when you called." She cleared her throat again. "I guess I'm still a little foggy." Not entirely untrue, but she hadn't really slept. She was too heartsick.

"It sounds like I called at a bad time."

"No, that's okay. How's the conference going?"

"Interesting and boring. Are you sure you're okay?" In Jackson, Wyoming, Spence stretched out in his bathrobe on top of the king-size bed in his hotel room. He missed his Rachel with a passion. The past couple of days away from her had only intensified his feelings. He wanted her with him in this lonely room, and her distant response to his call puzzled him.

"Yes, I'm okay. It's just that I had an exhausting day." He could hear her take a deep breath at her end.

He frowned at what sounded almost like an edge of desperation in her voice. But she'd said she was fine. Maybe he was reading too much into it. "You want to tell me about it?" he asked, wanting to share in her life, somehow ease the distress.

"No, that's okay. How about you? Do you guys really sit around all day discussing points of law or do you play golf and raise Cain?" A smile crept into her voice.

Spence grinned. Now that sounded more like Rachel. "Both. Have you talked to Katie today?"

"No, I crawled into bed as soon as I got home. Have you?"

"I'll be giving her a good-night call after we hang up." He thought Rachel really did sound tired. That must be it. He didn't want to keep her too long. "You sound like you need to rest."

"You're probably right."

Spence smiled to her over the phone. "I'll call you in a few days. Good night, darling."

Darling. The endearment pulled tears to her eyes. She squeezed her eyes shut. "Good night."

Spence laid the phone in its cradle. If it weren't so absurd an idea he'd swear he'd heard a misting of tears in her voice. For a long moment after they'd hung up, he lay awake, staring into the darkness, unable to shake the feeling something was amiss, something she wasn't telling him. But Rachel had always been forthright with him, pulling no punches. It was a part of what he loved about her....

He loved her. The thought came spontaneously, without deliberation, without doubt. And he wondered what she would say if he told her his feelings. But the acknowledgment was so new to him, he wanted to give it a little more time.

It was Saturday evening before he had the opportunity to call at a decent time again. He called Katie first, because it was so close to her bedtime.

"How's my Katie?"

"Okay, I guess." Katie's voice sounded small and disappointed.

"What's the matter?"

"Miss Rachel said she couldn't come over for the weekend like she said."

A very still feeling washed over Spence. Rachel knew how much Katie cherished their time together. "Did she tell you why she couldn't come?"

"She said she had something she had to do. She said she was sorry."

Something to do? Work? On a weekend? What in the hell was Rachel doing? "I'm sure she has a good reason, Katie," Spence said, trying to think of a plausible explanation to ease Katie's disappointment. "And I don't think she's been feeling very well lately."

"She isn't sick, is she?" Her little voice held the sound of tears. "Sometimes people die when they get sick—"

"No, no, Katie. It's just a cold, or something. People get them all the time. She isn't going to die." How could he have been so stupid? And what was going on with Rachel?

It was too late to stop the tears. "Uncle Spence, please come home. I miss you."

Spence ran a hand through his hair, then paced the floor as far as the telephone cord would allow. "It'll be okay, honey." But was it okay? He didn't know anymore.

"You promise?"

"I promise."

"I love you, Uncle Spence." Katie sounded better.

"I love you, too. Honey, let me talk to Mrs. Millican."

In a few minutes, Bea Millican came on the line. "Yes, Judge Garrett?"

"Did Rachel say why she canceled out the weekend?"

"Not exactly. Just that she had some business to take care of," Mrs. Millican told him in her discreet, low voice. "I would dare say, though, she didn't sound like she wanted to cancel."

"What do you mean?"

Mrs. Millican hesitated. "I realize this is none of my concern, Judge Garrett—"

"No, that's fine. What?"

"I think she's upset about something." Mrs. Millican sounded mildly reproving, as if she suspected a lovers' quarrel.

"Upset about what?" Spence was at his wit's end.

"She didn't say." Mrs. Millican's voice sounded as though she realized he was as much in the dark as she.

"Did she sound like she was getting sick, catching a cold, anything?"

"Judge Garrett, all I can say is she sounded different, and she couldn't tell Katie exactly when she could come to visit again."

Different? Upset? "Thank you, Mrs. Millican."

Spence immediately dialed Rachel's home number. It was ten o'clock Wyoming time, nine o'clock in Oklahoma.

"Hello?" Rachel sounded as if he'd awakened her from a dead sleep.

The anger that had been simmering just beneath the worry exploded. "What in the hell is going on with you?"

There was a shocked silence at her end.

"Rachel—" he prompted sharply.

"What are you talking about?" She sounded utterly confused.

"I'm talking about why you canceled your weekend with Katie, and why you've been stonewalling me."

At her end, Rachel's heart fell to the pit of her stomach. If only he could have waited until he was home and they could talk. She'd made a mistake, she realized now. And Spence's interrogative tone wasn't helping her think any more clearly. "I—" Her mind went blank. What should she say? Tears burned at the back of her eyes.

"You what?" Spence demanded, angry with her continued reticence. She was holding out on him and that made him mad. And it hurt. "You've been different since the day I left for Wyoming. And don't tell me you're tired. If you want out, you damn well better say so now."

Chapter Thirteen

Spence's caustic tone stung her, making Rachel realize just how angry he was.

She sat straight up, pulling the bed sheets around her like a prayer stole. The past days spent grieving had left her with the calmness she needed. "Spence," she began, her voice hoarse with emotion. "You and Katie mean the world to me—"

"You could have fooled me," he interrupted, every word jagged, he was so mad at her.

Rachel closed her eyes in despair. He thought she'd betrayed him somehow. And maybe in misguidance she had. Now he'd forced the issue. *I'm not ready for this,* she thought. But when was anyone prepared to give up the people they loved?

"Spence, listen to me," she said, her voice quiet, commanding, edged with sadness.

His answering silence told her she finally had his attention. "There's something I need to tell you." She paused, collecting her thoughts, suddenly feeling so tired.

Spence heard the hint of tears in her voice. "What is it?"

"The morning you left for Wyoming, your mother came to talk to me. She'd been drinking, I'm pretty sure. She told me not to tell you any of this, but I was going to tell you as soon as you got home." Rachel swallowed, feeling that odd numbness. "She hired a private investigator last spring to follow me...to dig up dirt on me. He took pictures of us, Spence."

"My God," Spence muttered, stunned.

"She said she would try to ruin me professionally if I didn't stop seeing you and Katie."

"Rachel—" Spence stopped, reeling from the shock of her revelations. "You're talking about extortion."

"She's afraid of losing you to me the way she lost Julia to Sam, I think. She thinks I'm after your money...that I used Katie to get to you." She gave a broken laugh. "At least now I know who broke into my apartment last spring."

"Why didn't you call me as soon as my mother made these threats?" he asked.

Rachel felt at a loss. "I see now I probably should have. But there was nothing anyone could have done about it right away. And I didn't want to have to talk about it over the phone. I wanted to think it through first."

"Did you really believe I wouldn't notice something was wrong? Especially after you canceled your weekend with Katie?"

"Oh, Spence, I didn't know what else to do. I was afraid of how your mother might react if I did see Katie.

I see now I made a mistake. I'm sorry, Spence, so sorry about everything."

"It's not your fault, Rachel," he said, his voice gruff. Anger raged through him. He'd be damned if he'd let Jacqueline get away with this. It had gone way too far. "I'm taking the next flight I can get out of Jackson. I'll try to be home by tomorrow morning. I'll call you as soon as I get in."

For a second, paranoia shivered through her. What if the private investigator was still watching her? But she knew at this point there could be no more secrets. "I'll be here," she murmured.

"Rachel—" The silence of hesitation traveled over the telephone wires between them. "This...this obsession of my mother's... She didn't used to be this way. I don't know how this got so out of control. I'm sorry she's trying to do this to you, to us."

"I know," she murmured. Rachel closed her eyes. Why did this have to be so hard?

Before Sunday-morning dawn, Spence took a commuter flight out of Jackson to Caspar to make his connecting flight to River Plains. By noon, the jet carrying him touched down at the River Plains airport. Within another thirty minutes, he'd arrived at Rachel's apartment.

Rachel stepped out onto the porch, waiting for him. She wore a white T-shirt tucked into blue jeans, leather slides on her feet. The mid-September sun shone warm through the branches of the trees, their leaves beginning to dry into rich color with the change of seasons. The air smelled of coming autumn and felt cool against the sunshine.

Spence cupped her face in his hands. Bluish shadows of fatigue underscored her dark eyes. "Rachel, are you okay?" he asked, immediately concerned.

"I'm okay," she said, welcoming him, but her smile was shadowed. She looked up into his face. His eyes beheld her with such tenderness, it nearly broke her heart. The sunshine played over his features, accentuating the curve of his lips, the stubble of unshaven morning beard on his chin, the strong lines of his jaw. The light picked out the gold streaks in his hair, the deep blue of his eyes, the muted greens of his plaid flannel shirt. He wore blue jeans and boots, making her think of hiking in the mountains, camping in the pines, things she would never share with him. But for this moment, he was here with her.

He dipped his head, brushing her lips with a kiss, and hugged her close. "I've missed you," he whispered against her hair.

Tears stung her eyes, but she closed her eyes against them, forcing them back. "Me, too," she murmured. She held him very tight, gripping his shoulders with her hands, then let him go.

Spence loosened his hold, sensing a reserve in her he didn't understand.

Rachel stepped back, holding the screen door open for him. "Come in."

He followed her up the stairs. Why this…this strained distance he felt from her? But then, his own mother was trying to blackmail her. What did he expect?

In the living room, Rachel sat in the chair next to the sofa, pulling her legs up to curl beneath her. Spence sat on the sofa, letting his forearms rest on his thighs, his hands clasped between his knees.

He spoke first. "What do you think, Rachel?"

She looked away with a mute shake of her head, then returned her eyes to his to answer him. "We have some decisions to make." She nodded at the manila envelope on the coffee table in front of him.

Spence picked up the envelope. He pulled out the photographs and sorted through them. The muscles in his jaw tensed into hard lines. The photos had been taken with telephoto lenses and a night-vision scope. He'd never wanted to beat the hell out of anyone more than that private eye. And he couldn't remember ever feeling so angry with Jacqueline. He dropped the pictures back on the coffee table with an angry flick of his wrist.

He bent his head, rubbing the back of his neck, trying to contain the rage pumping through him. "All this to get rid of you?"

"Yes." Rachel folded her arms across her chest and looked down, trying to avoid the surge of tears to her eyes.

"This is completely irrational."

"Yes, it is. And if it takes making a complaint to the national board to get my license revoked, that's what she'll do." Rachel looked back at him, refusing to let the tears fall, but heartsick. "She dug into my past, until she found what she thinks is some dirt on me—"

"What do you mean?" Spence frowned.

He needed to know. He'd probably hear about it from Jacqueline, and Rachel wanted him to know the truth, even though it wouldn't really change anything. She took a breath and shifted back into her chair. "About David, my brother... and how he died."

She could see the need to understand in his eyes, and the concern. "After our parents died, David and I were shuttled from one foster home to another. He was two years older than me. He always tried to take care of me...." She smiled at the memory. "We were what they now call 'special-needs' kids. That meant we were too old to be easily adopted out. We were lucky they never split us up. Finally, the welfare department placed us with Gerald and Carolyn Lyons. They had a sterling reputation in the community. They were a family as prominent as yours."

Rachel fell silent for a moment, surprised that after so many years the story still hurt so much in the retelling. "I was the lucky one. Gerald never touched me. But David caught it all. I tried to tell my caseworker, but she didn't believe me. Not about Gerald Lyons.

"Then David started using drugs. I think he thought it was the only way he could escape the pain...."

As a kid I imagined I had a secret garden I could escape to. Spence remembered her offhand comment, understanding it now.

"The night he died, it was storming. Gerald was in a rage about some business deal. David came in late, high as a kite on God knows what. They got into an argument. Gerald pushed him down the stairs. David broke his neck." She fell quiet. Tears burned in her eyes. "No one would listen to me. They blamed David, saying he fell because he was on drugs. He was only fourteen years old."

Spence felt his chest constrict. He reached for her hand. "Rachel, I'm sorry." Useless words, he knew, but he felt heartsick at the injustice of it. And he understood her now. "That's why you were so persistent with me, about the home study? About being objective?"

"Yes."

"Wasn't anything ever done about the Lyonses?"

"You can't fix a problem people won't admit to," she said, returning his gaze. "They gave up foster-parenting after that. Too much trouble, I suppose. Gerald died of cancer about five years later."

Silence settled between them for a few seconds. Rachel eased her hand from his and rubbed at her temple. She almost couldn't bear the compassion in his eyes. It gave her a sense of being taken care of. It was a feeling she hadn't known since . . . she couldn't remember when. It made saying what she had to say all the more painful. "Your mother dragged up the official version of David's death, so get ready to hear about it."

Spence sat in silence, trying to put things in perspective, to keep his anger at bay. Somehow the words *I'm sorry* just didn't cut it.

Rachel's eyes were sad as she asked, "The drinking, the jealousy. Is this what happened with Julia?" she asked.

"A part of it." He couldn't believe what he was hearing, and believed it all the same. "I knew Mother resented Julia . . . and held on to her at the same time." He looked at Rachel. He owed her what little of the truth he knew. He hoped it wasn't too late in the coming. "Julia was seventeen years old when she went to talk to our parents about marrying Sam. She was two months' pregnant with Katie. I wasn't there. All I have is Julia's side of the story, and Mother's. Julia said Mother had been drinking. They argued. I think my parents were pushing her to have an abortion or give up the baby. Julia just wanted to marry Sam. Dad had a heart attack in the middle of the fight. He died the next morning." He rubbed a hand over his face and shook his head. "Mother blamed Julia for Dad's death, unreasonable as burdening her with the guilt was. Julia simply couldn't tolerate the blaming any longer. So she left. She called and told me that much. She wouldn't tell me where they were going. She wanted to be sure Mother couldn't find her, couldn't control her life anymore.''

"Oh, Spence," Rachel murmured.

"Their fights were nothing new. Mother blamed Julia. Julia blamed Mother and Dad. There was no ending it. Julia was an angry teenager, always in trouble, always running away...."

"The family scapegoat," Rachel said softly.

"That's a good description. Mother was intolerant of Julia's behavior, Julia was intolerant of her. Julia wanted Mother's love, Mother didn't know how to show it. It was at a boarding school in Kansas that Julia met Sam. Of course, that didn't go over well, Sam having no family, in trouble himself...."

It all made a kind of twisted sense to Rachel. And it solidified the conclusions she'd come to. She wrapped her arms around herself, a futile effort to ease the ache in her heart, the hollowness in her stomach. "I don't think your mom is going to give in on this easily."

"This is going to stop," he stated unequivocally. "I'm just not sure how to do it."

Rachel looked down at her hands, clasped so tight her fingers hurt. This was the hard part. "I'm not the one to help you with this, Spence. There are several good treatment programs in River Plains that can advise you."

Spence's mouth tightened. "I'm just asking for ideas, Rachel." But a chill ran through him, her words foreshadowing something he couldn't define.

"I know. But whatever you decide to do, I think it has to come from you, not me. I do have this to offer you." She took a breath. "I think you'll have to confront her with the truth, with what's she's done, about the private investigator, the threats, everything."

Spence frowned. "But you said she threatened to have your license revoked. There's got to be another way."

Rachel shook her head. "I'll just have to take my chances on that." She looked away, then back at him. "I think that if I let you and Katie go, then you'll have a fighting chance to get this straightened out." The sentence came out with remarkable calm.

Spence stared at her. He couldn't believe what he was hearing, it was so inconsistent with what he felt, what he thought she felt for him. *I'm not the one to help you with this.* The thought nearly paralyzed him for a moment. She was looking at him with the same expression of emotional distance as she had the day Katie had moved in with him, months ago. He felt her pushing him away. And he didn't think she'd believe him if he told her he thought he loved her. She'd believe only that he was hanging on, needing her help... She'd tell him his feelings were some kind of misplaced transference. How could he make her believe it was so much more?

He got up from the sofa, feeling very unsure, very restless, the implications of her words sinking in. "What are you saying, Rachel? That it's over between us? Just that easily?"

"How can you think this is easy for me?" she asked, her shoulders slumping in despair. She could barely speak, her voice was so raw with emotion. "Please try to understand this. Without me to blame, she'll be faced only with you, Katie and herself. And maybe she'll finally see what she's doing. There's no place in this for me. I don't know what else to do."

"You don't think the strength of our relationship can weather this?" He couldn't contain his growing anger... and hurt.

"What about the strength of our relationship, Spence? How long will we be friends and lovers? A few weeks? A few months? A few years? Then what? Is that really enough to risk the pain, the emotional damage Katie could suffer from all this? What if your mother never gets treatment? When will it ever end?"

Spence could only stare at her. How could he answer that? Say, "I think I'm in love with you, Rachel? Marry me?" He really didn't think she'd believe him.

Anger billowed in his chest. "Is this really about my mother? Or are you afraid of this relationship?" He knew he was getting too angry, but he couldn't keep from asking.

Rachel's heart plummeted deeper into the darkness that seemed to be caving in around her. "That's not fair," she whispered.

"What's unfair about it?" He wanted to hear her answer, needed to hear it.

She wanted to say, *I'm letting you both go because I do love you, damn it.* But she couldn't bring herself to say it. From the anger in his eyes, she didn't think he'd believe her. And what did it matter? He couldn't give her a commitment, either. And that wasn't the only reason.

Rachel rose from her chair and faced him. "My work is the only thing that's given my life any meaning…that's let me make a difference in this world, to stop the pain, the suffering, no matter how small or insignificant a contribution it may seem to anyone else. It's the only way I can make up for David's death." The words quavered, but her voice was strong with conviction.

Rachel was dimly aware of Spence's attention to her every word, but she didn't wait for his response. The words just kept tumbling out.

"We're not kids, Spence. I can't just throw the kind of work I do away and say, 'Let's stay together and see where this relationship takes us, no matter what happens.' You and I both know that's not the way real life works. Your mother may try to get my license, but she can never take away my purpose. I won't help her hurt Katie. And by hanging on to a—a love affair, that's all I'll accomplish. Can't you understand that?'' The words sounded harsh, even to her, and her heart ached with despair.

They looked at each other in a long moment of silence. The mantel clock ticked away with hypnotic cadence. Rachel's cat jumped up onto the mantel and crouched, watching them from his perch. Outside the windows behind the sofa, the sound of wind rustling through drying leaves rose and fell.

Spence stared at her with the most peculiar, unreadable expression, then said, "Maybe you're right."

Rachel stared at him, uncertainty clouding her eyes. "About what?"

"That what we have won't work in real life." He studied her face for a quiet moment. He felt cheated—cheated out of the chance to love her. And he wondered if he had misread her, misread the depth of the feelings she had for him. Or was it that he could never convince her he loved her for herself . . . and not for what she could do to help him? He felt damned any way he went with it.

Bitterness and anger and an almost intolerable sense of loss overwhelmed him. She'd given him no other choice. "Goodbye, Rachel." Spence turned and walked out of the living room, out of her life.

Rachel sank into the chair and cradled her head between her hands. "Goodbye," she whispered. It was a broken word in an empty room, and she wept.

* * *

"Judge Garrett, I think calling your mother's bluff, as you put it, is the only option you have," Dr. Williams told him, chewing on the end of an unlit pipe. "She needs to understand you will cut off all contact with her until she gets help, and even then, your continuing relationship will be contingent on her actions."

Spence considered the suggestions. He sat across from the director of a well-respected alcohol treatment center. A little less than twenty-four hours had passed since he had talked with Rachel...since their relationship ended. Anger impelled him, driving aside the pain, leaving behind it only the raw determination to force change.

Dr. Williams tilted back in his chair and continued. "Make a list of everything she's done drunk you can think of and be very specific." He emphasized his words with a flourish of his pipe. "And you must be prepared to follow through with the consequences you've set for her, or it simply won't work. Understand, Judge Garrett, there are no guarantees she'll respond at all, but this is usually the most effective intervention."

"I understand." Impatience to get on with it propelled Spence from his chair. He shook the doctor's hand from across the desk. "Thank you. I'll be in touch."

Spence rubbed the scallop-edged paper napkin over the palms of his hands. He left his tea on the mahogany coffee table and moved restlessly to the center of his mother's living room. Through a window, the day's light faded on the horizon.

He thrust his hands into his pants pockets, his fingers toying with loose change. The muscles in his neck felt taut. He wanted it over with.

"Spencer, dear, I didn't expect you back from Wyoming so soon. I thought you weren't coming in until tomorrow night."

At his mother's voice, Spence turned to face her.

She stood, balancing herself with one hand on the back of the brocade couch. She held a drink in her other hand as familiarly as some would hold a cigarette.

"I changed my plans." He studied her shaky stance, then pulled a hand from his pocket and gestured toward the couch. "Let's sit down, Mother."

She returned his scrutiny through narrowed eyes. She looked wary but walked around the end of the couch. She sat, crossing her legs at the knee, letting one arm drape casually over the arm of the couch. "I'm sitting," she said unnecessarily, splaying her manicured fingers in a flippant gesture.

Spence sat in a chair across from her, his arms resting on the arms of the chair, his hands clasped at his lap. "I came tonight because I care about you enough, love you enough to give you...give us the chance to save what's left of our family."

She looked at him. The glass in her hands trembled, with anger or apprehension, he didn't know. "What do you mean?" she asked, pulling her chin up.

"I mean your drinking."

She bristled at his statement, her fingers flexing around her glass, her posture erect and rigid.

"Alcohol is poisoning your reason and judgment. You've hurt a lot of people with your drinking, Mother... Julia, Dad, me."

Jacqueline lifted a silencing hand. "Wait just one minute. I *never* hurt any of you. Everything I've done, all the sacrifices I've made have been in the best interest of my family, and if you can't appreciate that—'' She broke off, her voice filled with anger and resentment.

"Mother, appreciation isn't the issue. I realize you never intended to hurt anyone, but I also know you *have* hurt us." He tried to control his anger.

She set her glass down on the coffee table with a clink, "When have I *ever* hurt you? Tell me." Her voice filled with indignant hurt, her eyes brightened with tears.

"The night Dad died, you were too drunk to realize what was happening. Julia had to call the ambulance. That was the night she came to tell you she was pregnant, that she wanted to marry Sam."

Jacqueline began to tremble, defensiveness suffusing her face in red patches. "You weren't here. How can you know anything about that night? You were still living in Cambridge," she retorted, the pitch of her voice escalating.

"Tell me. What do you remember about that night?"

Silence met his question. His mother averted her eyes. She shook her head, trying to recall that night. "Julia had no business with that poor white trash...." Her voice lost some of its vehemence in her efforts to remember. "She upset your father.... She wouldn't listen to me.... I, I—''

"You can't remember?"

"The past is past, Spence. Talking about it isn't going to change anything," she said abruptly.

How many times had he said that, himself? "Sometimes, Mother, it's the past that helps us understand the problems we're having now," he replied, remembering Rachel's words. "This is one of those times. I don't think you *can* remember that night. I think you were too drunk to remember anything about it."

"You don't know anything! You don't!" Her voice became shrill with indignation.

"I know about your visit to Rachel, about the conversation you had with her. She showed me the photographs taken by the private investigator you hired." His voice was dead calm as he played his last card. It was his biggest gamble, gambling with Rachel's life's work. But he realized Rachel was right. He had no other choice if he was going to make Jacqueline understand.

Jacqueline stared at him. Her features went slack in stark surprise and shock. For a fraction of a second, he thought he saw naked vulnerability in her eyes.

He pressed forward. "It made me realize just how much trouble this family is in."

Jacqueline stared at him in uncertainty. "If this family's in trouble, it's because you've let that welfare worker take advantage of you. And if I drink, maybe it's because Julia and your father and…you have made my life so miserable." Her voice quivered with tears.

The blaming. He'd come to expect it, and he was ready for it. He ignored it. "And I don't know if I can forgive you for what you did. It will depend on what you do from here on out."

Jacqueline's cheek twitched. She clearly didn't know what to do with Spence's confrontation. "I had to do something…. She's just a gold digger. She was trying to take you and my granddaughter away from me." She sounded pleading, desperate.

Suddenly, Spence felt very tired. And suddenly, he knew with all his heart and mind why Rachel had let them go, why she had been willing to sacrifice her job, if necessary. "No, she wasn't, Mother. She was the best thing that ever happened to us. And she gave Katie and me up because she loved us so much. Sometimes, that's what it means to love someone, Mother. To let them go." And he realized just how much he had lost. The pain went so deep, he wondered how it could possibly heal.

Jacqueline fell silent, her mouth agape in confusion.

He reached into the breast pocket of his shirt and pulled out a folded piece of paper. "This is a twenty-four-hour telephone number for a treatment facility here in River Plains. You either get treatment for your drinking or never be a part of this family again, never see Katie or me again. The choice is yours. Do you understand me?"

His mother stared at him in horrified shock. "How can you say such a thing? After all I've done for you? You wouldn't treat me like this if you loved me!" she cried, her face flushed with fury and frustration.

He knew better. "This isn't a question of love. It's a question of life. You decide."

He turned to leave, then a thought stopped him. "And if you continue to have any ideas about ruining Rachel Moran, I'd think twice about it, if I were you. You try to ruin her and I'll assume you don't want anything more to do with this family. I will not tolerate your irrational, vindictive jealousy anymore. Do you understand me?"

Jacqueline only stared at him, a frightened look coming into her eyes as reality permeated her thinking. "Spencer..." She pressed her fingers against her lips, trembling.

"You decide."

There was nothing more to say, nothing more he could do. He turned and left, wondering if it had been enough.

The call came late the next day. "Judge Garrett, this is Dr. Williams at the treatment center. Your mother checked herself in for treatment this afternoon. She wanted you to know what her choice was."

Finally. He listened with relief.

"Judge Garrett, what happens from this point on is still up to Mrs. Garrett. How much she participates in treatment, how solid her commitment is."

"I understand." At least it was a beginning.

The relief eased only a part of him. Now, Spence wondered when the pain of losing Rachel, a feeling as desolate as mourning a death, would end.

He cradled his head in his hands. He couldn't think of a way to make her believe in his love for her, to make her understand it wasn't based on needing her help. It made him so mad . . . angry at her for . . . what? Not being able to read his mind? If she could, then she'd know he loved *her*.

He loved her. And there wasn't a damned thing he could do about it.

Chapter Fourteen

The last weeks of September dragged into October. Rachel lounged in her robe on the sofa with the Sunday-morning paper, sifting through for the article on the upcoming fund-raiser for the after-school support program. There it was. She skimmed the article, reading, "...black-tie fund-raiser to be held the second Saturday in October at the Museum of the Arts...Rachel Moran, a social worker in private practice in River Plains, is a member of the advisory board and will be the keynote speaker..." Pretty good article, she thought. She turned the page.

Her eyes riveted to the black-and-white news photo of Spence, then flicked over the caption, "The Honorable J. Spencer Garrett appointed to Oklahoma State Supreme Court judgeship." She touched the picture with her fingertips and closed her eyes. When would the hurting end? Getting over Hugh Mitchell had been so much easier. Hugh had given her plenty of reasons to let go of him. Spence had only given her reasons to love him.

He'd had the courtesy to call her a few weeks ago to tell her that his mother had checked into an alcohol treatment program and that there was no need to worry about any ramifications. Jacqueline had even sent her apologies to Rachel. Spence had sounded reserved. The call was short and to the point. She hadn't heard from him since.

She let the paper slump to the floor. *Got to stay busy,* she counseled herself. It's what she did these days, to not think about the judge and his niece, to not think about how much she loved them . . . still . . . to not feel the ache deep in her heart. But it didn't work, not really. If only he could have loved her the way she loved him, loving her for who she was, not for the help she could give him. If only, if only. Useless thinking.

"Dinner's in the oven, Judge Garrett." Bea Millican hoisted her handbag over her shoulder in preparation to leave. She'd set the bar in the kitchen with one place setting.

Spence gave her a thankful look. "You don't know how good that sounds." How many times after a long day had he come home to frozen corn dogs and a cola instead of a hot meal? "I appreciate your being so flexible about your hours, Mrs. Millican." It was eight o'clock and another week of jury docket.

"You're certainly welcome, Judge. I've missed having a family to care for, so I don't mind staying late when you need me." She started to turn, then she stopped. "By the way, did you see that lovely article on Rachel Moran?"

Spence looked up from peeking in the oven. "On Rachel? No."

"It was in last Sunday's newspaper." She put down her bag and dug through it. "Here. I have a copy of it." She handed it to him with a complete lack of guile.

"Very convenient," he commented, raising an eyebrow at her. He didn't hide the smile welling up. "You saved it for me, didn't you?" he accused mildly.

"I saved it for myself, thank you. But I thought you might be interested in reading about what she's up to these days. She'll be speaking at a benefit for an after-school..."

Spence listened to Bea with only part of his attention as he read over the article. Rachel would be at the Museum of the Arts this coming Saturday evening....

"You know, Judge Garrett, I've known Rachel since she first started at the welfare department. That was back when my Charles was still alive and we foster-parented for her. I can't think of anyone I've known who's as sweet and kind and caring as she is...."

Spence looked up from the paper. "You wouldn't happen to be trying to make a point, now, would you, Mrs. Millican?"

Mrs. Millican looked him straight in the eye with her faded hazel eyes. "Let's just say if you happen to need a baby-sitter some night soon, I'll be happy to stay with Katie."

"I hate to ask you to stay any more than you already do, Mrs. Millican," he said, hedging. What good was wishful thinking?

She waved away his statement. "Sometimes, we just have to decide what it is we want. Sometimes, it takes giving back to get. Sometimes, we just have to say what needs to be said. And I do know this—life's way too short as it is. Taking care of Katie is what I want to do. You let me know what *you* want to do."

Spence regarded her thoughtfully. With her sixty-plus years of life experience, her wrinkled wisdom and graying, old-fashioned ways... he knew she was right. And it made him understand something that had been eluding him. "I'll tell you what, Mrs. Millican. I may just take you up on that offer of yours to baby-sit."

Wispy stretches of orange-tinged clouds caressed the Saturday-evening sky. The wind cooled down the warmth at the end of the day. Rachel slowed her car to turn in between two pillars at a driveway. The renovated Italian Renaissance revival villa loomed ahead, a magnificent prelude to its fifteen acres of landscaped gardens. Once the home of one of River Plains's oil barons, it was now the Museum of the Arts, and tonight was the backdrop for the after-school support program benefit to be held in the elegant dining room.

Rachel parked her car. She adjusted her black satin headband, sweeping her dark hair away from her ears to show pearl earrings. She'd worn a black satin-and-lace dress, fitted to the curves of her figure with a length that showed off her slender legs.

She checked the notes for her speech, then poked them into her purse. The evening air smelled of autumn wood smoke and drying flowers. The grounds held an air of grace and peace. *So beautiful,* she thought, following the shady walk that skirted the villa, leading to the entrance.

In the dining room, white linen cloths covered the round tables. People arrived, some in couples, some alone.

"Rachel, dear, you look lovely." The blond, plumpish Mrs. Langley, draped in royal blue silk, approached from one of the tables and took Rachel's hand. "I think it will go very well tonight."

Rachel smiled at the older woman's enthusiasm. She looked positively radiant with anticipation. "I can't tell you how much I appreciate all the work you and the other women in the sorority have put into this fund-raiser."

Mrs. Langley waved her thanks away. "It's for an excellent cause," she interjected in a firm voice. She looked past Rachel. "Oh, I see some people I want you to meet." She led Rachel with her, taking her on a whirlwind of introductions.

Names flew by, faces became a blur, and after a while, Rachel thought her face would crack if she had to sustain her smile too much longer. But the people were courteous and interested in the project. She was surprised at how much she enjoyed meeting and talking with everyone. Maybe she had been cooped up too long and too alone, with work as her main companion. But of the single men there, not one erased thoughts of Spence Garrett from her mind.

After dinner, as dessert was served, Mrs. Langley stood and introduced Rachel as the keynote speaker. Rachel took her place behind the podium and began.

"I think that as adults, faced with the daily pressures and responsibilities of life, we sometimes look back on our childhoods as relatively carefree years. Sometimes, it's difficult to imagine the pressures that drive our youth to self-destruction—"

She lowered her gaze for a moment, then moved from the podium, leaving her note cards behind. "But they do. And many of our children are slowly dying in spirit, too discouraged and too fearful to face life as they see it." She met the eyes of her audience as she spoke. "The proposed after-school support program could be a lifeline to these kids, giving them a place to go, a place where they can be heard, a place where they can find healthy friendships . . ."

Rachel talked, feeling the attentive interest of the patrons seated at their dinner tables throughout her speech and to her closing words. "With your support, both financial and from the heart, I believe we can give our children back their hope and their future, which is ours, as well." She smiled, nodding her acknowledgment. "Thank you for your time tonight."

Applause rippled across the room in a crescendo of approval. She saw members of the audience nodding their support. And she made a point of smiling at the few stony faces in the crowd.

A movement at the back of the room caught Rachel's eye. In black bow tie and tuxedo, Spence Garrett stood in his familiar posture with his hands thrust into his pants pockets. He didn't take his eyes off her. A shimmer of excitement trembled through her. What was he doing here? She made herself look away, returning her gaze to acknowledge the audience. But the electric awareness of his presence stayed with her.

Mrs. Langley came back to the podium to thank Rachel and announce after-dinner drinks and dancing. She turned back to Rachel and gave her arm a squeeze. "You did a wonderful job. I think you might have converted a few skeptics who can do a lot to back this program."

"I hope so," Rachel murmured. She couldn't help but let her vision drift back to where Spence stood.

Mrs. Langley noticed the movement of her eyes and followed in the direction of her gaze. Her eyes raised in animated delight. "Why, Spencer, I didn't expect to see you here tonight," she called out to him, leaving Rachel. She walked toward him, both hands outstretched to take his as he met her halfway.

"Hello, Marian." Spence leaned down to bestow an affectionate kiss upon her upturned cheek. "I decided to crash your benefit after I found out it was for such a good cause," he told her with a teasing grin.

Rachel listened to his light banter. She didn't feel prepared to face him. She turned to gather her notes but Marian Langley's lilting voice rang out behind her. "Rachel, I'd like you to meet someone."

She couldn't avoid him, not without being rude. Swallowing her reluctance, Rachel turned around. Mrs. Langley beckoned her to join her and Spence.

It was all so unreal, Rachel thought, walking to meet them. She tilted her head to meet Spence's eyes, her hair cascading in a dark, silken waterfall between her shoulder blades. She knew he wasn't surprised to see her. That fact and the tenderness tempering the intensity of his gaze made her feel nervous.

Before she could speak, Spence surprised her by grasping her hand. "Ms. Moran and I have met before. She's the other reason I'm here." He excused himself courteously but quickly from an openmouthed Marian Langley. He pulled Rachel with him, letting go of her hand only to slip her arm through his as he escorted her through the double doors and outside onto the patio.

Rachel couldn't speak. She was mute with the surprise of Spence's appearance and his obvious determination to see her. He anchored her hand over his arm with his free hand, sensing, she supposed with a pinch of irritation, her reluctance to go with him.

He led her to a small, round wrought-iron table and chairs, intimate by design. Her knees brushed his legs from where she sat. She shifted her posture self-consciously to break the physical contact, the electric connection between them, without much success.

He gazed at her with an expectancy she didn't understand, and that only increased her discomfort. She found her voice. "What are you doing here, Spence?"

"I wanted to see you."

The straightforwardness of his words unsettled her.

"Why?" she asked, equally straightforward.

He leaned closer. For a second, she thought he was going to reach for her hand, but he didn't. Her heart thrummed under the intensity of his look.

"Several reasons."

"Which are?"

"First off, I wanted to tell you what I've learned over the last months."

The statement pulled a smile of curiosity from Rachel. "What have you learned?"

He looked away, his brow creasing with thought. "I've learned when a fever is high enough to call a doctor and when it's not." He turned back to her, a smile softening his expression. "I've learned Katie and I both like Walt Disney and Dr. Seuss. And I've learned to send her to her room if she calls me a stupid-head."

Rachel ducked her head and compressed her lips to stifle laughter, then looked up at him with a grin. "Why did she call you a stupid-head?"

"A few weeks ago, she decided she wanted riding lessons every day. I said no. She called me a stupid-head. She spent about half an hour in her room trying to decide whether or not to apologize."

"And?"

"She apologized. And then she started renegotiating the deal...but that's another story."

Laughter bubbled up in Rachel at Spence's dry version of life with Katie. They sat smiling at each other in a moment of closeness, a meshing of hearts and souls. It felt so special, so rare.

The sunset was at that point on the western horizon where it glowed firelight golden over the earth. It cast rich, sensual shadows over Spence's face, his lips, his eyes. The effect was surreal, magical, compelling. And futile. Rachel's smile faded with the thought.

Watching her change in expression, Spence grew more thoughtful. "And I've learned that I'm not good at keeping meals on a regular basis, and that I can't give her the mothering she needs from a woman.... Mrs. Millican takes care of those problems for me. I've learned I don't need you anymore for those things, Rachel." The smile left his eyes, leaving in its place a question she didn't understand.

A bittersweet combination of pride in Spence and disconsolateness filled Rachel's heart. She tightened her lips in a flat smile to keep them from trembling with the tears inside her. She'd thought she was over the pain of him. But now she knew it would never go away, not with him popping in when she least expected him, making her miss him all over again. "Well, good... I'm glad to hear that," she replied with all the sincerity she could summon, her voice faltering.

Spence studied her face. "That's what I needed to know," he replied, his voice velvet deep and soft as the touch of the evening's breeze.

"What do you mean?" she asked, staring at him in confusion. She hated the feeling he could read her mind.

The last rays of the sunset brought out the rosiness of her mouth, her skin, making him want to lean in closer to her. But he didn't, not just yet. "That maybe you'll accept my help."

"What?" She continued to stare at him, her dark eyes wide with wonderment, confusion, and more than a little pique.

"If I'm going to back your program, I needed to at least know you'd accept my help. After everything that's happened, I just didn't know."

"You want to back the after-school support program?" she repeated, feeling as if she were losing IQ points with every passing minute. What was he doing?

"That, and more."

Rachel could only look at him, her eyes wide in surprise, in confusion. "You don't need me anymore, but you're here to help me? Why?" She nearly choked on her question. She didn't think she could bear a casual relationship with him, even one that would benefit the program.

"Rachel, a wise old woman told me that sometimes you have to think about what you want, that sometimes you have to give to get back.... I don't need your help any longer. I'm here because I want to be here, because I want to help you with whatever you're doing...because—" He closed his mouth and studied her face with open scrutiny. "Because I love you. And I think, at least once upon a time, you loved me. What I don't know is whether I'm too late."

She understood, then, with a peace and joy she'd thought she'd never have, everything he was trying to say. "I never stopped loving you," she whispered, her heart filled with emotion.

He reached for her hand and pulled her up to stand with him, taking her into his arms. He held her close, one hand tangling in her hair, the other pressed against her back, unwilling to ever let her go again. "I love you, Rachel," he murmured again, brushing her forehead with a kiss, her skin soft as the petal of a rose against his lips. "I was afraid I'd lost you . . . after everything—"

She tilted her head to look at him, her arms curled around his waist, her heart melting.

He regarded her as though she were a fragile dream that could slip through his fingers.

"I love you, too," she murmured, being able to say the words to him a freedom she'd never thought she'd have.

He touched his forehead to hers and said, "Marry me." He lifted his head, waiting for her answer, barely breathing.

She tilted her head up to look at him. Her dark eyes misted. "Yes."

Finally. Spence pressed his mouth over hers in a hard kiss, the joy of loving her threatening to consume him.

Rachel laced her fingers through his hair, lost in the sweet caress of his lips against hers, in his touch, in the loving that bound them together.

And they held each other in a communion of human need and enduring love, a love with the strength to last a lifetime.

Epilogue

On the first Saturday of December, the afternoon sun chased away the late-autumn chill. The last of the rust, gold and scarlet leaves swirled to the ground. The bare boughs of sweet gum and maple trees gleamed silver-gray in the sunlight. Guests arrived, strolling down the walk leading to the crimson double doors of the church.

In the soft light of the sitting room in the church annex, Jacqueline Garrett carefully secured the wreath of flowers holding the chapel-length veil in Rachel's shining dark hair.

"There now," Jacqueline said as she finished, her jade satin jacquard dress rustling with her movements. "Turn around and let's take a look."

Rachel moved gingerly in a half turn, toward the full-length mirror. She ran her hands over the bodice of alençon lace. Its embroidered iridescent seed pearls glittered with her movements.

"Careful, now," Jacqueline cautioned, moving behind her to pick up the ivory satin train of Rachel's gown. "These things just aren't meant to be worn, really, just to stand still in or walk forward."

A bubble of laughter welled up in Rachel's chest as she listened to Jacqueline's accurate assessment of wedding dresses. Her mirth faded into shyness. "What do you think?" she asked, feeling a tremor of nervousness.

Jacqueline let the satin fall in a cascade behind her. She moved to one side of Rachel, looking at their reflection in the mirror. Her lips quivered unexpectedly, and her eyes glistened with the brightness of unshed tears. She regarded her soon-to-be daughter-in-law standing beside her, so beautiful and radiant and filled with nervous expectancy. "I think you look just lovely," she began valiantly, her voice trembling. "I'm truly happy for you both . . . and I'm proud to have you as my daughter."

Rachel turned to her. "Oh, Jacqueline," she whispered, her eyes misting with tears. She held out her arms to the other woman and gave her a brief hug.

Jacqueline stepped back again to hold Rachel at arm's length. "I think you look perfect."

Rachel's heart filled with emotion, knowing recovery for Jacqueline continued to be an uphill struggle. But their tenuous friendship, born over the past few months, grew stronger with each passing day.

Jacqueline pursed her lips. "Except for one thing."

Rachel looked at her. "What?"

"I have something for you." She lifted a hand, signaling Rachel to wait. She turned and crossed the room to the cherrywood table covered with boxes of flowers and personal items.

She picked up a rectangular box covered in blue velvet. She looked at it, lost in a moment of thought, her fingers stroking the velvet covering. Then she turned back to Rachel, her expression a curious mixture of sadness and understanding. "While I was drinking, I did things that were unthinkable." Her voice grew hoarse. "Perhaps unforgivable." She swallowed. "I hurt the people I loved...I hurt people I didn't even know...you especially."

Rachel looked at her, not knowing what to say.

Jacqueline spared her the necessity of a response. "I kept remembering something Spencer told me that night. He told me you loved him and Katie so much that you'd given them up." A hint of tears thickened her voice.

Rachel felt her throat tighten with emotion, and she asked gently, "Why are you telling me this now?"

"Because what I did was wrong. Because I admire you for the strength of your love for my son and granddaughter. Because I learned from it. I just hope you have it in your heart to someday forgive me."

"Jacqueline—"

Jacqueline shook her head, not wanting Rachel to say anything. She opened the box and lifted up a diamond-and-pearl chevron necklace set in gold. "This belonged to my grandmother. She gave it to my mother when she married, who in turn gave it to me when I married," she explained in a quiet voice. She held the necklace draped between her fingers for a few silent seconds. Her blue eyes filled with tears. "I never had the opportunity to give it to Julia when she married...." She swallowed back her tears. "Please, accept this necklace, with the promise you will pass it on to Katie the day she marries."

"Oh, Jacqueline..." Rachel's voice quavered with shared tears of sorrow and joy.

Jacqueline fastened the necklace around Rachel's neck. Rachel looked into the mirror at the brilliant fire of the diamonds in the light, alternating with the opalescent glow of the pearls. She touched a hand to her neck. "They're beautiful," she murmured, awed by the significance of the gesture. She turned to Jacqueline. "This means so much to me. You have my promise."

Jacqueline pressed her lips into a shaky smile. "Thank you," she whispered. She cleared her throat. "It's something old for you to wear," she added in a stronger voice.

The door opened and Leslie poked her head around the door. "Can we come in? Need any help?"

Rachel smiled. "You can come in. I think I'm almost ready."

Leslie came in then, followed by Katie. They made a precious picture, dressed in identical, ankle-length sapphire velvet dresses, drop-waisted and trimmed in crocheted ivory lace at the collars.

"Aunt Rachel, we're ready to get our bouquets," Katie announced. "Miss Leslie says it's almost time!" Excitement made her voice rise an octave.

Leslie went to the table and sorted through the boxes. She handed Katie one of the two hand-tied bouquets of peach roses, irises and Queen Anne's lace. She carefully lifted Rachel's bouquet from its box and handed it to her.

Rachel held the traditional bouquet of peach roses, white freesia, Queen Anne's lace and ivy at her waist. She took a deep breath. "Is it time?"

Leslie nodded, growing teary-eyed. "Oh, Rachel, you look beautiful," she said, her voice cracking with the emotion of the moment.

They both laughed as Leslie wiped a tear from the corner of her eye with a tissue.

Katie looked up at the three adults, puzzlement bringing a frown to her features. "Why is everyone crying and laughing?"

Jacqueline touched her head in comfort. "Because we're all so happy."

Katie's expression was less than understanding but she shrugged. "Okay."

A woman with the church altar guild came to the door. "The organist is playing Pachelbel's *Canon in D*. It's time to seat Judge Garrett's mother."

Rachel's heart quickened in anticipation. Jacqueline gave her hand a squeeze before she left.

Leslie looked at her. "Shall we go?"

Rachel took a deep breath and nodded.

When they walked into the arched, stone walkway leading to the church sanctuary, they could hear the classical strains of the pipe organ drifting from within, regal and melodic. Within moments, the majestic chords introducing Purcell's *Trumpet Voluntary* resounded through the sanctuary. The exuberant notes carried first Leslie, then Katie down the aisle in a cadenced walk.

Rachel moved alone into the back of the church. She had no one to give her away, but when she looked beyond the sea of guests seated in the pews, she found Spence's eyes seeking hers. Serenity swept away any wedding nervousness.

He stood tall in the front of the church in his gray tuxedo, next to Harry Rubin, his best man, waiting to receive her.

Rachel walked down the aisle, guided by the love they shared, aware only of the man waiting for her, waiting to make her his wife, forsaking all others.

And then she was there. The priest took her hand, and then took Spence's hand, joining them together. Together, with Katie beside them, they promised their love to each other, promising a family to cherish for a lifetime.

* * * * *

BABY BLESSED
Debbie Macomber

Molly Larabee didn't expect her reunion with
estranged husband Jordan to be quite so explosive.
Their tumultuous past was filled with memories of
tragedy—and love. Rekindling familiar passions left
Molly with an unexpected blessing...and suddenly a
future with Jordan was again worth fighting for!

Don't miss Debbie Macomber's fiftieth book,
BABY BLESSED, available in July!

She's friend, wife, mother—she's you! And beside
each **Special Woman** stands a wonderfully
special man. It's a celebration of our heroines—
and the men who become part of their lives.

TSW794

Take 4 bestselling love stories FREE

Plus get a FREE surprise gift!

Special Limited-time Offer

Mail to Silhouette Reader Service™

3010 Walden Avenue
P.O. Box 1867
Buffalo, N.Y. 14269-1867

YES! Please send me 4 free Silhouette Special Edition® novels and my free surprise gift. Then send me 6 brand-new novels every month, which I will receive months before they appear in bookstores. Bill me at the low price of $2.89 each plus 25¢ delivery and applicable sales tax, if any.* That's the complete price and—compared to the cover prices of $3.50 each—quite a bargain! I understand that accepting the books and gift places me under no obligation ever to buy any books. I can always return a shipment and cancel at any time. Even if I never buy another book from Silhouette, the 4 free books and the surprise gift are mine to keep forever.

235 BPA ANRQ

Name	(PLEASE PRINT)	
Address	Apt. No.	
City	State	Zip

This offer is limited to one order per household and not valid to present Silhouette Special Edition® subscribers. *Terms and prices are subject to change without notice. Sales tax applicable in N.Y.

WHAT EVER HAPPENED TO...?

Have you been wondering when much-loved characters will finally get their own stories? Well, have we got a lineup for you! Silhouette Special Edition is proud to present a *Spin-off Spectacular!* Be sure to catch these exciting titles from some of your favorite authors:

HOMEWARD BOUND (July, SE #900) Mara Anvik is recalled to her old home for a dire mission—which reunites her with old flame Mark Toovak in *Sierra Rydell*'s exciting spin-off to ON MIDDLE GROUND (SE #772).

BABY, COME BACK (August, SE #903) Erica Spindler returns with an emotional story about star-crossed lovers Hayes Bradford and Alice Dougherty, who are given a second chance for marriage in this follow-up to BABY MINE (SE #728).

THE WEDDING KNOT (August, SE #905) Pamela Toth's tie-in to WALK AWAY, JOE (SE #850) features a marriage of convenience that allows Daniel Sixkiller to finally adopt...and to find his perfect mate in determined Karen Whitworth!

A RIVER TO CROSS (September, SE #910) Shane Macklin and Tina Henderson shared a forbidden passion, which they can no longer deny in the latest tale from *Laurie Paige*'s WILD RIVER series.

**Don't miss these wonderful titles, only for our readers—
only from Silhouette Special Edition!**

by
Laurie Paige

Maddening men…winsome women…and the untamed land they live in—
all add up to love! Meet them in these books from Silhouette Special Edition
and Silhouette Romance:

WILD IS THE WIND (Silhouette Special Edition #887, May)
Rafe Barrett retreated to his mountain resort to escape his dangerous feelings
for Genny McBride…but when she returned, ready to pick up where they
left off, would Rafe throw caution to the wind?

A ROGUE'S HEART (Silhouette Romance #1013, June)
Returning to his boyhood home brought Gabe Deveraux face-to-face
with ghosts of the past—and directly into the arms of sweet and loving
Whitney Campbell.…

A RIVER TO CROSS (Silhouette Special Edition #910, September)
Sheriff Shane Macklin knew there was more to "town outsider"
Tina Henderson than met the eye. He saw a generous and selfless woman
whose true colors held the promise of love.…

Don't miss these latest Wild River tales from Silhouette Special Edition
and Silhouette Romance!

SEWR-4

by Christine Rimmer

**Three rapscallion brothers. Their main talent: making trouble.
Their only hope: three uncommon women who knew the way to
heal a wounded heart! Meet them in these books:**

Jared Jones

hadn't had it easy with women. Retreating to his mountain cabin, he found willful
Eden Parker waiting to show him a good woman's love in MAN OF THE MOUNTAIN
(May, SE #886).

Patrick Jones

was determined to show Regina Black that a wild Jones boy was *not* husband
material. But that wouldn't stop her from trying to nab him in SWEETBRIAR SUMMIT
(July, SE #896)

Jack Roper

came to town looking for the wayward and beautiful Olivia Larrabee. He never
suspected he'd uncover a long-buried Jones family secret in A HOME FOR THE HUNTER
(September, SE #908)....

**Meet these rascal men and the women who'll tame them,
only from Silhouette Books and Special Edition!**

COUNTDOWN
Lindsay McKenna

Sergeant Joe Donnally knew being a marine meant putting lives on the line—and after a tragic loss, he vowed never to love again. Yet here was Annie Yellow Horse, the passionate, determined woman who challenged him to feel long-dormant emotions. But Joe had to conquer past demons before declaring his love....

MEN OF COURAGE

It's a special breed of men who defy death and fight for right! Salute their bravery while sharing their lives and loves!

These are courageous men you'll love and tender stories you'll cherish...available in June, only from Silhouette Special Edition!

CAN YOU STAND THE HEAT?

SUMMER Sizzlers '94

You're in for a serious heat wave with
Silhouette's latest selection of sizzling
summer reading. This sensuous collection
of three short stories provides the perfect
vacation escape! And what better authors
to relax with than

ANNETTE BROADRICK
JACKIE MERRITT
JUSTINE DAVIS

And that's not all....

With the purchase of *Silhouette Summer
Sizzlers '94*, you can send in for a FREE
Summer Sizzlers beach bag!

SUMMER JUST GOT HOTTER—
WITH SILHOUETTE BOOKS!